## Wild Kingdom

'Be assured that if I planned to kill you, Rianna, I'd find a far less public place than this damnable forest to dispose of you. Anyway, my plans are of a far more intimate nature.' Niska ran a finger across Rianna's cheek.

'Intimate?' Rianna shrank back, feeling trapped.

'You had a female lover in the seraglio. Sarin encouraged you to enjoy the pleasures of others of the same sex. I recall one incident when he ordered you to wear the harness –'

'And I refused, and suffered a beating,' interrupted Rianna.

'You were braver and stronger then, my dear. The fire has left you now,' purred Niska. 'You do not have the strength to refuse me anything!'

# Wild Kingdom
Deanna Ashford

**BLACK LACE**

This edition published in 2007 by
Black Lace
Thames Wharf Studios
Rainville Rd
London W6 9HA

Originally published 2000

A catalogue record for this book is available from the British Library.

*www.black-lace-books.com*

Typeset by SetSystems Ltd, Saffron Walden, Essex
Printed and bound by CPI Bookmarque, Croydon, CR0 4TD

The paper used in this book is a natural, recyclable product made
from wood grown in sustainable forests. The manufacturing process
conforms to the regulations of the country of origin.

ISBN 978 0 352 33549 4 [UK]
ISBN 978 0 352 34152 5 [US]

Distributed in the USA by Holtzbrinck Publishers, LLC, 175 Fifth Avenue,
New York, NY 10010, USA

1 3 5 6 7 9 10 8 6 4 2

# Chapter One

The grey swirling mist was like a living entity, swallowing up the forest and the path ahead. Lady Rianna of Harn shivered, feeling as though she and her armed escort had strayed into some strange netherworld, where nothing existed but endless gloom. All she could hear were the muffled chink of armour, the rhythmic noise of the horses' hoof-beats and an occasional strange, unidentifiable screeching from the forest that set her nerves on edge. The fog was so dense she could barely see the mounted man-at-arms in front of her, let alone the thick banner of trees which lined the narrow road.

The chill dampness invaded Rianna's weary limbs, numbing her fingers as she clutched on to her palfrey's reins. They had been on the road for three days now and the journey had been long and hard. She was unused to riding so far and so fast in such inclement weather. She was close to exhaustion and dusk was approaching: it was imperative that they reach a safe place to spend the night.

Captain Leon, and his small troop of well-armed soldiers, had been charged by her betrothed, Prince Tarn of Kabra, to escort her to the safe refuge of her father's kingdom of Harn. With Tarn's army increasing in size by

1

the day, the final assault to drive the Percheron invaders from Kabra would soon be underway. This forest, which snaked along the borders between Kabra and Harn, was a haven for vagabonds and bandits. Captain Leon did not trouble to hide his concern as he constantly scanned the trees, which were still almost hidden by the drifting fog, looking for the slightest sign of anyone who might be about to attack.

'It's not far now, my lady,' Captain Leon said, glancing over at Rianna. 'The castle of Dane is close by.'

As Leon spoke there was an unholy yell and a number of savage-looking creatures, dressed in outlandish garments and brandishing swords, leaped from the trees. One lunged towards Rianna's palfrey. Startled, she gave a sharp scream and her mount began shying nervously. The horse surged forwards as Leon hit it hard across the rump with the flat of his sword.

'Go!' Leon shouted. 'Ride for the castle.'

Leon and his men were fighting for their lives. Rianna heard the resounding clang of metal against metal, punctuated by hoarse shouts and the loud cry of a wounded man. Yet she had no chance to even look back as her mount galloped wildly along the path and everything behind her was swallowed up by the mist. Filled with fear and anguish she struggled to control her horse, her heart beating out of control. She did not know how far it was to the sanctuary of the castle. The hood of her cloak fell from her head and tendrils of her red-gold hair escaped from their pins and whipped against her face as she prayed that Leon and his men would survive.

The ominous thudding sound of hooves approaching behind her made Rianna dig her heels into her mare's flanks, urge it into an even faster gallop. Then she saw the walls of the castle loom out of the fog just ahead. The gates were open but there were no men-at-arms on guard nor any sign of life at all. She galloped into the deserted bailey.

She pulled agitatedly at the reins, her horse's hooves

sliding on the damp flagstones as she whirled around to face her pursuer. To her relief it was one of Leon's men. He jumped from his horse and ran towards the gates, shouting loudly for someone to help him as he attempted to push one of the heavy oak doors shut.

The soldier, who Captain Leon had sent ahead to announce their arrival and have the place properly prepared for Rianna, ran from the stables and was followed by a grubby, poorly dressed servant who wearily rubbed his eyes as if he'd just woken up. They put their shoulders to the oak gate, heaving one side into place but leaving the other partly open; they were ready to slam it shut if the bandits reached the castle before Captain Leon and his men.

Rianna's heart was still pounding as she clung to the reins of her weary mount and watched the gate as more servants appeared brandishing an assortment of weapons. She heard the drumming sound of horses approaching, then Leon appeared, holding aloft his bloodied sword, followed by a number of his men-at-arms. Rianna counted them as they entered the bailey, relieved to find that they were all safe. Leon rode straight over to Rianna and stopped his mount a few feet from hers. Foam flecked the horse's mouth and steam rose from its flanks.

'As soon as they realised what they were facing, the bandits retreated in disarray, dragging their wounded with them,' Leon told Rianna, as the gates were slammed shut and barred by a heavy wooden beam almost the length of two grown men. 'They were a ragged, poorly armed band, who would never dare attack this castle,' he added reassuringly.

'I was concerned for you all,' Rianna said breathlessly, as she glanced around the bailey. The fortress was old and unimpressive: little more than a tall stone tower, surrounded by thick outer walls, and built, like many others, to protect the borders of Kabra. It was permeated by a very visible air of neglect. Chickens foraged amid the piles of rubbish heaped against the outer walls and,

3

judging by the foul odour, excrement from the midden had not been cleared for many a long month. In the height of summer this place would be swarming with flies and disease, thought Rianna. For the first time on this journey, she was thankful that it was winter; it was so cold that every breath she expelled was visible in the chill air. Her horse snorted and lowered its head as she struggled to recover from her fright. She watched the soldiers dismount. They were still exhilarated from the brief battle and talked cheerfully among themselves as they led their horses to the stables.

'My lady,' Captain Leon said worriedly, 'we must get you inside. It is cold and damp, if you remain here you'll be chilled to the bone.'

Rianna pushed back the stray strands of hair that had fallen across her face. Her ivory skin looked even paler in contrast to her still-flushed cheeks, and there were dark violet smudges of weariness under her large green eyes. Yet her dishevelled state only served to enhance her fragile beauty.

'These last three days have not been an experience I would like to repeat often,' she confessed. They had been forced to take a tortuous route in order to avoid groups of enemy soldiers, as the invading army of Percheron still retained control of large parts of Kabra despite Prince Tarn's determined efforts to drive them from his land. 'I will be glad of a hot bath and a good night's rest in a comfortable bed,' she continued, her voice trembling with tiredness.

Rianna always rode astride, and as she tried to dismount her movements were hampered by the weight of her velvet cloak, which was now saturated by the heavy moisture in the air. She almost fell into Captain Leon's waiting arms and his strong hands closed protectively around her waist. 'I fear I pressed you too hard,' he said softly, his handsome features etched with concern.

'Prince Tarn ordered you to make haste and escort me to Harn with expediency, did he not?'

4

'He did.' Leon smiled tenderly at her, his hazel eyes filled with far more than just loyalty and concern. 'And the sooner I deliver you to your father, the sooner I can return to fight by his side.'

'And may the gods protect you all,' Rianna said, leaning against Leon's firm chest for a moment, comforted by his strength and the hardness of his muscular form.

Most soldiers stank of leather, dirt and sweat, but she had noticed that Leon was fanatical about cleanliness and the odour of lemon verbena always scented his clothing. As his warm breath brushed her cheek a familiar lust flooded Rianna's veins. She and her lover, Tarn, had barely spent a private moment together for weeks and she craved the loving caresses of a man's hands and the joy of a hard male body in her bed at night.

Rianna pulled away from Leon. He was charming and very attractive but no real substitute for Tarn – the man she loved and wanted to be with for the rest of her life. 'We should make our way inside.' She glanced around the gradually darkening bailey. 'I trust that the inside of the keep is an improvement on this!' she added.

'Sir Olaf suggested his castle would provide a comfortable refuge on our journey east,' Leon commented. 'His staff have clearly grown slack and slovenly since his departure.' Keeping a firm hold on her arm, he escorted Rianna up the slippery stone steps and into the castle.

The great hall was dimly lit by smoking torches that gave off an acrid smell. It was sparsely furnished and the rushes were almost ankle deep on the floor. One layer had been laid upon the other and, judging by the musty, greasy odour of rotting food, they'd not been replaced for some time. Close to the large soot-stained fireplace two scrawny hounds scrabbled and snarled over pieces of meat.

A stooping, grey-haired man shuffled forwards and bowed low before her. 'I am the steward, Bayliss. Welcome, Lady Rianna,' he said in a quavering voice. 'A chamber has been prepared for you. The maidservants

5

are young and unused to attending a noble lady, but they are all I could provide at such short notice.'

'I am certain they will be more than able; my needs tonight are simple.' Despite her disappointment at the state of the place, Rianna felt rather sorry for the old man. He looked ancient, and well past working age. If he were her servant he would have been assigned far lighter tasks than caring for this castle. She turned to glance at Leon. 'I'll see you on the morrow, Captain.'

'On the morrow, my lady,' he agreed with a warm smile. 'If you have need of me, you have but to call,' he added, then strode off, glancing back at her again for a long penetrating moment before he left the great hall.

'My lady, your chamber is this way,' the steward said, shuffling forwards to slowly ascend the broad stone staircase. Rianna followed him, moving stiffly, her damp skirts clinging to her legs.

When Rianna reached her bedchamber she was pleasantly surprised to find the room spacious and spotlessly clean, with a welcoming fire blazing in the hearth. The bed, with its fresh linen sheets, looked comfortable, despite the fact that the red velvet curtains were worn and faded. What pleased Rianna most was the large wooden tub, placed close to the fire, filled almost to the brim with steaming water.

A servant entered the chamber, carrying Rianna's small travelling chest. He then left, along with the steward, while the two young maidservants, waiting to attend Rianna, just stood there staring at her nervously, not daring to say a word. They were cleaner than the other servants Rianna had seen, with spotless white aprons covering their simple woollen gowns. Judging by their red, work-roughened hands, they were more used to heavy household tasks than attending to a lady's needs.

Rianna smiled, sensing their nervousness. 'Your names?' she asked.

'Hiller, my lady,' the taller dark-haired one said, curtseying clumsily.

'Agnes, my lady,' added the younger and prettier of the two.

'Hiller, you unpack my chest,' Rianna ordered. 'I shall need a nightgown and my rose-scented soap,' she added, having noticed the bar of coarse lye soap that had been left beside the tub. 'I'll bathe and then retire,' she added, longing to be rid of her damp clothing and luxuriate in the hot water.

She went to unfasten her cloak, but her fingers were too stiff and cold to undo the heavy clasp. 'Let me,' Agnes said, rushing forwards.

The maidservant lifted the sodden cloak away from Rianna and draped it out to dry across a chair near the fire. Then she unlaced the back of Rianna's plum, woollen dress. As it fell in a pool at Rianna's feet, Agnes uttered a faint gasp of surprise.

'Have you not seen a woman in breeches before?' Rianna asked with a soft laugh. She wore supple form-fitting leather breeches beneath her long skirts. Usually she wore men's clothing when riding, not caring if it shocked those who saw her. Last night they'd slept out in the open and she'd put on her dress as well in a vain effort to keep warm.

'I have not,' Agnes replied. She seemed unable to keep from staring curiously at the garment which clung very tightly to Rianna's long, shapely legs.

'Help me off with my boots,' Rianna said, leaning back against a chair while lifting her left foot.

Agnes eased off one boot, then the other. Rianna stepped on to the rug of wolf-skin pelts, which partially covered the cold stone floor. The thick fur felt warm and tickled her bare feet as Agnes awkwardly helped Rianna unfasten her breeches and peel them off. Rianna was left wearing only a very brief silk shift – one far more revealing than the heavy linen shifts most noble ladies wore. Feeling more comfortable devoid of her damp clothing, she moved closer to the fire to allow the heat to start warming her stiff limbs. As the maids fussed around the room, unpacking her garments and gathering up linen towels left warming by the fire, Rianna stared pensively into the flickering flames, thinking of Tarn and praying that he would remain safe.

'Should I take down your hair?' Agnes asked, touching the thick red-gold coils that had not escaped from their pins.

'Leave it.' Rianna repressed a shiver as Agnes's callused fingers brushed the nape of her neck and a tingle of desire slid slowly down her spine. They reminded her too much of the hot purpose of Tarn's sword-roughened hands when they'd last made love. 'I'll manage it myself. You may both leave now.'

'Do you wish for something to eat? The cook has prepared a light repast,' Hiller said. 'After such a long journey, my lady, you –'

'No,' Rianna interjected impatiently. 'Just leave.'

Agnes and Hiller seemed to be relieved that their duties were over as they hurried off, pulling the heavy wooden door shut behind them. Once she was alone, Rianna removed her shift to revel in the feeling of nakedness as the flickering flames cast dark inviting shadows over her pale skin. Gently she cupped her full breasts, running her thumbs over the soft tips of her nipples, imagining it was her lover's hands caressing her. She teased the tiny peaks until they hardened and felt an answering tug in the pit of her groin.

Rianna did not handle enforced celibacy with ease. Lately she'd resorted to pleasuring herself. She climaxed easily enough but she was always left feeling partially unfulfilled. Soon she would be with Tarn again, she thought, as she picked up her precious bar of scented soap and stepped over the rim of the tub into the steaming water. It was warm, but not uncomfortably so. She sat down, her back pressed against the smooth wooden side, her knees bent and slightly apart.

A faint sheen of perspiration formed on her brow as the heat seeped slowly into her muscles, easing her weary limbs. The water lapped comfortingly against the narrow valley between her thighs and cradled the undersides of her full breasts. This tub in front of the fire was a far cry from the elaborate bathing facilities of her former husband's palace in Percheron, but in Rianna's estimation it was infinitely preferable. She had been forced by her father into a marriage of convenience with Sarin, the ruler of Percheron, in order to prevent him invading Harn as he had Kabra. But that episode in her life was now over. Sarin, the man she'd come to loathe and despise, was part of her past and Tarn was her present and future. Yet still, even now, memories of Sarin and his erotic sexual excesses invaded her dreams at night.

Tonight she would dream only of Tarn. She would close her eyes and see every inch of his tall muscular body and imagine that she could feel his magnificent cock sliding deep inside her. Tarn was even stronger and braver now than when they'd first met; he had been toughened by the time he'd spent as Lord Sarin's prisoner and slave. Tarn had suffered at Sarin's hands but now he was free and Sarin was the slave. Unknown to the people of Percheron, who believed their ruler dead, Sarin was a captive in Freygard, the land of Rianna's mother, Kitara. In Freygard women ruled, while men were consigned to being mere chattels and slaves. Rianna felt no pity for Sarin's plight, only relief that he would never be free to hurt her or Tarn again.

Rianna picked up the muslin cloth, which had been draped over the side of the tub, and covered it with her rose-scented soap. Her thoughts still centred on Tarn, she rubbed the cloth over her arms and breasts, down over the swell of her stomach and between her legs. She pressed the cloth against her sex, and the dull ache of longing increased into a restless fire. The red-gold hairs of her pubis tickled her fingertips as she discarded the cloth and gently caressed the thick bush of hair. In Percheron she had been forced to have all her intimate

9

hair denuded, but thankfully it had grown back thicker and silkier than ever.

Her fingers stroked the valley of her sex, where the flesh was as soft and supple as the finest velvet, and she began savouring the first faint flutters of pleasure. With Tarn's image vivid in her mind, she touched her clitoris, rubbing it gently at first and then harder. Soon it became firm and tight, the heat of her desire magnified by the subtle sensations of the warm water gently caressing her open quim.

A sudden blast of chill air crossed her shoulders, blowing out the candles, leaving only the flickering fire-light to illuminate her room, but Rianna was too lost in her fantasies to care. She was almost able to smell Tarn's familiar musky male scent and feel his strong fingers sliding deep inside her, his knuckles brushing her warm moist folds, while his lips nuzzled her breasts. She barely heard the sudden gust of wind that howled noisily around the castle walls, like a banshee haunting the night. All her attention was centred on pleasure as she slid the tip of her finger into her soft, welcoming opening.

The wind died as suddenly as it had appeared, and the silence of the chamber was filled with the quick, sharp sound of Rianna's agitated breathing as she strained towards the climax that remained just out of her reach. Then the skin on the back of her neck began to prickle, as she was filled with the knowledge that she was no longer alone.

'Who's there?' she stuttered, her heart beating out of control. Suddenly she feared that the castle was haunted by some unhappy restless spirit who had come to do her harm.

Rianna tensed nervously as a hand touched her shoulder, but it was no ghost: the flesh was firm and warm. Terrified for a moment, her mind froze into abso-lute stillness. The faint scent of lemon verbena drifted towards her as she willed her numbed limbs to work. It could only be Captain Leon, but surely he would not be

10

so bold, she considered, knowing that she should speak out, order him to leave. Yet for some unidentifiable reason she could do nothing but remain where she was as warm fingers moved caressingly across the nape of her neck. Her skin prickled with pleasure as the hand moved seductively up and down the line of her spine. The alluring sensation was just too delicious to resist.

'Fear not, my lady. I come to worship at the altar of your loveliness,' a deep voice whispered in her ear. 'Would you deny me that small pleasure?'

'How could I?' she gasped, her heart leaping at the familiar sound of his voice. She was hardly able to believe this was happening as he cupped her left breast, and tugged teasingly at her rosy nipple. Wine-tainted breath brushed her cheek, as she inhaled his musky odour, now overlaid with the rich aroma of lemon verbena that clung to his clothing. 'You surprised me,' she added, in a voice trembling with emotion. 'How came . . .'

'Hush, my sweet lady,' he murmured, his mouth caressing her neck, his warm tongue tracing a line to her ear, before he pulled the tiny lobe between his lips and sucked on it gently.

Rianna was hungry for this man. He was all she wanted. Her pussy ached with need for him and she was desperate to feel him driving deep into her tight core. 'Please,' she whimpered, as his hand slid into the water, stroking her stomach and the tangled curls of her pubic hair. 'I want to feel you inside me.'

'Soon,' he murmured, pulling away from her, ignoring her soft moan of displeasure.

Rianna heard the faint sound of movement as he pulled off his clothes. She waited, tense with excitement, not daring to turn her head and look at him, unwilling to break the circle of sexual magic that surrounded them.

She shivered with excitement as he eased her forwards and stepped into the tub behind her, lowering his bulk into the water, which began to spill over the sides of the tub, gathering in puddles on the cold stone floor. Rianna

11

gasped as she was pulled back against his warm naked flesh until her buttocks rested on his muscular thighs and her back pressed against his firm chest. She was faint with desire as the hard line of his cock pressed demandingly between her bottom cheeks.

She was so aroused she could barely breath, and she wanted him inside her so much it was like a physical pain. Yet she also needed to savour every precious second, every sweet moment. She glanced down at the hands that cupped her breasts. In the flickering firelight his flesh looked dark against her pale skin as he rubbed her nipples, squeezing them roughly until she moaned with pleasure.

Rianna ground her buttocks against the hardness of his groin, forcing his cock further between her arse cheeks as she heard his breathing quicken.

'So eager,' he said, with a soft chuckle of amusement. 'So greedy for me, my sweet.'

'Why not?' she asked breathlessly. 'I've been starved for so long,' she added as his hand slid downwards, tracing the smooth curve of her belly. Her legs opened of their own accord as he ran his fingers through her crisp pubic curls and caressed the wet valley of her sex.

The fleeting pleasure she'd managed to arouse with the pressure of her own hand was nothing compared to the hot rush of bliss as the rough pads of his fingertips stroked and teased her clit. He played her body as a master of music would his instrument, his touch setting her nerve endings alight and sending wheeling arcs of pleasure through her. Then he slid two fingers inside her, and began thrusting them in and out of the slippery wetness.

'How I've longed for this moment,' he said softly, his voice taut with passion as he lifted her, tipping her buttocks away from him so that he could slide into her with one smooth stroke. He jerked her back against his rigid stomach, filling her with the hot hardness of his flesh as he held his hand across the soft swell of her lower belly. The pressure of his fingers further increased the sensation of fullness she experienced as he began to roll his hips and thrust at the same time. A low moan escaped Rianna's lips as he compounded the assault on her senses by lightly tugging at her clit, rolling the swollen flesh smoothly between finger and thumb.

The water swirled and eddied around them, splashing over the sides of the tub in a steady stream as his movements became faster and more vigorous. All Rianna's attention was focused on her relentlessly rising pleasure as she felt his body power harder and deeper. She had no wish for this to end, yet all too soon her stomach contracted as the sensations erupted into an orgasm so sweetly profound that she felt faint from its power as it ripped through her flesh.

Panting breathlessly, she remained motionless, listening to the ragged sound of her lover's breathing. She was still feeling weak in the aftermath when he gently eased her round to face him. Rianna smiled, feasting her eyes on his handsome face; she was filled with indescribable joy.

'Fie on you,' she teased. 'Intruding on a lady's privacy unannounced. For a moment, you scared me near half to death.'

Tarn smiled lovingly. 'I had no intention of frightening you, my sweet.'

'At first, when I sensed a presence, I feared you were a ghost. Once I realised you were flesh and bone, I was unconcerned,' she said, with a soft teasing laugh, not about to confess she'd not known for sure it was Tarn until he had spoken. 'Who else would it have been? Your soldiers guard me well, they would never have allowed a stranger to enter my chamber.'

'Perhaps some poor fool captivated by your charms?' he gently jibed. 'Captain Leon, for instance. He seems very taken with you, my love.'

'You are the one who has cast a spell over my senses and captured my heart,' she swiftly countered. 'Although

13

I confess that the scent of lemon verbena confused me for a moment. I know you prefer not to have it near you as the smell reminds you too much of Sarin's palace.'

'I had no choice.' He shrugged his wide shoulders. 'My own clothes were soaked, I'd ridden so long and so hard to reach you. Captain Leon's shirt was a tight fit, but it served me well enough.' Tarn chuckled. 'I fear I've taken the last clean garment he had with him.'

'No matter,' she replied, dismissing her brief attraction for Leon from her thoughts.

'The water grows cold,' Tarn said. 'If we stay here much longer, you might catch a chill,' he added, easing away from her and standing up. Water streamed from his tall, muscular body as he stepped out of the tub and took hold of one of the linen towels, wrapping it around his waist.

He scooped Rianna out of the water, and set her down on the fur rug in front of the blazing fire.' 'Tell me,' she said, unable to hold back the question that now consumed her thoughts. 'Is the battle won or lost?'

Tarn laughed as he set about tenderly drying her. 'Do I look like a fugitive fleeing for my life?'

'You do not, my lord.' Rianna touched the livid bruise on his sword arm. Praise the gods she could see no other damage to his flesh apart from a few very minor scratches and bruises. 'So you won, but at what cost?'

'None,' Tarn replied with a confident smile, seeming very cheerful for a man who had just fought a terrible battle. 'There was no need to fight. Orders came from Percheron for the army to withdraw and return home.'

'Why?' she asked in confusion, as he busied himself unpinning her hair, running his fingers through the silky red-gold strands and fanning them down across her back.

'It appears that once Lord Sarin was deemed to have perished during his sortie into Freygard, there was a struggle to gain control of Percheron. Sarin had no legal heir, and at first the army remained in total control. Less than a month ago, Chancellor Lesand and his supporters

14

managed to gain the upper hand. Lesand now rules Percheron as regent, and it was he who ordered the withdrawal of his troops from Kabra.'

Lesand had proven to be a loyal friend to Rianna during her time in Percheron and had eventually helped her and Tarn escape Sarin's clutches. 'He's a good man. I'm pleased to hear that he is safe and in a position of such authority,' Rianna said with relief. 'Now there can be peace at last.'

'We can hope for nothing else.' Tarn swung her into his arms and carried her to the bed. 'We can concentrate on rebuilding Kabra, making it a happy and prosperous land. But first there are more important matters to attend to, are there not?'

'If you say so, my lord,' Rianna said meekly, but she was far from meek as she jerked off his towel and pulled him down beside her. Then she pressed tender kisses to each bruise, each tiny mark that marred his golden flesh, as she ran impatient hands over his body.

She trailed her fingers slowly over Tarn's cock. 'Rianna,' he growled softly as she felt his balls tighten and saw the shaft twitch excitedly.

'Are you ready to pay your dues to me?' she teased.

'What dues,' he gasped as she wanked him with smooth firm strokes.

'I've waited for this moment,' she told him. 'Kabra is free and you can be mine at last.'

'I have always been yours in my heart, Rianna,' he replied, his voice trembling with the depth of his feeling.

She milked him harder, easing her grip as she reached the tip, tightening it as she slid her fingers down to the less sensitive root. Tarn's blue eyes narrowed with passion as she smiled wickedly, then leaned forwards to trail the tip of her tongue over the taut cock head, running it teasingly around the sensitive rim, knowing the gentle touch would drive him insane with lust as it always did.

'Please,' he begged.

15

Rianna moved astride Tarn's hips. 'Do you submit?'

'Do as you will with me,' he groaned as she impaled herself on him, grinding her pelvis hard against his.

Tarn stood on the battlements of the castle oblivious to the chill breeze that stirred his long blond hair. He narrowed his blue eyes; the sun's rays were bright, yet its heat was barely discernible on this cold winter morning. The forest looked far less threatening in daylight now that the wind had blown away the last vestiges of the heavy mist.

Sunlight pierced the leafless branches of the trees, bathing the roots where the first flowers of the approaching spring were stirring into life. Soon Kabra would be reborn also, stronger and more prosperous than it was before the invasion. Life was full of hope at last, Tarn thought, as he leaned against the icy moss-covered stone of the battlements.

He had woken just before dawn and lay by Rianna's side watching her sleeping, her glorious hair splayed across the pillow. She looked so innocent, her beautiful features so pale – almost as if they were carved from the finest alabaster. She had the face of a goddess, yet when she was awake her beauty was even more moving, more profound, because it was enhanced by the fire in her green eyes and the warmth of her smile.

Tarn blessed the day he had found her – that fateful moment when, as a helpless captive of Lord Sarin, he had opened his eyes to find this glorious creature bending over him. In his fevered confusion he had thought her a faerie or some forest wraith come to lead him to paradise. Then he had discovered she was Sarin's betrothed. He soon realised that in many ways she was as much a prisoner as he was. It had been both the best and worst time of Tarn's life. He had found Rianna then she had been torn from his grasp, and he had almost lost himself in the dark carnal excesses he was forced to indulge in as Sarin's personal body slave.

16

'You seem troubled,' said a gentle voice.

Tarn turned to look at Rianna as she stepped on to the exposed walkway. 'I was wondering what the future now holds for us,' Tarn replied, pulling her close.

Rianna's hair was loose around her shoulders, and she wore his thick, fur-lined cloak over her nightgown. The garment was far too long for her and fell in heavy folds around her slippered feet. 'Nothing but good,' she said confidently.

In the distance an eagle swirled majestically across the clear blue sky. It flew towards a narrow plume of smoke, which came from the village barely a league from the castle, then turned and rose high into the heavens aiming for a distant mountain peak.

'Soon spring will be here and with it the promise of new life.' Tarn smiled lovingly at her. 'A life filled with nothing but happiness.'

'Tell me,' Rianna prompted. She knew Tarn well enough to sense that something still troubled him.

'My father's condition worsens,' he admitted. 'A messenger arrived just before dawn. His doctors fear he will only last a day or so longer.'

After the invasion King Brion had been allowed to remain on the throne of Kabra, merely as a puppet dancing to the tune of his new masters. He had even been forced to send his only son as a hostage to the court of Lord Sarin, and his health had started to decline from that terrible moment. He was already gravely ill when Tarn had returned home. Brion had managed to cling on to life all these months, but now Kabra was free he appeared to have given up the struggle to survive.

'You must go to him,' Rianna said. 'Be with him at the end.'

'When I am declared king, I want you beside me,' Tarn said and hugged her even closer, unhappy at being forced to leave her again so soon. 'But I will not allow my future queen to be placed at risk. I have ordered Leon to despatch most of his men into the forest to flush out

17

any bandits remaining in the area. Once he deems it safe to proceed, you can follow me.' Rianna was stubborn and self-willed at times, but Tarn was certain she would not disagree with this decision.

'I wish I were a warrior like my mother,' Rianna said frustratedly. 'Then I could bear arms and always remain by your side, even in battle.'

'Kitara was raised to be a warrior; you were not, my love,' Tarn pointed out. He had great respect for the women of Freygard and even more respect for the beautiful Kitara. 'Once matters are settled I can arrange for my swordmaster to tutor you – teach you to fight.' He gave a soft laugh. 'You already have the heart of a warrior, Rianna.'

'But not the constitution.' She shivered. 'It grows colder. Come inside.'

'If you wish it.' Tarn guided her through the arched opening and shut the sturdy wooden door. The narrow stone-flagged corridor was far from warm, but at least they were protected from the chill breeze. 'Come,' he said, pulling her closer. 'Break your fast with me. Then I must ready myself for the journey, tis getting late.'

'Not yet,' Rianna stared thoughtfully up at him.

'What ails you, my love?'

'Nothing.' She smiled. 'I was just thinking how blessed I am to have you, Tarn. Now kiss me, then tell me how long we have before you plan to depart.'

'Long enough,' he growled, his mouth covering hers. Tarn kissed her hungrily, his lips locked fiercely on hers, his tongue probing and plundering her mouth.

He slid one hand inside her cloak and cupped her breast. The heat of her flesh seared its way through the fine fabric of her nightgown, warming his icy palm. Kissing her with unrestrained passion, he stroked and kneaded her breast, feeling her nipple stiffen with excitement as she became more and more aroused.

Rianna moaned, her breathing becoming ragged as she pressed herself against him, twining her arms around his

18

neck. He pulled roughly at the thin fabric of her night-gown, ripping it apart in his haste to expose her body to his hungry gaze. He felt her tremble as the cold air of the passageway hit her bare skin, yet she seemed too aroused to bother with such minor discomforts as she whispered sweet words of encouragement in his ear. Tarn tore the fragile garment further and thrust his hands between her thighs. His cold fingers invaded the slit of her sex and began burrowing into her warm depths. Her flesh felt hot and moist as he thrust his fingers deeper until she gave a breathy moan of bliss.

'Tarn,' she gasped, straining urgently against his invading hand as her juices began to flow in abundance.

Hot tremors ran though his body as Rianna pulled at the laces fastening his breeches together. They were only loosely tied and she easily jerked them apart to free his cock, which reared majestically out of the opening. Clutching hold of the rigid shaft, she wanked it until he gave a faint, almost despairing groan.

'I want you now,' he whispered, still continuing to rub her clit with rhythmic thrusts, while she milked his cock with long smooth strokes. He felt as though it would soon be ready to explode.

'Then take me,' she pleaded, trembling with passion. 'Right here. Right now.'

Tarn cupped her buttocks in his hands and lifted her until her belly was level with his. Rianna clutched on to his broad shoulders, uttering a small animal sound of pleasure as he jerked his hips, forcing the entire length of his swollen cock deep inside her. Pulling her hips closer, he paused for a second to savour the delightful sensations of her body tightly embracing his.

Rianna's head meanwhile was pulled back by the heavy weight of her fur-lined cloak, the metal clasp digging cruelly into the skin of her neck. Supporting her with one strong hand, Tarn unfastened the clasp. She gave a faint gasp of relief as the heavy fabric fell on to the stone floor at their feet. Rianna didn't seem to care that she was left almost naked, the remnants of her nightgown hanging in useless tatters away from her.

'Now,' she demanded, digging her nails into the skin of his shoulders.

Tarn began to thrust into her with deep powerful strokes, feeling the weight of her body bearing down on to his straining cock. His movements became faster and he knew by the tightness of her cunt and the small whimpering sounds she was making that she was close to her climax. Her pale cheeks grew flushed, her lips trembled and her green eyes darkened as passion overwhelmed her. She burrowed her face into the base of his neck, nipping at the skin with her teeth as her internal muscles contracted in orgasmic waves.

Tarn climaxed immediately, giving a loud resounding roar that echoed around the narrow corridor, totally drowning out Rianna's mutual gasp of pleasure.

Queen Danara was nowhere to be seen as Sarin was dragged into her anteroom by two burly female guards. He shivered nervously. He had been here many times before in the six months he'd been in Freygard and he never knew what to expect from the beautiful cold-hearted Queen.

Sarin made no attempt to struggle as he was man-handled to the centre of the room and forced to his knees on the dark polished-wood floor. In a fair fight Sarin suspected he could probably have defeated both these female guards. Despite their muscular build they were still women and no match for a skilled warrior such as he. He couldn't fight them today, however, because his hands were fastened behind his back with metal restraints, while his ankles were hobbled together by a short length of timber, which made it difficult to walk in anything but a slow stilted shuffle.

One of the guards thumped him on the back and Sarin couldn't stop himself falling face down on to the boards with a loud smack, only just managing to turn his head in time to stop his nose from getting smashed on impact. The guard gave a sarcastic chuckle and muttered something derogatory about men under her breath, then left along with her companion. Sarin knew that they would not go far, they would remain on guard just outside the door of the chamber, ready to come to the Queen's aide in a second if she needed them.

Sarin struggled to his knees, cursing every woman in Freygard to perdition, presuming he was about to be punished once again. At least this time it would not be for some insignificant fault conjured up by the slave mistress because his lack of servility infuriated her. This time he had stubbornly refused to do as he had been ordered. He might be a captive here, and an unwilling slave, but he hadn't forgotten his heritage; he was still of royal blood. Sarin had fallen low, but not low enough to shovel stinking shit from the midden and heap it into carts to be carried away.

Sometimes he found it hard to clearly remember his former life, beyond the borders of Freygard. This stone fortress set on a nameless peak was home for him now and in the foreseeable future. Nevertheless, he had not yet surrendered his spirit, or allowed himself to be totally subjugated. He was determined to somehow find a way to escape, or if necessary perish in the attempt. Death was infinitely preferable to this life of subjugation and slavery.

When he'd first been imprisoned he'd expected a rescue mission from Percheron, even though Queen Danara had laughingly told him that a message had been sent to his people stating that after he and his men had left the protection of her fortress they had been waylaid and butchered by bandits. Sarin had been certain that his people would not believe such falsehoods and would send a large contingent of soldiers to discover his true fate. But the rescuers had never come; he had been abandoned and betrayed by his courtiers and subjects.

Sarin was a brave man but Danara frightened him far

more than he cared to admit. She had reached into his soul and found a deep dark part of him that actually found pleasure in being enslaved and abused. In Percheron he had been the master, now he was experiencing the other side of the coin. He was a helpless victim.

He heard footsteps and all thoughts fled his mind. Turning his head he saw Danara walking towards him, looking as chillingly beautiful as ever in a filmy violet gown. A shiver of terrified excitement slithered down his spine and he felt his belly tighten; his cock stirred beneath his blue thigh-length tunic, which was the only garment the male slaves in the castle wore. The Queen had spent hours in the past teasing and torturing his senses almost beyond endurance. Sarin was obsessed with Danara; the more she abused him the more he wanted her. Sarin never knew what to expect when he was summoned to her presence. Sometimes it was pleasure; more often than not it was punishment, or an exquisitely tantalising mixture of both. She might just beat him, allow him to pleasure her, or even tease and caress him with her own hands. Yet in all the many hours he had spent with her, he had never been permitted to couple with her as a man would with a woman. Sarin was determined that one day, before he left this place, he would do just that.

'The slave mistress tells me that you have performed some of your tasks very well.' Danara tapped the leather bound switch she carried against the filmy skirt of her gown. 'You have proved to be the best and most productive stud in the coupling chambers.'

Men were of use for only two things in Freygard: as slaves or providers of seed. Coupling was to be endured in order to provide offspring. It was considered an uncomfortable chore by most of the women, who preferred to find their sensual enjoyment with those of their own sex. If a girl child was born they rejoiced, while a male child was raised in a separate settlement and upon reaching adulthood took his place among the other slaves.

Over the years the bloodline of the male slaves had grown weak and any new captives were welcome additions to the coupling chambers, especially powerful warriors such as Sarin. At least a dozen of Danara's best soldiers were now pregnant by Sarin, and he had to admit that this part of his life was reasonably pleasurable. He had even managed to persuade some of them to relax and take their time, to enjoy the sensual delights of having sex with a man. One in particular, Zene, a member of the Queen's personal guard, enjoyed herself so much she had met secretly with Sarin and repeated the experience a number of times. He knew that she'd grown fond of him and she had already tentatively offered to aid his escape as long as she could travel with him to Percheron. Zene was eager to taste what the world could offer her, away from this rigidly controlled female community.

'The slave mistress honours me,' Sarin said, his lips twisting into a sarcastic smile.

'Your manner is insolent.' Danara stepped closer and stared coldly down at him. 'Slaves must be submissive and do as they are told. It appears you forget that far too often.'

'I will never surrender.' Sarin stiffened, reminding himself of his noble heritage as he continued to stubbornly stare at her, even though slaves were supposed to keep their eyes lowered when in her presence.

'Will you never learn?' She shook her head reprovingly, then used the tip of the switch to lift up the hem of his tunic. 'It seems not,' she added with a cruel smile as she caught sight of his semi-aroused cock.

'You are a woman and I'm a man. Why should my body not automatically show desire?' he replied, grinning insolently. 'Men are the conquerors and true masters – born into this world to control women. We always have been the stronger sex and always will be.'

'Still after all this time you chafe against your chains,' she muttered, half to herself.

'Why not?' he proudly challenged. 'I'll never truly be enslaved.'

'Eventually you will submit,' she sneered.

'Never,' he vehemently vowed. 'One day I swear I'll force you to your knees, and you'll rue the day you tried to subjugate Lord Sarin of Percheron.'

'Bold words for one in your position, but they are just the empty threats of a helpless slave,' she replied with chilling confidence. 'However, *my* threats are far from empty!' She slapped the switch across his upper arm, leaving a thin red weal on his olive skin.

Grabbing hold of Sarin's long dark hair, Danara jerked his head back and stared into his eyes. His stubborn pride kept him strong, enabling him to stare boldly back at her, and hide the sudden apprehensive fear that flooded his veins. She tugged at the thin ties that held his garment together at his shoulders, and the blue linen fell in untidy folds around his knees, baring his body to her gaze. Sarin was even more firmly muscled now than when he'd been the ruler of Percheron as his body had been honed and moulded by the hours of heavy labour he did under the merciless gaze of the slave mistress. Sarin missed the long, lazy, sunny days in the luxurious surroundings of his palace. The endless nights he had spent being pleasured by both his male and female slaves. Now he was the one who had to perform, and try to please the many different women who visited the coupling chambers at night.

'Stand up,' Danara snapped. 'Move over to the table.'

Sarin struggled to his feet. he did not dare to disobey, knowing that if he did not do as he was told he would be humbled into obedience by the guards. He shuffled forwards, his movements hampered by the cruel hobble attached to his ankles. Danara smiled, amused by his stilted gait as he approached the table with its smooth polished-wood top and leather padded edges. Sarin had often wondered how many other slaves had been forced to bend their upper bodies across this object, which masqueraded as a table but was actually a punishment block.

He did not wait for her command, just leaned obediently forwards so that the padded edge of the table dug into his belly and his upper torso was laid against the cold oak slab. Then he felt her hands on his wrists, unfastening his bonds. As he moved his arms, stretching them across the tabletop, the blood surged through his cramped limbs. His muscles tingled into life, but before he could regain his full strength, Danara had fastened his wrists to the restraints, set in opposite corners, close to the edges of the table. His upper body was spread-eagled across the wood, and he pressed his cheek to the smooth surface, both fearing and anticipating what would come next. So many times in days gone past Danara had chained him here and shown him, in a variety of ways, how pain could subtly be transformed into aching pleasure.

With his legs held apart by the hobble, his balls and cock were even more exposed than usual, hanging defensively down between his parted thighs. Sarin felt the trickles of fearful excitement slide down his spine and lodge heavily in his groin as he waited. Standing directly behind him, Danara drew back her arm and hit him hard with the leather switch. Using just the right amount of force, she expertly employed the switch, crisscrossing Sarin's taut buttocks with kissing weals of pain. Sarin clenched his teeth, conscious that with the stinging agony came the slow subtle sensations of arousal. He was determined not to cry out as the beating continued, ever aware that part of him welcomed each lovingly applied stroke. His breathing quickened as each starburst of agony sent lust pounding through his veins. He felt his cock twitch and stiffen, spurred into life by the cruel caress of the lash.

The tension in his loins increased and his cock, which

grew harder from the painful stimulation, longed for the gentle feel of hands, lips, or better still the hot moistness of Danara's cunt. The beating continued until the skin on his arse turned an angry red.

'You deserve this punishment, don't you, slave?' she said softly. She stopped hitting him and ran her fingertips over the mesh of red lines that now decorated his skin, her gentle touch serving only to further magnify the delectable agony.

'Yes,' he gasped as her cool fingers slipped between his thighs.

She cupped the soft sac of his balls in her hands. 'I am told by the slave mistress that your seed is proving to be very powerful,' she purred, her fingers closing possessively around the root of his penis. 'That heartens me, even though your continued disobedience displeases me greatly.'

Sarin's legs trembled; his senses were focused on a knife-edge of lust. He wanted to beg her to stimulate him; he was desperate to feel those cool, slim fingers sliding caressingly up and down his cock. Yet he still had enough strength to remain silent. He could smell the warm scent of her jasmine perfume and it reminded him painfully of the fragrant gardens of his palace in Aguilar – a place he did not allow himself to think of too often. He desired Danara so much that the powerful need almost overwhelmed the throbbing pain in his buttocks. Discomfort paled into insignificance compared to his passion for this cruel bitch. As she began to stimulate him in a gentle stroking motion, he failed to stifle the sobbing, 'Please,' that somehow escaped his lips.

'What are you asking for, slave?' she taunted, wanking him until he grew iron hard and a single dewdrop seeped from the tip. 'Do you want me to whip you again until you climax from the pleasure, or shall I make you wear the harness you both crave and despise?'

Danara was often able to read Sarin's thoughts, sense the powerful and often bizarre fantasies that crowded into his mind, but on this occasion she was entirely wrong. His only desire was to tie her down, bind her as thoroughly as he now was, then fuck her until she was forced to acknowledge that he was her master and she was his willing slave.

'The choice is yours,' he grated. 'I have no say in the matter.'

'No, you do not,' she said, and he tensed apprehensively at the menace in her voice.

Danara had ordered a special harness to be fashioned especially for Sarin. The garment, made of leather and metal, was designed to fit perfectly around the base of his engorged penis, keeping it permanently erect, while tightly containing his balls. When he wore it, Danara would chain him to a post in her bedchamber and amuse herself by keeping him tantalisingly close to climaxing for what seemed like hours on end. The need to come would drive Sarin almost insane before Danara was finished with her cruel game. She had told him that this carefully administered sexual torture would increase the strength and potency of his seed, ensuring that all the children he sired would be female.

'I have a mind to try something different today,' she purred, running her cool hands over his abused flesh. 'But first I must ensure that your body will bear no marks of your beating. If I ever decide to sell you in the slave markets you must be healthy and your skin unblemished. Obvious lash marks lower the price. They show the prospective buyer that the slave in question is surly and disobedient.'

Danara began to anoint his buttocks with a sweet-smelling ointment that she'd often used on him in the past. It cooled his reddened skin, and for a moment he allowed himself to enjoy the soothing sensation. But he tensed again when her hands, still slippery with the ointment, ran teasingly up and down his cock, flooding his loins with the familiar lustful submission. Sarin felt the dark pleasure expand and grow as she expertly

27

masturbated him until he was breathing heavily and was dangerously close to coming.

Sarin gave a soft moan.

'Not yet, slave,' she hissed, knowing his responses all too well. She dug her fingernails into the sensitive skin on his cock head and the pain cut through his pleasure like a sword thrust, quashing his desire in an instant as he struggled to stifle the scream that rose in his throat. Danara let go of him and patted Sarin's buttocks as a master would his favourite horse. 'Fulfilment has to be earned,' she told him, heaping fiery coals on to his pain and humiliation.

Sarin slowly expelled a breath, while a string of vile curses filled his thoughts. He was consumed with frustrated anger and hate. Danara was accustoming his body to a diet of pain mixed with carefully applied pleasure. If she continued long enough she was bound to achieve her objective and subjugate him completely. Sarin knew how well such measures worked; had he not used the selfsame methods on Tarn? His strength and his self-respect were steadily being sucked out of him, and he knew that he had to find a way to escape or lose both his body and his soul to Danara.

# Chapter Two

$D$anara released Sarin's wrists but he made no attempt to fight her when she refastened them together in front of his body with a short length of chain. There was no point in physical resistance, her guards were within earshot and could be called upon at any time.

He heard her walk away as he straightened his back, easing the discomfort in his cramped muscles. Sarin was infuriated by his own weakness, knowing he could not fight her forever and fearing that one day soon his resolve would give way. Uselessly, he pulled at the chain that held his wrists together, knowing full well his bonds were far stronger than his own self-willed determination.

'Come into my bedchamber, slave,' he heard Danara say.

Sarin turned and shuffled awkwardly towards her, gritting his teeth at the discomfort as the hobble chafed the skin of his inner ankles. Hatred of Danara filled every fibre of his being, yet even now he was consumed by desire for this cruel bitch as he followed her into the adjoining bedchamber.

As she turned, the light from one of the tall arched windows streamed through her dress and beneath the filmy garment she was totally naked. Sarin's heart began to beat faster. He anxiously scanned the room, looking for any sign of the harness or the other painful instruments she had used upon him in the past, but he saw nothing sinister at all. Yet he could still feel the burning ache of need in his groin, the slight stinging discomfort where her fingernails had dug into him, and he knew he was far from safe.

The women in Percheron surrounded themselves with elaborate fripperies but Danara's bedroom was spartan in its simplicity, apart from the brocade-draped bed. She was so very different from the beautiful, submissive females of his seraglio. Sarin was certain that buried deep inside her was the soul of a true woman, one he could tame. He tried to keep his mind focused on that one thought as he paused apprehensively at the end of her bed.

'Do you know,' she said softly. 'I've never found the company of a man stimulating before.' She ran her hands over the well-defined plains of his muscular chest, then paused to tease each small flat brown nipple in turn until they stiffened into tiny peaks. 'All the other male slaves are weak and servile creatures. Only you Sarin, and Tarn before you, have had the strength and determination to resist enslavement. I find such resolve challenging. Would that I had you both here to serve me.'

'You could have refused the Lady Kitara's request to free Tarn, could you not?' Sarin retorted. He constantly regretted his decision to follow Tarn and Rianna into Freygard when they had fled from Percheron. Danara had given Rianna refuge willingly enough, but had then proceeded to imprison Tarn in the slave quarters and force him to serve in the coupling chambers. It was only at the instigation of Rianna's long-lost mother that they had both been allowed to leave. Kitara had gone with them to be reunited with Rianna's father, Gerek – the Protector of Harn – while Sarin had been left behind as Danara's slave.

'Kitara is my kinswoman, and of noble blood. She had the right to demand Tarn's release into her custody,' Danara said, failing to hide the resentment she held towards her cousin. Sarin knew she had never forgiven Kitara for falling in love with a man. 'It appears, Sarin, that I will have to be content with just you to serve me.' She reached inside her gown and removed one of the decorative clamps she had attached to her nipples.

In Freygard women rarely wore any jewellery apart from the highly prized decorative clamps which were gifted to them by a close relative when they reached the age of majority. The gold was still warm from the heat of Danara's body as she imprisoned Sarin's left nipple in its tiny teeth. Then she pulled at the clamp, stretching the sensitive flesh until the discomfort caused an answering tug in the pit of his groin. 'So you will,' he agreed, his desire increasing as it always did when she teased him, while he wondered when the true extent of her cruelty would surface again. Danara's moods could change like the wind: hard and fierce one moment, soft and gentle the next.

'You both irritate and amuse me, Sarin. You appear to want to resist at all costs, yet you also secretly enjoy the punishments you are forced to endure at my hands.'

'I do not,' he insisted.

'You try to deceive yourself as well as me,' she countered, running her hands over his chest, and underneath his dark hair, which had grown so long that it hung in tangled disarray around his shoulders, partially concealing the leather collar he constantly wore. This was his badge of servitude, which had been placed around his neck by Danara during the first few hours of his imprisonment.

Danara took hold of the length of chain she kept permanently fixed to her bedpost and fastened it to the back of his collar, just as she always did when she intended to keep him in her chamber all night.

'You may free your ankles,' she said coldly, watching

31

as he bent and struggled to unfasten the buckles of the hated hobble.

It wasn't easy to unfasten them with his hands chained together but he managed to free himself and kicked the hated object away in disgust. Danara frowned in annoyance when she saw the red and inflamed patch on each of Sarin's ankles, where the skin had been rubbed raw by the ends of the wooden bar.

Sarin glanced pointedly at the chain tethering him to her bed, then at his chained wrists. 'Do I frighten you so much that you feel you have to keep me confined in your presence?' he sneered.

'The warriors of Freygard do not fear anyone,' she said proudly. 'But I would be a fool to even chance trusting you to behave as you should.'

'I have no wish for you to *ever* feel you can trust me,' he replied with a wry twist of his lips. 'Once you do so, I will know that I am lost.' He stared boldly back at Danara, and it was she who turned away first.

Sarin enjoyed his brief moment of power as she walked over to a carved cupboard placed close to the side of her bed. 'See this?' she said, removing a dildo attached to a prettily tooled white leather harness. 'Do you know what it is?'

'Yes.' Sarin nodded. 'Only too well. Do you wear it when one of your warriors shares your bed, or do you prefer it to be used on you, Danara?' he jibed with a trace of his former arrogance. 'Does it feel good when it is thrust inside you? I assure you the hot hard flesh of a man is far better, far more satisfying.'

'I doubt that,' she countered. 'And the way I take my pleasure with those of the sisterhood is none of your concern, slave!'

She tossed the object on the bed. There was a protrusion on the inside as well, so that both she and her partner would be stimulated at the same time.

'One of my women in Percheron gained pleasure from such an instrument. I sometimes allowed her to use it to

32

punish my recalcitrant male slaves,' Sarin said, fearing that Danara intended to use it on him. When he'd watched the slaves writhing beneath Niska's thrusting hips, he had almost envied them, and wondered what it would feel like to have such an object powering deep inside his own anus, yet he had never tried it himself.

'I should like to meet her,' Danara said. 'She sounds a woman close to my heart.'

'Not close enough. Niska was one of my wives. She lived only to serve me.'

'While *you* serve me, Sarin,' Danara reminded him as she slowly removed her gown.

Sarin's blood grew hot with fearful anticipation. He had seen her naked often, but her beauty never failed to move him. Danara's training as a warrior had given her the most perfect body. Her limbs were long and slender, her torso well toned, and her breasts full, firm and luscious. As Danara moved, her full breasts jiggled slightly and the tiny chains dangling from the remaining nipple clamp swayed enticingly, reminding Sarin of the teeth tightly clamped to his own nipple. Sarin swallowed hard as she sat down on the edge of the bed and opened her thighs. It had been the custom in Percheron for the women of his seraglio to be denuded, and the sight of Danara's thick dark auburn pelt excited him. It reminded Sarin of how much of a barbarian she truly was – this bitch who drove him almost to the edge of insanity.

'Kneel,' Danara haughtily ordered, beckoning him forwards. 'Pleasure me with your mouth.'

The familiar yielding lust flooded through Sarin's veins and he couldn't deny that he wanted to do as she commanded. Sweat pooled in his armpits and between his thighs as he stepped forwards and fell to his knees between her open legs.

Hungrily he pressed his face to her cunt, burrowing his nose in the auburn curls. Her musky odour was more inviting than a bowl of sweet-scented roses, more intoxicating than the finest of wines. He kissed her hungrily, sliding his tongue teasingly between the pink petals, running it along the moist valley of her sex.

Sarin knew that goading and provoking him secretly turned her on. Why else would she be so wet and ready each time she allowed him to touch her? Today the moisture was even more copious than usual. As he ran his tongue along the soaking folds, he drank her dew, savouring its familiar musky taste. Danara gave a soft, unconscious groan as his mouth burrowed deeper, while his tongue circled the root of her clit. The flesh there was already tight and swollen. He pulled the firm berry between his lips and sucked on it hard.

Danara pressed herself closer to Sarin's face as he tentatively probed the entrance to her vagina, feeling the hot welcoming moistness. Forcing his muscles to stretch to their fullest extent he probed deeper, thrusting into her with sharp stabbing movements that made her moan aloud with pleasure.

Sensing that she was close to coming, Sarin bunched three fingers together and plunged them into her, mimicking the movement his cock longed to make. He mouthed her again, thrusting even harder with his bunched fingers, ignoring her sudden growl of fury and rubbing his thumb over her clit. Too overcome to resist, Danara surrendered to her steadily rising pleasure. Sarin thrust faster, deeper, until he felt her internal muscles tighten in rhythmic waves as her climax came.

Filled with the most intense feeling of satisfaction, Sarin no longer cared how angry she would be as he pulled away from her and crouched in a foetal position, close to her feet, his hands reaching for his aching prick. He grabbed and pumped furiously, desperate to come before she recovered enough to begin punishing him again. Somewhere in the distance he heard Danara's angry shout, but he was too caught up in his own lust to care as he vigorously masturbated his cock. His pleasure built swiftly and he wanked harder, barely aware of the sound of running feet, followed by the sharp sting of the lash on his back and buttocks.

He was tantalising close to his climax, but before he could come, he was yanked to his feet, pulled so hard that the chain at his neck stretched taut and the collar dug into his throat, stifling his frustrated yell. The desperate pressure in his groin increased as he was flung face down on the bed, arms stretched above his head. His legs were pulled apart, held wide open by tightly tied ropes, while he writhed and struggled, trying to find purchase on the soft mattress to stimulate himself further and achieve the orgasm he so desperately craved.

Consumed by fearful frustration, he found himself tightly confined, barely able to move a muscle. Then he felt a steady trickle of oil being directed down the slit of his buttocks. As it pooled warmly around his anus, Sarin gave an unconscious pleading whimper. He raised his head to look at Danara. She was strapping on a phallic appendage that looked almost twice the size of the one she'd shown him earlier. The black phallus was smooth, shiny and frighteningly huge. Abject terror pulsed throughout his veins, accompanied by a dark excitement that turned his limbs to water. The wild sensations swamped his senses and he tensed apprehensively as Danara mounted the bed and crouched over him.

He was too scared to even shiver as he felt the cold hardness pressed against his tightly clenched sphincter muscles. Danara pushed hard, and with the help of the oil it began to enter him. Sarin had never been penetrated in such a crude manner. The sensation was strange, terrifying, and yet superbly pleasurable. He held his breath, feeling the cold hardness force his internal muscles to stretch and expand. The sharp, sweet pain of innocence turned to the dark viscous pleasure of submission as it thrust deeper, until it was buried to the hilt inside Sarin's helpless flesh.

Danara placed her hands on the small of his back to aid her stability as she began to move her hips, powering in and out of him with hard thrusting movements. The sensations were indescribably cruel but infinitely perfect, and Sarin lost himself in the steadily deepening pool of dark, aching bliss.

He pushed his pelvis into the soft mattress, unable to escape the relentless thrusts that set each nerve ending alight. The forceful movements made the sensitive skin of his cock-shaft rub sensuously against the soft linen sheets, increasing his arousal even more. A sudden, violent orgasm ripped through his body from penis to anus, every muscle in his pelvis clenching spasmodically as wave after wave of it swept through his flesh. Sarin was so overcome, he was barely able to take a short, sobbing breath, let alone realise that tears were sliding from his eyes and running down his flushed cheeks.

Leon lingered in the bailey, enjoying the last remnants of the weak afternoon sunshine. He loathed the air of neglect that permeated the castle, and the stale mustiness of its faded furnishings. It was good to be outside in the fresh winter air. He could understand Lady Rianna's frustration at being forced to remain here after Prince Tarn had left that morning. It wasn't a place Leon would choose to stay in for long, but he had no choice – he was under specific orders from his sovereign lord to remain here until it was safe to proceed. Leon had already sent most of his soldiers into the forest to flush out any bandits in the area. He had kept only three men-at-arms to help guard the castle walls, which were thick and high enough to protect them against anything but the most determined assault.

'My lord,' Leon heard someone call. He turned his head to see a young maidservant running toward him.

'Yes?' he asked as she halted breathlessly in front of him.

She blushed, and bobbed a curtsey. 'A message was brought here by one of the local peasants. 'Tis from a lady lodged in the village.' She held out a piece of folded parchment.

The thick parchment crackled as Leon turned it over and examined the heavy seal, recognising it at once. He was half-afraid to believe that what he was seeing was true. 'You may go,' he said distractedly. The crest belonged to the Baroness Crissana, a beautiful noble-woman he'd met just over two months ago in Ruberoc, the capital city of Kabra.

Regardless of the recent conflict, many travellers still chose to use the trade route that cut across Kabra, mainly because the land to the west was often near impassable and the land to the east was dangerous to travellers of any kind. The ruler of Freygard did not allow strangers across the borders of her land and most men refused to travel there, fearing that they might be captured by the wild warrior women and enslaved.

Leon had been captivated by the wealthy baroness and she had appeared equally taken by his charms. The lady was recently widowed, and had been travelling north to visit her family when the fighting had become too heavy for her to continue in safety. She had take refuge for a short time in Ruberoc, and had been residing in the same inn as Leon, where they'd met, quite by chance. He'd done his best to entertain her, and soon they had become embroiled in a passionate affair. Leon had fallen deeply and foolishly in love. He was of noble blood, his father was an advisor to King Brion, and he had truly hoped their liaison might eventually lead to marriage. But she had told him quite determinedly that she had no plans to remain in Kabra, and as soon as it was safe enough she intended to continue her journey north.

It was the first time Leon had ever fallen in love, and he still dreamed of her at night, hoping against hope that one day he'd see her again. Yet he'd never expected to come across her in the middle of the damnable forest. He opened the letter, scanning it quickly. The gods had been kind to him after all. The baroness was now less than a league away from here in the local village.

He had to see her now, he thought, as he stuffed the letter inside his metal-studded leather doublet. He walked swiftly to the stables and waited impatiently until his horse was saddled. The bandits were far from his thoughts as he rode at a fast gallop along the narrow track through the forest, consumed by the need to see his ladylove again.

The village was even more run-down than the castle, a small huddle of wattle-daubed houses in a large clearing. Leon was surprised that the baroness hadn't called at the castle and asked for rooms for herself and her servants as it was the custom for landowners in Kabra to offer wealthy travellers lodgings for the night.

The inhabitants of the local village were peasants who scraped a meagre living from the small patches of open land to the east of the settlement, and they looked even dirtier and scrawnier than the servants in the castle did.

Leon noticed a small group of heavily armed men sitting on some rickety benches in front of a run-down tavern. A skinny young woman was serving them beakers of wine, but the rest of the villagers were giving them a wide berth, which wasn't surprising as their clothing and armaments showed them to be mercenaries. Some wore the elaborate breastplates and thick, brightly coloured, striped breeches of the western plainsmen; their long frizzy red hair was held back by thin bands of metal across their brows. Others came from the Seminite Mountains. Their skin had a yellowish brown tinge, their eyes were dark, mere thinly lidded slits, and their hair was pulled back so tight in long pigtails that their skin seemed to stretch even more tautly across their high cheekbones. Their individual castes were denoted by the different designs of their heavy gold armlets and the number of thick gold rings piercing their ears. There were others, fierce-looking men in strange unidentifiable costumes, and Leon had no idea from whence they came.

The mercenaries ceased their laughing and joking to stare pointedly at Leon as he rode towards them. Leon could only suppose that the baroness had hired the men to protect her on her journey north, but he questioned the wisdom of such a decision. Before they'd parted, she had told Leon that she planned to travel north with a caravan of merchants who had obtained a promise of safe passage from the two warring factions in Kabra. Leon wondered what had caused her to change her mind. He didn't trust mercenaries. From what he knew of them, they were likely to turn on those they were hired to protect if the price was right.

One man, with dark skin, a scarred face and almond eyes, stood up, pulling a heavy purple silk cloak around his wide shoulders. He looked Leon squarely in the eye. 'Captain Leon, I presume?' he said in an oddly accented voice, with no trace of the deference Leon expected from a common soldier. 'My mistress is expecting you.'

Leon nodded. He let his reins fall across the neck of his mount and rested his right hand casually on the pommel of his sword as he slowly followed the man, guiding his horse with his knees. The brightly coloured tents of the mercenaries' encampment were at the eastern edge of the village. More mercenaries, many more than Leon had expected to see, lounged around the tents and sat by the campfires. They were all just as well armed and as threatening as the others were. Some looked curiously at Leon as he rode past them; others ignored him and carried on their conversations or busied themselves sharpening their vast array of weapons.

He noticed two who stood out from the rest of the fiercely disreputable group. Half a head taller than anyone else, and far more muscular, they had skin that looked almost jet-black. Leon had heard tales of these dark-skinned races, but he had never actually seen such a man in the flesh.

He dismounted, still feeling uneasy at the presence of so many mercenaries, and followed the man towards the largest of the tents. It was very luxurious by Leon's military standards, with a thick, brightly patterned carpet covering the floor, lush silken pillows and gold lamps set on low wooden tables. The tent was heated by hot coals burning in large braziers and was pleasantly warm. Leon found it far more appealing than his quarters in the castle.

When he at last caught sight of the woman he longed to see again, his heart beat faster. She was even more stunningly beautiful than he remembered. Her blonde hair, so pale it looked almost silver, was coiled tightly atop her head, and the heavily embroidered azure-blue gown she wore emphasised the strange colour of her eyes. The irises were the most extraordinary pale blue, like limpid pools of moonlight with darkly defined rims.

'My love,' he said, stepping forwards to kiss her hand. 'I had not thought to see you again.'

'Leon,' she replied in her husky, sensuous voice that made his knees grow weak. 'Fate is strange, is it not? You may go, Chang,' she told the mercenary.

Once they were alone, she removed his sword from its scabbard and placed it beside one of the braziers, then led him towards a low couch covered in thick white fur. Leon's breath caught in his throat as they sat down and she turned towards him. The thin blue silk clung to her shapely breasts and he could have sworn she was wearing nothing underneath as he could see the outline of her pale nipples; one of which he knew was pierced by a ring from which dangled a perfect tear-shaped diamond. He had never known anyone like this woman, her presence made him feel excited and wildly alive. She was a proud and wilful noblewoman, yet in bed she was loving and passionate, more knowledgeable about pleasing a man than the most experienced courtesan.

She turned towards a side table, intending to pour him some wine, but Leon could not wait. Giving in to his most base urges, he grabbed hold of her and pulled her close, covering her lips with his and plunging his tongue

40

deep into her mouth. She tasted of honey, and sweet-scented cloves. The feel of her soft body, coupled with the scent of her exotic perfume, made his senses swim and spurred him onwards. Roughly Leon forced his hand into the front of her gown, ripping the small silver buttons from their loops. He cupped her breast, feeling the cold harness of the diamond attached to her nipple pressing against his palm. She gave a soft moan and melted against him, returning his kiss with passionate abandonment, while he eased his hand lower. Urgently Leon ripped open the front of her gown, baring her entire torso. He stroked the swell of her belly and the smooth, naked skin of her mons. He had always found her lack of bodily hair exciting. It made him think he was making love to an innocent young virgin, who responded to his caresses with the expertise of a whore. The contrast was tantalisingly sensual and fired his lust.

Blood rushed to his head. 'I've missed you,' he growled, holding her close, his fingers digging into her flesh as she tried to pull away from him.

'I have missed you also,' she said breathlessly. 'Now desist, Leon. Tis not the time; we need to talk.'

Leon could not ignore the rigid hardness of his cock pressing against the constricting tightness of his breeches. 'No,' he grunted, his desire spiralling out of control. He ripped her dress fully apart, pushed her prone on the couch and leaped astride her hips. Invigorated by the yielding wetness of her flesh, he thrust his fingers deep inside her.

When she moaned and worked her hips against his invading digits, he pulled away from her, jerked open his breeches and mounted her in one swift movement. As he buried his cock deep into the soft warmth, she gave an angry squeal and resisted, trying desperately to buck him off her. Leon was far stronger and he ignored her struggles. She raked her nails down his cheek, and the pain only served to incite Leon even more. Filled with a powerful craving to vanquish her completely, and driven by the basest of urges, he powered into her, each pounding thrust slamming his pelvic bone hard against hers.

She squirmed beneath him, and the smell of her, the feel of her, drove him into a wild frenzy. All of a sudden she stopped struggling and gave a submissive moan as she twined her legs around his hips. It felt as if he was somehow sliding deeper into her with each violent thrust, and Leon lost himself in the straining bliss. The pressure gradually began to build inside him, until the blood roared in his ears, his entire body a tight mass of pleasure. Then his orgasm came, exploding with a powerful wrenching spasm that forced a triumphant cry from his lips.

His limbs trembling and rationality slowly returning, Leon looked down at the lady he adored. During their wild encounter she had dug her sharp little teeth into her lower lip and it was covered with bright beads of blood. She smiled, pursing her blood-spattered mouth, and pulled his head down to kiss him. Leon tasted the metallic, saltiness of her blood as her tongue squirmed erotically into his mouth.

Leon was filled with the sudden longing to bury his head between her thighs and savour the nectar of their union, suck her dry and feel her come against his open mouth. But first he had to put matters right between them. He pulled away from her and collapsed limply at her side. 'I am sorry,' he muttered awkwardly. 'I was crude and brutal.'

'What is there to apologise for?' She unfastened his doublet and eased it off, then took the dagger from his belt and held the blade to his chest, close to his beating heart. 'Should I punish you for giving me pleasure?' she teased as she cut the laces of his shirt, pulling the fabric apart so that she could trail her mouth over the hard planes of his chest. She caressed his body, working his nipples, nibbling and nipping at them with her sharp little teeth.

42

'I only thought of my own needs,' he gasped, writhing with pleasure.

'Not so,' she purred with a wide sensuous smile. Leon had always found it strange that her small upper incisors were filed into sharp points. He could only presume it was the usual custom in Vestfold, the land of her birth. Like most of his peers, he knew little of the cold lands north of Kabra.

'I never knew you could be so wild, so savage,' she added, running her fingers over the long red wheal she had carved on his cheek. 'Your passion pleased me more than you'll ever know.'

'I've never met anyone like you,' he confessed. Leon had never bedded a female, let alone a noblewoman, who enjoyed being treated in such a violent manner.

'I should hope you have not.' She lapped up the layer of salty perspiration that lingered on his skin. Trailing her lips lower she circled his belly button, then dipped the tip of her tongue into the shallow well.

'That's good,' Leon gasped, as she moved closer to his cock, which lay limp on its crisp brown bed of curls. He was unable to quell a soft groan as she touched it with her tongue, licking the shaft with long strokes as a cat would when cleaning itself. Leon's flesh was still over sensitised by his recent climax, and he shuddered as she circled the tender tip. 'I can taste your essence mingled with mine,' she murmured, pulling the head into her mouth.

Even though she was being extraordinarily gentle, Leon could hardly bear the feel of her lips. His body had not yet recovered from his recent climax, and pleasure was tempered by aching discomfort, but despite everything he was becoming more and more aroused.

Keeping him trapped in the hot wetness of her mouth, she swivelled round, until she was sitting astride his waist. Leon was faced with the delectable sight of her pale buttocks bobbing sensuously up and down as she mouthed his cock. He grunted and shuddered as she

43

gradually eased her body upwards, and her firm buttock cheeks opened enough to allow him a brief glimpse of the rosy brown ring hidden inside. Leon had never considered penetrating that orifice before, but he did now, overcome by the eroticism of the sight.

Soon she was crouched astride his head, her open quim poised tantalisingly above his face. Her strong musky odour excited Leon as he stared up at the gaping rosy flesh. 'Taste me,' she begged, pressing herself hard against his face.

Leon kissed her, sliding his tongue along the soft folds, while he felt her mouth continue to work on his aching shaft. Burrowing his lips deeper he found the hard pip of her clitoris and pulled it into his mouth, sucking on it sensuously until he heard her muffled groans. He felt his cock grow rigid, but at the same time the acute discomfort increased. No matter how hard he tried, he knew that he would be unable to respond to the need to climax again. With increased urgency his lips worked their magic: sucking, licking and nibbling until he felt her body tense against his mouth. She shuddered, pushing her body hard against his face as her orgasm came.

Leon gently eased her away from his aching loins. 'I'm not yet ready,' he told her. 'However much I may want it to be,' he added, pulling her round and cradling her in his arms.

'There are advantages to being a woman,' she said with a soft laugh. 'We have the unique ability to reach the peak of pleasure again and again.'

'I had not thought of that before,' Leon confessed, then he remained silent for a moment, before adding, 'How came you here, my love? This is not the road north.'

'Once we had parted I came to realise that I could not face the future without you. I heard tell that you were charged with escorting the Lady Rianna to Harn, so I hired these mercenaries to protect me and followed you. We would have been hard pressed to catch up with you if you had not paused to rest in the castle of Dane.'

'You say that you cannot face the future without me?' Leon asked, hardly able to believe that all he had wished for might be about to come true.

She smiled lovingly. 'Indeed, my lord, I cannot. Now that the battle to free Kabra is over, you can look to the future. Is that not so?'

'So *we* can,' he agreed. 'Nevertheless, I did not think that the news of Prince Tarn's victory would travel so swiftly.'

'It did not,' she replied. 'We heard the joyful news when we arrived in the village a few hours ago. One of the peasants had delivered fresh produce to the castle early this morning and the servants there were all too eager to share their good news. When I learned you were to stay at the castle a few days more I decided to send word to you immediately.'

'Once my men-at-arms return from scouring the forest for the last remaining bandits, we can travel back to Ruberoc together,' Leon said, thinking that the first thing he must do on their return was speak to his father. He was certain that his parents would be delighted with such a match.

Leon knew the baroness was a very rich young woman. Not only did she own vast tracts of land in Percheron, she had in her baggage a chest full of the most magnificent gems he had ever seen. She had told him that most were gifted to her by her late husband and the rest had been part of her own dowry. Once Tarn was King, Leon expected to be rewarded with honours and lands of his own. With the lady he loved at his side, his future now looked better than he had ever expected it to be.

'As you wish,' she said compliantly. 'But first this . . .'

Rising to her knees she straddled Leon again. Gently taking hold of his partially erect cock, she stuffed it inside her, wiggling her hips, burying it deeper and deeper.

\* \* \*

45

Sarin awoke with a start, unsure what had disturbed his slumber. Most probably it was the hardness of the floor coupled with the cold – he had nothing to protect him from the chill night air, apart from his own scanty tunic which he'd used in a useless effort to try and cover himself.

He shivered and sat up, pulling his tunic up over his legs, fastening it as best he could around his waist. Moonlight streamed through the windows and Sarin calculated that there were at least two hours until dawn, maybe even more. He rose stiffly to his feet; his body felt bruised and battered, and there was a dull ache between his buttock cheeks, which served as a permanent reminder of his brutal possession by Danara. Once she had tired of using him in any number of perverse ways she had thrown him out of her bed, commanded him to sleep on the floor as he always did when he spent the night in her room.

Sarin looked at Danara sleeping peacefully in her bed. He was filled with hate and loathing for her. Yet he couldn't ignore the fact that in a bizarre way he'd obtained pleasure from the many cruelties she had inflicted upon him. He took a step back, realising that he could not feel the weight of the chain pulling at his neck. The guards had unfastened it when they had spread-eagled him across the bed, and it appeared that Danara had forgotten to tether him to it again.

Hope leaped within him, this was the opportunity he had been looking for. At this time of night the guards would be far less vigilant, most probably half-asleep. He had to figure out a way to free his hands, then he just might be able to find a way out of the castle. The metal cuffs around his wrists had been welded into place by the castle blacksmith, but for his captors' convenience the chain that held them together was only threaded through a heavy link attached to each bracelet, then fastened together with a simple padlock. It would probably be far quicker to try and force the lock, than find out where

Danara had hidden the key. For all he knew it might not be in her room, she may even have given it to one of the guards.

Sarin prowled silently around the chamber until he found what he needed: a sturdy, sharp-ended hairpin that had been left with a number of others on a low table close to the bed.

A few years ago a thief had been brought before Sarin for judgement. The young man had already been found guilty of a number of crimes and the law decreed that he should be taken to a place of execution and publicly beheaded. Sarin had taken a liking to the handsome youth and instead of sending him to his death had kept him at court as one of his personal body slaves. Their relationship had been very close; the young thief had displayed a passionate enthusiasm for pleasing Sarin in any number of ways. During their time together he had showed Sarin some of the secrets of his former profession. Sarin had watched him pick a variety of different locks and had even tried to do it himself. Eventually he had succeeded, but only with the thief's help, and he knew it was not as easy as it appeared to be.

Once he'd tired of the thief's presence, Sarin had rewarded his loyalty by transmuting his sentence to life imprisonment. He had been sent to the galleys to spend the rest of his days chained to an oar, forced to toil endlessly, and Sarin was all too aware that few galley slaves survived for more than a couple of years.

His body tense with concentration, Sarin inserted the tip of the pin in the keyhole, trying to find the internal mechanism of the lock. Unskilled as he was, he knew it would take a fair amount of patience and determination to locate just the right spot. He struggled on for what seemed like ages, and even began to wonder if he might fail, until he felt something give way inside and heard the faint, encouraging click. Cautiously he pulled at the hasp and it came away in his hands.

Sarin unthreaded the chain and placed it on the floor,

wincing at the faint clinking sound of metal coiling upon metal. As he flexed his arms, he glanced apprehensively towards the bed and was relieved to see no sign of movement from Danara. Feeling more confident, Sarin walked over to a pair of large, carved-wood chests, set against the wall close to one of the tall windows, and eased open the lids. One contained women's clothing, which was of no use, but the other chest was filled with an assortment of garments and weaponry – presumably battle trophies taken from those Danara had killed or enslaved.

Not wanting to make too much noise, Sarin selected the first weapons he came upon: a sturdy serviceable short sword and an ornate dagger with a finely wrought silver hilt. He also found a pair of leather trousers and a fur-lined doublet. He smiled wryly as just beneath them he discovered a long sky-blue, silk pennant, bearing the arms of Percheron, which had not that long ago deco-rated the lance of one of his men-at-arms.

Sarin placed the garments and sword in a pile on the floor. Then, draping the silk pendant around his neck, and clutching the dagger in his hand, he walked silently back to the bed. Danara was still sleeping peacefully, her auburn hair splayed across the pillow, the bedclothes rucked around her naked hips. She was beautiful and he wanted her, perhaps now more than ever. Good sense told him to leave straight away, to make his escape while he could, but Sarin hadn't forgotten his vow – the thought that had helped to keep him defiant and stead-fast all these long months. He was determined to fuck her no matter what.

Letting the blue tunic slip to the floor, he crept to the foot of the mattress. The ropes that had been used on him were still attached to the bed-posts, and it was easy enough to loop them gently around Danara's ankles without waking her. Sarin picked up the braided silk girdle she'd discarded along with her dress, and moved to the side of the bed to look thoughtfully down at the sleeping queen.

Gently he brushed the tips of his fingers across her nipples. They appeared to be slightly elongated by the near permanent pressure of the clamps, which now lay discarded on a bedside table. She moaned and moved her head as Sarin tied the silk girdle around her left wrist. Cautiously he moved her other arm, fastening her wrists together. Fortune was on his side, because she hadn't woken, but he knew he must act swiftly now to achieve his desired objective; he had to be in full control before she came to and realised what was happening. Leaping astride her waist, he held her down with the weight of his body as he placed a hand across her mouth to stifle her surprised screams, and pressed the tip of the dagger to the pulse at the base of her throat.

Danara awoke. Her eyes fluttered open, then widened in terror as she saw Sarin crouching menacingly over her. 'Not a sound,' he warned, pressing the blade harder to her throat until he drew forth a bright bead of blood. 'Call the guards and you'll be dead before they even enter the room,' he continued, inflamed by the raw fear in her eyes.

She was wise enough to heed his warning, knowing better than to chance crying out as he eased his hand from her mouth. 'You'll regret this,' she hissed, before her words were stilled as Sarin gagged her with the silk pennant bearing the arms of Percheron.

Never taking her eyes from her captor, Danara moved slightly to gauge how securely she was confined and Sarin knew by her tense expression that she was scared. To be at the mercy of a mere man was her worst nightmare. Determinedly he forced her arms above her head, and tied them to the rope she'd used not so long ago to secure him in a similar fashion.

'Perfect,' he said softly, his lips twisting in the parody of a smile. 'Just how I like to see my women,' he added, pulling off all her remaining bedclothes.

The many hours she'd spent abusing him were now about to be paid back in abundance. He ran his hands over her naked body, feeling even more empowered as he saw her limbs tremble slightly at his touch. He looked back at her face, heartened by the raw fear in her green eyes, as he played with her nipples, stroking and squeezing them until they hardened and grew even more pronounced. Then he ran his hands caressingly over her flat belly, sliding them between her thighs. 'Not so long ago I was the slave, now you are my captive. Does that frighten you, Danara?' he purred menacingly as he tugged at her abundant curls. 'I confess, I do not like my females to have body hair, it offends me. It's crude and ugly. At home in Percheron, I always insisted that my women have it removed because it distracts from the beauty of the female form.'

Sarin picked up the dagger, holding it in front of her face for a moment, before he ran the flat of the blade slowly over her lower stomach, tracing the line of her pubic hair. An unconscious shiver ran across her belly, then she froze in terror as he angled the blade and started to scrape away the curls. Sarin shaved her pelt slowly, employing great care, having no wish to cut or nick her pale flesh. Of course the women of his seraglio would never have employed such crude methods; the slaves of the hammam used sugaring or plucking to remove the offending hair.

Danara gave a pleading whimper, which was half muffled by her gag, as the cold metal moved closer to her most intimate parts, shaving every inch of her until her quim was as naked as the day she was born. Sarin smiled as he tossed the handful of auburn curls on the sheet beside her, certain that the humiliation of this moment would stay with her for far longer than her pelt took to grow back. 'Much better,' he said to Danara, amused by the expression of helpless fury on her face as he surveyed the result of his endeavours, admiring the way her rosy inner lips peeped out of the innocent-looking little slit.

She squirmed and struggled as he stroked her denuded flesh, sliding his fingers into the pink valley of her sex, surprised at how soft and moist she felt. His own desire increased as he skilfully teased her clit. He didn't want this to be rape, he was determined to make her body respond to him. Then her humiliation and self-anguish would be even more acute.

Sarin was well used to seducing frightened and unwilling females, those who had been gifted to him and were destined to spend their lives pandering to his every need. Most had ended up worshipping him, eager to do anything and everything to please their master. Danara's eyes were still full of hate but her struggles gradually lessened and her hips moved seductively, almost as if she were secretly enjoying the experience.

'You deceive yourself when you say you do not desire a man. However, your body does not lie,' Sarin commented with lustful amusement, feeling her moisture increase until it slickly coated her sex, allowing him to easily slide his fingers inside her. 'You're wet, and *so* ready for me.'

Kneeling between her outstretched thighs Sarin stimulated himself, making sure she could see his every movement, masturbating until his cock hardened into a rigid rod. Danara desperately bit at the silk gag, trying uselessly to force it from her mouth, bucking her hips and wildly shaking her head as Sarin crouched over her, his lust growing. Now he would possess her as a man should a woman, and she would learn to enjoy the pleasure-filled experience. This one supreme act would destroy Danara – once he'd fucked her, the Queen of Freygard would never be quite the same again.

As he tried to enter her, he felt her muscles tense, but even so he managed to slowly force his cock inside her. Her struggles became even more desperate, even more urgent as he inched deeper, until he was almost fully embedded. Suddenly she relaxed and stopped fighting the inevitable. Sarin felt triumphant as he gave a final thrust, then paused, allowing himself time to savour the unique perfection of this moment.

'This will be so good,' he promised Danara. She briefly closed her eyes and Sarin took it as a vain gesture of submission. Amused by her hate and confusion, he wondered how he could both loath, despise and want her all at the same time.

Sarin angled his body so that she would experience the most intense stimulation with each powerful thrust. Then he began to move his hips slowly and seductively, employing all of his skills in order to give his unwilling partner the most profound pleasure, withdrawing occasionally and rubbing the head of his cock over her clit. At first Danara just lay there, meek and acquiescent as if made of stone, but he was determined to overcome her passive resistance as he kept up the relentless rhythm. The room was cold, but a thin layer of perspiration still formed on his skin as his vigorous jerking over her clit became faster and even more demanding.

His arousal increased, his orgasm growing steadily closer. He could stand the suspense no longer, and plunged back into her cunt just in time to feel her internal muscles tighten and see her eyes glaze over as her breathing became ragged and uneven. He fought to hold back on his own release, knowing he was close to winning this battle. Bending his head Sarin pulled one of Danara's nipples into his mouth, sucking on it hard as he sensuously rotated his hips, still keeping up the relentless thrusting rhythm.

Danara gave a muffled moan, her limbs trembling as her climax overwhelmed her, and her cunt tightened around his cock in powerful waves. He could hold back no longer – pulling out of her, he spilt a creamy stream of seed over her belly and breasts. Sarin had no wish for a child to result from this encounter; no female offspring of his would ever rule this accursed land.

Hate and disgust flared again in Danara's eyes, and Sarin knew that she would loathe him even more now that he'd shown her that no matter how much she despised his sex, she could still gain pleasure from coupling with a man.

'I doubt you'll ever forget this encounter,' he said with a taunting grin, wiping his cock clean with a hunk of her hair. 'I would love to stay and remind you of it often, Danara. But sadly I must depart.' He laughed bitterly. 'When we meet again, it will be on a battlefield at the head of our respective armies. One day soon I intend to invade and conquer Freygard, enslave you, Danara, just as you have me!'

If she'd not been gagged venom would have poured from her mouth. Instead Danara gave a muffled grunt and pulled at her bonds so hard that the rope dug deep into her flesh, almost drawing blood. Sarin didn't care much what happened to her now as he sprang from the bed and put on the close-fitting leather trousers and fur-lined doublet, which felt far better than his scanty tunic. He had no boots and he doubted that the sandals he'd worn as a slave would be sturdy enough to survive a long journey, but they would have to do for the present. Picking up the sword, and tucking the dagger in the top of his trousers, he headed towards the far wall of the chamber, which was half covered by a fretwork screen.

Zene had told him that there was a door hidden behind the screen. It led to the great hall and Danara used it when she wanted to spy unseen on her warriors. He glanced back at his Nemesis, still lying bound and gagged on the bed. 'Farewell. You do not realise what a dangerous enemy you've made, Danara,' he coldly warned. Then he stepped into the narrow passageway, which led to another door – hidden by the massive tapestry, depicting scenes from Freygard's history, that decorated the wall of the great hall.

# Chapter Three

*F*ortunately for Sarin, the great hall was empty and silent. In most castles it would have been full of sleeping retainers, bedded down on the cold marble floor. Only the lord and his immediate family would have their own personal bedchambers, but in this castle even the lowliest servants had their own bed to sleep in at night. The women of Freygard did not conform to what others did, they were a law unto themselves.

Moonlight streamed through the large, arched windows. Sarin kept to the shadows, creeping along close to the walls, aiming for the main doors which, according to custom, were always left partially open. The castle guards were mainly for show, because in an isolated kingdom such as this, there was little chance of an enemy breaking into the castle. The only guard on duty outside the hall entrance sat slumped on a chair, fast asleep. Such dereliction of duty in Percheron would result in brutal punishment, but Sarin knew he should be grateful that discipline here was so slack.

Holding his sword at the ready, he inched past the sleeping guard, wincing when he eased open the heavy oak door of the keep and heard it creak. Still undetected, he ran down the stone steps and across the deserted bailey. There were guards on the battlements but their eyes were turned towards the distant forests and mountains, ready to defend the castle, not on the lookout for someone trying to escape.

Sarin jogged swiftly across the cobblestones towards the stables. He'd been working there of late, and had befriended a coal-black stallion, who was rarely ridden by any of the warriors. The horse was exceptionally strong and needed a firmer hand than most of the women could provide. Even if he'd still been king, Sarin would have chosen just such a mount for the long journey which lay ahead.

There was a faint glimmer of light from the stables, but that wasn't a troublesome sign, for a lantern was always left burning in one of the far stalls at night. As he opened the door, someone stepped unexpectedly from the shadows. Before the warrior realised who he was, Sarin grabbed her and wrestled her to the ground. He struggled to put a hand across her mouth, determined not to let her call out and warn the guards, but she fought so hard he was forced to clamp his fingers across her windpipe and half strangle her instead. Gasping for breath, and barely conscious, she fell limply back, doubtless fearing that if she resisted again he would kill her without a second thought.

Sarin dragged his captive inside the stables, kicking shut the door behind them. In Percheron men did not indiscriminately slaughter women and even after all he'd suffered in Freygard he still couldn't bring himself to kill the guard. He looked around for some rope to tie her up. He would find a place to hide her so she wouldn't be discovered until he was far away.

She gave a faint groan and for the first time he looked down at his captive. 'Zene!'

'Sarin?' she croaked in surprise, her hand going to her bruised throat.

'I'm sorry,' he said. 'I didn't know it was you,' he

added, relieved that he'd not chosen to kill her as soon as she'd attacked him.

'How did you get out of the slaves' quarters?' she asked, as he pulled her upright and examined the finger-marks he'd left on her tanned flesh.

'You will be a little hoarse for a few days but you'll recover.' He half carried her towards the black stallion who was lodged at the far end of the stables. 'I'm leaving,' he added, noticing that the spirited chestnut Zene often rode was in the adjacent stall. 'Are you coming with me?'

'Now?' she asked stupidly, still looking dazed. 'How did . . .'

'Yes, now,' Sarin interjected impatiently as he sat her down on a bale of straw, and grabbed a halter and bridle. 'Are you with me, or not?' he asked, hoping she wouldn't refuse as she knew the countryside and he did not.

'I am with you.' She gave a shaky smile, still rubbing her bruised neck. 'As long as you promise not to throttle me again.'

'That was a mistake and you know it,' he replied as he set about saddling his mount.

'I'll take the chestnut. Saddle him as well,' she commanded, as if he were still a slave.

Sarin chose to ignore the curtness of her tone. She would be forced to change her ways once they were safely away from the castle. 'Where are you going?' he asked, as she stood up and walked towards a door at the rear of the stables.

'We need extra clothing and provisions. I may find something of use in the tack room,' she explained, disappearing through the narrow doorway.

Sarin set about saddling both horses, knowing he would have to try and put his full trust in Zene despite the fact he barely knew her. It would be far easier to get out of the castle with her help.

He was just tightening the black stallion's girth when she returned. 'Here.' She tossed Sarin a pair of well-worn boots. 'I hope they'll be big enough. They belong to Gelar,' she added, her voice still sounding a little strained.

Gelar was in charge of the stables. She was almost as tall as Sarin, three times as wide and as ugly as sin. She had taken a liking to Sarin and, even though she was probably well past child-bearing age, he had been haunted by the fear that she might turn up at the coupling chamber one night and ask for him. He was certain that he'd never manage to get an erection if he saw Gelar naked.

Sarin gratefully pulled on the boots, which were a tight fit but would be better than riding in sandals. 'They're fine,' he said as Zene put on one of the heavy, black woollen cloaks she was carrying.

She handed the other cloak to Sarin. 'Pull the hood low over your head. It will help hide your face from the guards on duty at the gate,' she said, taking hold of the chestnut's reins and throwing a pair of bulging saddlebags across its back. 'And if you want to survive, let me do the talking.'

Sarin followed her from the stables, mounted the black stallion and adjusted the cloak he now wore so that it hid the majority of his face. With luck the guards wouldn't even realise Zene's companion was a man, he thought, as he followed her towards the small postern gate in the west wall, which was the only exit at night. There were two guards on duty, and one automatically moved to bar their way. 'Let us through,' Zene snapped. 'We carry urgent despatches from Queen Danara to the eastern settlements.'

'Safe journey to you sisters,' they said, not even bothering to glance at Sarin, as they pulled open the gate.

Sarin followed Zene, hearing the gate slam shut behind them. It was the most comforting noise Sarin had heard for a very long time. Urging his horse into a gallop, he followed Zene down the narrow road that led into the valley below. The escape had been easier than he'd ever imagined, but they had many leagues to travel before they would be safe.

Dawn was breaking over the mountains when Zene stopped her horse at the crossroads and looked at Sarin. 'We'll take the road south,' she said. 'Then turn south west on to a little-used track that leads directly to the borders of Percheron.'

'That'll be the route they'll expect us to take,' Sarin pointed out, throwing back his hood and taking a deep breath of the cold morning air. It smelled different now that he was free.

'The Queen is unlikely to send many warriors after an escaped slave – even such an important one as you. We can easily evade a small group of warriors if we are careful,' she replied. 'We go south.'

'No!' Sarin said curtly, his former arrogance returning in an instant. 'I know that the Queen will be determined to recapture me at all costs. If needs be she'll send every warrior she has after me. I'd stake my life on that, Zene. We have to head due north, then turn west after we pass the mountain range.'

'Into Kabra?' Zene asked in surprised confusion, appearing unsettled by the fact that he'd had the temerity to disagree with her.

'My army occupies Kabra. There is a large garrison stationed close to the border. They will be able to provide protection for us even if any of Danara's warriors do manage to track us down and follow us into Kabra itself. Although with luck we will evade our pursuers, because Danara will not expect us to travel in that direction. It is the safest choice.' Then without waiting for her approval, he turned his horse and headed due north into the forest.

Zene frowned and shook her head, then urged her chestnut forwards to follow Sarin.

Lady Rianna tapped her foot impatiently; it was getting colder by the minute as she stood at the top of the steps that led into the keep. She had been up before dawn, and had been waiting for some time for Captain Leon and his companion to arrive. She was eager to leave the castle and return to Ruberoc, having endured three days of soul-destroying boredom before Leon had announced it was now safe to depart.

The soldiers Leon had sent into the forest had returned after slaughtering most of the bandits and driving the rest back towards the distant mountains. Leon had immediately begun to plan their departure and he had suggested they travel with a friend of his, the Baroness Crissana, who was also on her way to Ruberoc. There was always the chance they might come upon small groups of Percheron soldiers who had not yet heard of their army's retreat. He had pointed out that as the baroness had a large body of soldiers in her retinue, their combined forces would ensure that they could travel in perfect safety.

Leon had not said much about this mysterious baroness, other than that she was recently widowed and very wealthy. However, he had been spending an inordinate amount of time with her over the last three days. One of the maids had heard tell that the woman, who was very beautiful, had arrived in the local village soon after they had reached the castle. Rianna could only presume that the baroness had been following Leon because they were romantically involved. Now that the war was over, Leon, like other noblemen, could think seriously of settling down. Rianna hoped they would be happy together, while she wondered whether she and the baroness might become friends. There had been little time for socialising since she and Tarn had arrived and she knew few people in Kabra.

Rianna had originally intended to travel on horseback, but because the weather had turned so damp and drizzly again, Leon had suggested that she might be more comfortable riding in the baroness's carriage. Rianna was inclined to refuse the kind offer as carriage travel on these rough roads could be bumpy and uncomfortable.

Yet she had agreed, mainly because she was curious about the baroness.

The baroness's coach trundled through the castle gates and Rianna looked at it in amazement. The body of the coach was fixed to the wheels and chassis by thick leather straps, which she presumed were designed to cushion against jolting and jarring on the rough roads. The woman must be very wealthy for the elaborately painted and gilded conveyance was fit for a queen.

Leon was riding alongside the carriage. Dismounting, he ran swiftly up the steps. 'Forgive our tardiness, my lady. The baroness's men took longer than we had expected to break camp.'

'So it appears,' Rianna said. She was chilled to the bone, despite her heavy cloak. The coach might not be much warmer on this chill morning, but at least she'd be protected from the damp, cutting breeze. She accompanied Leon down the steps, while her meagre baggage was loaded on to the wagon that had followed the carriage into the bailey. 'I want to reach Ruberoc as soon as possible.'

'As do we all,' Leon replied, opening the carriage door and helping Rianna inside.

The interior of the carriage was surprisingly cosy and it was occupied by two women: a plump rosy-cheeked maidservant and a lady wrapped from head to foot in a black velvet cloak, with her head covered by the hood and a thick veil hiding her face.

'Is your mistress unwell?' Rianna asked the plump maidservant, feeling a little disappointed as the lady made no attempt to acknowledge her presence.

'She is sleeping,' the young maidservant whispered. 'She spent a restless night.'

Wondering if the baroness's lack of sleep had anything to do with Leon, Rianna settled herself more comfortably on the seat. The warmth in the carriage was generated by a small copper stove filled with hot coals, which was just as strange to Rianna as the design of the carriage.

Leon had mentioned that the baroness was born in Vestfold. She'd heard that it was populated by uncivilised barbarians but, judging by the unfamiliar comforts this lady surrounded herself with, that was not so.

The carriage began to move, and Rianna found the rocking motion quite pleasant after the bone-shattering carriage journeys she had endured in the past. As they turned out of the castle gates, Rianna caught her first glimpse of the baroness's men. When Leon had spoken of them he had failed to mention that they were mercenaries. The heavily armed barbarians looked more dangerous than the bandits that had attacked them *en route* to the castle.

Rianna reassured herself with the thought that the baroness was obviously happy enough with the way the mercenaries served her, as she stared at their strange clothing and the infinite variety of their facial features. When one of them, an ugly creature with long frizzy red hair and bright-coloured garments, looked straight at her with a lewd leering grin on his face, she sat back and pulled down the leather blind until it half-covered the window, feeling unsettled by his penetrating glance.

Trying to forget her instinctive concerns, Rianna relaxed back on her seat, and looked over at the sleeping baroness. The veil fluttered fractionally as she breathed, but it was so thick it was impossible to make out any of her features beneath it. Rianna smiled at the plump maidservant. 'I trust your mistress will feel better soon.'

'A rest will soon put her to rights,' the maidservant replied as she glanced over at her sleeping mistress, then back at Rianna.

'This carriage is most comfortable to travel in. I've never seen such a design before. And the stove,' Rianna added, looking towards the contraption that generated such warmth. 'Do they come from Vestfold?'

'I believe so,' the maid confirmed. 'My lady once told me that they have to have such comforts because in the middle of winter it can become so cold in her land that a

61

person could freeze to death in minutes. I confess even the thought of travelling there fills me with alarm, but my mistress has expressed a wish to see her family again.'

Rianna frowned. 'You say that your mistress plans to return to Vestfold, but we are on our way to Ruberoc, are we not?'

'Indeed we are,' the maidservant said quickly, her cheeks turning even pinker. 'The baroness plans to stay there a while, then travel north to Vestfold in the summer months when the mountain passes are clear of snow.'

'That would be better,' Rianna said thoughtfully.

'Yes,' the maidservant agreed. 'During these journeys my mistress likes to have ready some spiced milk. She finds it most palatable and it helps to settle the stomach during such long journeys,' she gabbled, appearing a little uneasy. 'It is probably some time since you broke your fast. Would you like to try some, Lady Rianna?'

'Yes, I would like that.' Rianna's stomach already felt quite empty. The cook in the castle was unskilled and had a heavy hand with the honey cakes Rianna usually ate after she'd woken. But she'd barely tasted them this morning because, half-stale, they had been so unappetising.

'It will take but a moment.' The maid removed a silver jug from a small alcove in the side of the carriage and set it atop the stove. It was designed with a rim, which fitted neatly over the stove and stopped the jug from toppling even when the coach hit a rough patch of road. Within moments the smell of honey and spices filled the small space.

'That smells good,' Rianna said, her stomach growling with hunger as she watched the maid pour the posset into a horn beaker.

Rianna took the cup and tasted the spiced milk, which was even sweeter and more delicious than she'd expected. She sipped it slowly, feeling the warmth revive her as a sensation of wellbeing spread through her body.

Handing the beaker back to the maidservant, she chanced lifting the blind to look out of the carriage window again.

After a time the unrelenting view of trees, coupled with the swaying motion of the carriage, made Rianna feel very weary, and she yawned behind her gloved hand.

'You look tired, my lady. We have a long way to go yet,' the maidservant said in a soothing voice. 'Why not do as my mistress does, and sleep for a while? I'll close the window blinds so that you can rest in more comfort.'

Rianna was indeed having great difficulty in keeping her eyes open. Her lids felt incredibly heavy, 'Yes,' she agreed with a deep sigh. Laying her head back against the padded seat rest, she gave up the battle to stay awake.

Rianna awoke, no longer able to feel the rocking motion of the carriage. She was lying on a soft mattress in a tent. A latticed lantern hung high above her head, casting patterns of light and shade on the soft blanket that covered her, and it looked to be dark outside. Also, someone had removed her clothes and her shift had slid from her breasts and was rucked untidily around her slim waist.

She could hear the familiar sounds of a military camp, something she'd become accustomed to over the last few months, and she could see the flicker of campfires through the thick fabric walls of the tent. It had been early morning when she'd entered the baroness's carriage, now it appeared to be night. Surely she hadn't slept all those hours?

Rianna wondered why she had slept so long and so deeply. Of late her slumbers had been very disturbed and she'd awoken at the slightest sound. 'This is strange,' she muttered, sitting up to loosen the pins that held her hair up and which seemed to be contributing to her dull throbbing headache that was gradually becoming more pronounced.

'I agree.'

Rianna tensed at the sound of the all too familiar voice. 'Surely not?' she murmured, her heart feeling as though it had plummeted to her stomach. She turned to look at the lady who entered. How came she to be here of all places? The last time she'd seen Niska had been in Sarin's seraglio in Percheron. 'You are the baroness?' she stuttered.

'Who else would I be?' Niska asked haughtily, as she smiled in her usual chilling manner. Rianna pulled up the blanket to cover her breasts as she stared at Niska in confused concern. She looked as lovely as ever in a loose scarlet robe that fell open as she walked slowly forwards to reveal her long shapely legs. 'A fortuitous coincidence that we meet again, is it not, dear Rianna?'

'Fortuitous?' Rianna echoed. 'I think not. I had hoped never to lay eyes on you again, Niska.' She drew back in alarm, pulling the blanket closer to her breasts, as her former enemy sat down beside her.

'Well we are here together whether you like it or not,' Niska replied, smiling in the familiar cruel predatory way that set Rianna's teeth on edge. 'So you'd better get used to it.'

'I doubt I can,' Rianna replied, recalling her relationship with Niska when she had been in Percheron. Rianna had arrived, as a very unwilling bride, to discover that Sarin was already married to Niska. Rianna had not even known that it was the custom for the ruler of Percheron to take more than one wife. Without consulting Niska, Sarin set her aside, made her a secondary wife, so that he could marry Rianna and make her his queen. Not surprisingly Niska had been furious. She blamed Rianna, not Sarin, and from then on had done all she could to harm and discredit Rianna. 'Especially as you now masquerade as someone you obviously are not.'

'It is no masquerade,' Niska retorted, still staring coldly at her with eyes that always uncomfortably reminded Rianna of a wolf. 'I *am* the Baroness Crissana. Soon after it was learned that Lord Sarin was dead, brutally slaughtered while in pursuit of his adulterous wife and her traitorous lover, his military leaders assumed control. They decided to sell off most of the members of his seraglio – even me, Sarin's poor grieving widow. I was purchased by Baron Crissana, a lecherous old creature who was as ugly as sin and twice as depraved. He wanted a beautiful young wife to share his bed and bear his children.' She smiled. 'Unfortunately, the baron expired after only a few weeks of marriage, leaving me a *very* rich widow.'

'How sad that must have been for you,' Rianna said sarcastically, wondering if she had murdered her husband. 'Now you've seduced Leon. Is he your next victim, perchance?'

'Leon is an attractive young man, an ardent lover and of noble blood,' Niska replied thoughtfully. 'Also he adores me, and will do whatever I ask of him. As yet he is only a captain, but I understand his father is one of King Brion's closest advisors, and one day Leon will inherit both his position and title.'

'That is true,' Rianna agreed with a tight smile. 'But you clearly do not know that King Brion lies on his deathbed and soon Tarn will be king. After all that happened in Percheron, Tarn would never welcome you to his court, he may not even allow you to remain in Kabra. You helped his cousin, Cador, plotted with him to steal Tarn's birthright. Tarn loathes you and all you stand for, Niska.'

'Will you not persuade him to let bygones be bygones?' Niska asked, leaning towards Rianna, her warm breath brushing her cheek. She gently untangled a lock of Rianna's long hair, laughing softly as Rianna winced, instinctively pulling away from her.

'Never,' Rianna hissed.

'That is a pity,' Niska mused. 'Why do you continue to hate me so? In Percheron did I not offer to help you both escape?'

'It is *you* who have always hated me,' Rianna retorted.

'You only recall what you choose to, Niska. You only offered to help us because you planned to lead us into a trap and have us both killed,' she added icily. 'If it were not for Chancellor Lesand's help, Tarn and I would be dead by now.'

'All lies,' Niska insisted. 'It was Cador's plan to offer to aid your escape, not mine. I had no intention of harming you or Tarn. I just wanted you out of the way and Tarn for myself.'

'I wager that Leon does not know of your past life, before you became a respectable widow.'

'It is best forgotten and you'll not speak of it,' Niska said threateningly. 'Not if you know what is good for you, Rianna.'

'What would Leon think of you, Niska, if I told him the truth about you?' Rianna asked, smiling sarcastically.

'I doubt he would believe one word, even if he heard it from your sweet lips, Rianna. Leon loves me, his heart would never allow him to believe wrong of me.'

She was probably right, men could be inordinately stupid when they were in love. Rianna decided that she would have to find a more subtle way to reveal Niska's true nature to Leon, while feeling very uneasy about the situation she found herself in. Niska had many mercenaries in her employ and they probably outnumbered her soldiers four or five to one. It would be better to appear to accept Niska's presence with a modicum of good grace. 'I'll not say anything,' Rianna confirmed. 'Leon would most likely not accept the truth anyway. Nevertheless, when we reach Ruberoc circumstances may well change. Tarn is more outspoken and has a less forgiving nature than I. He'll not keep quiet about the past. It might be best if you did not plan to remain too long in Kabra after his coronation. Your maid tells me you were eventually intending to return to Vestfold. It would be wiser to consider going there sooner rather than later. Perhaps you could persuade Leon to accompany you to Vestfold before he learns the truth from Tarn?'

'That might be a wise move,' Niska agreed, far too obligingly for Rianna's peace of mind. Suddenly she meshed her fingers in Rianna's long hair and pulled her closer, until their faces were almost touching. 'For the time being, Rianna, we will agree to appear friends – good friends.'

Catching her totally by surprise, Niska kissed her, plunging her tongue deep into Rianna's mouth, while her other hand pushed aside the blanket and roughly caressed her breasts. For a moment Rianna found her treacherous body responding to Niska's unwanted touch. Sarin had trained her well and taught her to enjoy the sexual pleasure another woman could give her. The lessons were so ingrained that still after all these months Rianna found them hard to resist.

Summoning all her strength she pulled away from Niska, ashamed of the sudden swell of moisture that had formed between her closed thighs. She had learned from Sarin that she could even feel desire for those she loathed. Had she not willingly welcomed Sarin into her bed even when she knew he was torturing Tarn by forcing him to be his personal body slave? Sexual response wasn't something Rianna found easy to understand or explain.

'Still playing your hedonistic games, Niska?' she said sarcastically, as she pulled the blanket higher up her body, clutching on to it even harder as she tried to hide how readily her body had responded to Niska's lechery. 'I pity Leon. You will never ever be content with one man.'

'I am so different from you, Rianna. I may have shielded Leon from the full truth of my past but I have never pretended to be something I'm not.' Niska rose to her feet. 'In time Leon will come to accept that I need different and very varied pleasures to remain utterly content. He has a lusty appetite, and eventually he'll be only too happy to join me in my sensual games.' She looked Rianna disdainfully up and down. 'It is Tarn I pity. He loves you and plans to make you his queen. But in truth you are a whore better suited to the lowest bordello than to be seated on a throne at his side. Accept your true nature, Rianna. I know full well that you'd spread your legs for any man who wanted you.'

'That isn't true, you bitch.' Rianna shook with fury. 'You know nothing of my true nature.'

'I know you well enough,' Niska said coldly. 'And in future you best watch your tongue. You will remain safe Rianna, only as long as I want you too. Never forget that my mercenaries greatly outnumber your small group of soldiers. If I gave the orders the throats of every one of them could be slit while they slept, this very night,' Niska said with a chilling laugh that sent a shiver of apprehension through Rianna.

'You'd not do that because of Leon,' Rianna challenged.

'But if you tried to poison his mind against me, I would be forced to do it, would I not? So you need to consider your behaviour very carefully if you want to be reunited with your beloved again. It is not such a lot to ask in exchange for the life of you and your soldiers, is it?'

Feeling invigorated by her confrontation with Rianna, Niska walked out of the rear of her tent on her way to speak to her trusted lieutenant, Chang. He always chose to camp apart from the other men, as he preferred his own company.

She found Chang sitting naked in front of the fire, eyes closed in silent contemplation. Niska had been fascinated by him ever since she had laid eyes on him in the slave market of Aguilar. His shaven head, dark, slanted eyes, yellow-tinted skin, and lean body had taken the interest of a number of buyers. Yet many noble ladies had been repelled by the strange tattoos decorating most of his body and the gill-like line of scars on his angular cheeks, but these were the very attributes that had forced her to bid such an exorbitant sum to possess him for herself.

Her soft slippers made little noise on the rough ground, but Chang's senses were as sharp as a cat's and his eyes snapped open to stare at her as she approached. He did not speak or even acknowledge Niska as she joined him, sitting cross-legged on the hard ground, careless of the way her loose robe slid open to reveal her bare legs. Stones stuck in her buttocks as the cold night air caressed her open quim. Moisture still lingered there and her sex felt hot and swollen. The need for satisfaction stabbed her deep in the belly as she stared at Chang's lean naked body; sex with him was the best she'd ever had.

'Did I disturb your meditation?' she asked.

His inscrutable features revealed none of his true thoughts as he inclined his head. 'I was almost finished, it matters not,' he said in his strangely accented voice, which had a sing-song quality that Niska had always found charming and quite compelling.

She still lusted after him, still wanted him, but the time of sexual congress between them was long past. Their relationship had deepened and changed beyond the physical. Niska had considered it a meeting of two like minds on a higher plain, or that was how she'd thought until this moment. But now the old familiar lust for him ate away at her vitals, and made her nipples tighten in anticipation.

They were similar in many ways, both had suffered harsh conditions and cruelty during their youth, but in others they were very different. Niska was proud of her strong sense of self-preservation which often made her appear heartless and extraordinarily cruel, but she could be very loyal to those who served her well, as long as they were strong enough to stand up to her demanding nature. Yet she knew that this inherent hardness bore no relation to the greedy insidious serpent that lurked deep inside Chang. He was strong and he kept this dark side partially suppressed by means of meditation, determined will and, for the time being, a constant vow of chastity.

Even so Niska trusted him implicitly; he'd sworn to protect her with his life ever since she had saved him from execution in Aguilar.

'When I saw you just now I was reminded of the day I first laid eyes on you in the slave market,' she confessed. 'I knew then that you would come to be of great importance in my life, but I didn't know how or why.'

Chang's smile did not reach his obsidian eyes. 'You may have felt those things but most of all you wanted me to fuck you. Your cunt was wet for me and that was more than enough to make you bid so high. I also remember that day all too well. The sun was so bright I could only see you as a small veiled figure, yet I could sense the lust you felt for me,' he added in a soft sensuous voice. 'Just as I can sense it now. I can smell the musky odour of your arousal. You're soaking. You'd love me to bury my face between your thighs and suck you until you came against my lips.'

Niska's legs shivered and felt weak as she moved them slightly, and her robe fell open from the waist. It was dark, the flickering firelight could not reach into the blackness between her open thighs, yet she could feel Chang's eyes caressing her there. The strange sensation sent the blood pounding through her veins, and made every nerve ending tremble with the promise of untold pleasure. She felt like a vixen in heat; her cunt hungered for his cock. Recollections of their violent couplings in the past made her limbs feel weak and just once more she wanted to savour the pleasure of fucking him. Nevertheless, if everything was to proceed as planned she could not allow that to happen. 'I wish . . .' she began.

'I know.' He laid a finger against her lips, letting the unspoken words increase the sexual tension until it was a palpable entity in the cold night air.

The baron had been away on business the day she had first taken Chang home from the slave market. Her steward had feared the fierce-looking warrior and advised against removing his chains, but Niska had

70

insisted. Chang had said nothing on his release, just sat down on the floor of her chamber and stared meditatively into the distance. Niska had left him there and gone to her bed, but later he had come to her, moving so swiftly and silently that she'd not even heard him until he had pounced. Chang had fucked her hard and brutally, using her in ways no other man had dared, not even her half-impotent husband. She had been sore for nearly three days, but the pleasure he gave her had been worth every second of the subsequent discomfort.

'If only matters had turned out differently,' she murmured, unable to keep her gaze from roving his naked body.

Blue tattoos of strange serpents ringed his arms and a winged creature that could only have existed in the most terrible of nightmares was pictured on his back. It was designed in such a way that its clawed feet and spine-tipped wings appeared to move of their own volition as he walked or flexed his muscles. Serpents also twined erotically around his upper thighs, their fanged jaws reaching ravenously out towards his cock. That was also decorated with tattoos, and the elaborate pattern was even more impressive when he was fully aroused.

'The fault was mine,' he said softly, his gaze never leaving the dark valley of her quim, seeming to caress the silken folds until clear fluid began to dribble from the hungry opening. 'I was jealous, knowing that you were forced to warm the baron's bed. The beast within me burst free as I imagined his boney fingers exploring your body, and his shrivelled organ forcing its way inside you. I sought out something, anything, upon which to slake my resentful lust, and I came upon the baron's favourite slave. Possessing her felt like sweet justice at the time.' For once his troubled emotions showed on his face. 'If she had not struggled, not fought me so hard, she might well have lived. It was her reluctance, her fear and her terrified pleas that allowed the loathsome beast to cloud my mind, fill it with dark obscene thoughts, desires I thought I'd long conquered.'

Niska shivered as she recalled that fateful night. She had woken in the baron's arms to hear the anguished screams and she'd followed her husband into the garden. By the light of the full moon, in those tranquil surroundings, she had seen Chang rutting with the slave, his hands locked around the terrified girl's throat. It was too late even then for anyone to help her. Chang had climaxed at the exact moment his straining fingers had drained the last ounce of life from her body.

He'd not even bothered to fight as he was forced away from the corpse by the baron's soldiers. Niska would never forget his eyes: they'd been as cold and lifeless as if he too were dead. Then she'd watched in painful disbelief as Chang was dragged away to be incarcerated in a cell until his punishment was decided.

'How can you blame yourself?' she asked. 'You told me that the urge to kill at the moment of sexual release was not born in you. It was a curse inflicted on you by one of your greatest enemies.'

'I was foolish, because I thought I'd learned to master it, but I have been forced to accept that I cannot ever be sure of controlling it.' He smiled sadly.

'Yet you hold it in check now,' she pointed out, noticing that his cock had grown hard.

'On occasions with great difficulty,' he confessed with a grimace. 'I want you even now, Niska. But if I tried to take you I could not be sure you'd be safe. The curse grows even stronger because my lust consumes me, eats me up inside.' He ground his nails into his palms, finding a kind of peace in the infliction of pain on himself.

Guiltily Niska covered herself, knowing that she had contributed to his agony. She had the means to alleviate the desires that simmered inside her, Chang did not – all he had was his own self-will. 'I am sorry, I did not think,' she muttered.

'Often I think that you should have allowed me to die. You could have let the execution go ahead!'

'I could not have done that.' Niska had gone to the prison the day before he was due to be beheaded for his crime and bribed the guards to allow Chang to escape. She had kept him safely hidden, so that he could help her murder the baron, while making her husband's death look like nothing but a tragic accident.

'The future is not as bleak as you think it to be, never forget that. In Vestfold you can confront and fight the demon who dwells within you. There are many skilled Necromancers there, and others who use the power of magic. You will be able to find someone to help you lift the curse,' she told him.

'So you say.' Chang folded his arms and looked down at his cock, watching it slowly return to its generous natural size. 'It may be possible to find a way,' he agreed, sounding less than convinced. 'But first we have to reach Vestfold.'

'Have you ascertained how many of Leon's men might choose to join us?'

'Less than half his troops at the most,' Chang replied. 'As long as the price is right. We will have to find ways to rid ourselves of the rest. Three or four can disappear slowly over the next few days. Now that the war is over, it would not be surprising if they stole secretly away in the night – deserted in order to return to their families.'

'And the others?'

'In a day or so I will send a small party to scout ahead – it will be composed of our most trustworthy men and the rest of Leon's loyal soldiers. Once they are well away from us, they will unfortunately be set upon by bandits and none of Leon's men will survive the attack.'

'It might be more convincing if we lose one or two of our own men.' Niska smiled encouragingly.

'I agree.' Chang nodded. 'There are a couple I would be happy to be rid of – troublemakers of the worst sort.'

'So we dispense with them at the same time?' Niska

shivered, realising how cold it had become. Chang was never troubled by the vagaries of the weather, withstanding heat and cold with equanimity. 'You must arrange it with the mercenaries you have taken into your confidence.'

'Will Leon prove any problems to these plans?' Chang watched Niska pull her robe more firmly around herself, then blow on her icy hands in a vain attempt to warm them.

'I can handle, Leon.' She rose stiffly to her feet. 'I'll keep him busy so that he doesn't realise what is happening until it is too late. It won't take me long to convince him to accompany me to Vestfold. I can persuade him to do anything I want him to. Compared to you and I he is but a helpless child.'

'Even children can prove to be disobedient and uncooperative at times,' he said sagely, then closed his eyes as Niska walked away from him.

As Niska entered her tent it felt deliciously warm in contrast to the chill night air. She stepped over to the large portable brass stove filled with glowing coals and held her frozen fingers out to the welcome heat.

'My lady, your skin is like ice,' her maid, Tanith, said as she gently placed a soft cashmere shawl around her shoulders.

'Do you think I should send for Leon to warm me up?' There was a teasing note in Niska's voice that made Tanith blush.

'Is that your wish?' she asked. 'I can send for him now?'

Niska still ached for Chang. Leon's lovemaking was feeble in comparison. The first time they'd been reunited a few days ago, he had shown a glimmer of promise, which had raised her hopes, but since then he'd been irritatingly gentle with her when she had allowed him to her bed. The brief hint of brutality he'd displayed just that one time was a far cry from the cruel pleasure Chang could give her.

'I am in no mood for Leon yet,' she replied with a dismissive wave of her hand. 'His loving-demands irritate me when I am feeling tense. Undress me, Tanith, then I'll get into bed.'

Tanith removed the cashmere shawl, then Niska's loose robe. Her fingers felt incredibly comforting as they brushed against Niska's icy flesh. 'I could massage you with scented oils, or just try to warm you with my hands,' Tanith suggested with a slight catch in her voice.

Niska turned round to face her maid, feeling the heat from the stove caressing her buttocks. 'Do you want to touch me, Tanith?' She gave a soft husky laugh.

'You know I do.' The maidservant's bottom lip quivered as she tentatively lifted her hands. She ran her warm palms up and down Niska's arms and over her shoulders, nervously sliding them down towards her breasts. 'Please let me massage you, my lady,' she begged, her fingers brushing Niska's pale nipples.

'Not tonight,' Niska said dismissively as she stretched her arms upwards, rolling her shoulders. The casual movement gave extra emphasis to the firm swell of her pert breasts, while the diamond that pierced one of her nipples caught the light, sparkling enticingly against her pale flesh.

'I beg of you.' Tanith ventured to press her hand against Niska's belly, letting it slide cautiously downwards to stroke her mistress's naked mons.

'You're a greedy little bitch.' Niska's eyes gleamed as she opened her thighs to allow Tanith's fingers to invade her damp slit, shuddering as the maid's pudgy fingers slipped inside to tentatively caress the sensitive interior.

'Enough!' She slapped the girl's hand away. 'Be assured, Tanith, if you behave like that again I will punish you.'

Tanith sank to her knees, her shoulders shaking as tears started to slide down her plump cheeks. 'Forgive me,' she wailed.

Tanith was a plump young woman, and as she

crouched there her skirt moulded to her body, revealing tight little rolls of fat round her belly. Niska dug her toe in the plump mounds, sliding it slowly downwards until she was pressing her foot hard against Tanith's pussy. She smiled as she heard Tanith's hungry groan. She found the maid's soft plumpness an interesting contrast to the firm hard bodies of the men she welcomed in her bed, but she was not in the mood for Tanith's gentle caresses tonight. She needed stronger and more vigorous stimulation.

'I always do forgive you, don't I, Tanith?' she said irritably. 'Now get up and find me a nightgown!'

Tanith sprang to her feet and scurried to do Niska's bidding, sliding a finely embroidered lawn nightgown over her head, then covering it with an ornate velvet robe. 'Would you like me to prepare you something to eat or drink?'

'Has our guest been fed?' Niska enquired.

Tanith nodded. 'She ate little, and now she sleeps again. I fear the potion we gave her this morning was too strong.'

'At least while she's sleeping she is not a problem to us,' Niska said thoughtfully. She often spoke her thoughts aloud to Tanith, although usually the maidservant had little or no idea what she was talking about. 'She appears compliant, but I'm not sure I can place any trust in what she says. She promised me she'd not speak of the past to Leon, but she always was a liar and if the opportunity should arise I am sure she will.' She walked over to a brass table and snapped open a delicate silver box, withdrawing two similar vials. One held a greyish powder, which she handed to Tanith. 'One pinch of this in her food tomorrow morning. It will cloud her mind, make her more amenable. And this . . .' The other vial contained shimmering, green viscous liquid. 'It is a potion from Cimmera, so precious it cost me a hundred pieces of gold just for this small amount. One drop only, every day.'

The potion was an aphrodisiac and Niska had often used it on Sarin to ensure his interest in her never waned. Although it had not stopped him from arranging a marriage of convenience with Rianna. The union had destroyed Niska's hopes of becoming Queen of Percheron. Then somehow Rianna had managed to worm her way into Sarin's affections, and he had cast *her* aside. When she had plotted her revenge, and made plans with Cador to gain possession of Tarn, and keep him as her slave, Niska had intended to use the potion on him. Then he would have forgotten his hopeless love for Rianna and come to her bed all too willingly. But the bitch had helped Tarn escape, and foiled all her carefully thought-out plans. Now at last she was about to have her revenge.

'Is it very precious?' Tanith asked nervously.

'Immensely, and so rare I can obtain no more of it,' Niska warned her.

As Tanith scuttled away to place the vials in a safe place, she wondered what would happen when she reached Vestfold. She was unsure of the welcome she would receive, but both her older brothers were dead now, and during their childhood Ragnor had always been her friend. Surely he would be more than happy to see his long-lost half-sister, especially if she brought with her the beautiful daughter of the Ruler of Harn, the intended bride of the King of Kabra, as his slave.

# Chapter Four

When Rianna awoke again it was still night, and she had no idea how many hours had passed. Her thoughts were still confused and, even though she'd slept for a day or more, she still felt extraordinarily tired as if all the energy had drained from her body. Rianna was well versed in the art of caring for the sick and skilled in the use of herbs. She was convinced that the drink she'd been given had been laced with something to make her fall into a deep sleep.

She sat up, trying to make some sense of her muddled thoughts. It was Niska who had done this, probably so that she wouldn't discover the baroness's true identity until it was too late. If she had found out near the start of this journey, she could have refused to travel with Niska and insisted that Leon take her back to the castle. Now she was here, in the middle of this inhospitable forest, and Leon and his men were totally outnumbered by Niska's mercenaries.

She would have to find a way to speak to Leon in secret, and warn him about Niska. Rianna couldn't believe that Niska really planned to remain in Ruberoc, especially not as Leon's wife. He was only a minor nobleman of little importance, and he was far too kind and gentle a man to keep Niska happy for long. She must have other plans, and Rianna knew she had to try and find out what they were.

The dim glimmer of campfires was still visible through the fabric walls of the tent, and Rianna could hear odd snatches of muted conversation and the clank of weaponry as a sentry walked by. She shivered, she had been so consumed by her concerns she had ignored the fact that Niska was only a stone's throw away, in another portion of the warm, opulently furnished tent. She could hear her, or rather she could hear the soft moans and groans of lovemaking.

Rising to her knees, Rianna crept towards the heavy curtain that separated her small section of the tent. A thin line of light showed under the hem. Rianna cautiously eased some of the thick fabric aside, and saw two naked figures reclining on a fur-covered mattress. One was Niska, the other she was certain was Leon, even though he had his back to her.

Leon's brown hair clung damply to the nape of his neck, and his lean, muscular back glittered with sweat. He had small firm buttocks, which were moving in a smooth rocking motion as he thrust into Niska. With a soft grunt, he rolled on to his back pulling Niska with him, their bodies still locked together.

Niska gave a husky laugh, tensing her slim thighs as she straddled Leon and rode him vigorously. Her fingers grabbed hold of his flat brown paps, pinching and twisting them until he winced in discomfort, then groaned as Niska ground her pelvis harder against his.

Despite her loathing for Niska, Rianna could not fail to be aroused by the sight, and the soft wet sounds of their coupling. She tensed, clenching her thighs together as Leon reached up Niska's writhing form and kneaded her pert breasts. He twisted the glittering diamond, straining her pale flesh alarmingly as Niska gave a low feral growl of bliss. Rianna knew how much the bitch enjoyed pain, almost as much as the pleasure she derived from inflicting it on others.

Niska began to move faster, lifting her hips higher before each thrust. Rianna unconsciously held her breath for a moment as she caught a brief glimpse of Leon's damp shiny shaft, before it disappeared deep inside Niska again. She felt a stab of need deep inside her own sex as Niska's thrusting body devoured Leon like a hungry animal feeding on its prey. He moaned and rolled his head from side to side, his fingers still pulling urgently at Niska's nipples, until she arched her back and gave a strangled cry.

Just as Leon came, Niska rolled off him. His cock jerked wildly as a white stream of semen pumped from its head, spattering his stomach and upper thighs. Niska smiled and began to lap greedily at his leavings like a cat hungrily devouring cream.

Rianna was aroused and yet sickened by the sight as she crouched behind the curtain trying desperately to ignore the hot fire in her groin and the sticky trail of her own desire that glued her legs together.

'I adore you,' Leon gasped, pulling Niska to him, cradling her lovingly in his arms.

'And I you,' Niska replied, her voice sounding just a little shaky as she pressed her face to his chest.

'Does something ail you?' he asked worriedly. 'You sound upset.'

'Nothing ails me,' she whispered, lifting her head to reveal unshed tears sparkling in her pale eyes. 'I am just a little concerned. There are things I must tell you, Leon. Things about me you may not like.' She sighed, one single tear sliding down her cheek. 'I have no wish for your opinion of me to change . . .' her voice faltered again. 'Or lose your love.'

'I'll always love you, no matter what,' he said with so much depth of feeling that it made Rianna feel even more uneasy. 'Nothing you can tell me would ever make me change my opinion of you Niska, or prevent me from loving you.'

'You promise?' Niska asked in a childlike voice that made Rianna want to slap her face. She was a good actress, even Rianna had to admit that. She was playing with Leon's affections, drawing him in like a fish on a line.

'I promise.' Leon kissed her gently on the lips. 'Now what is it you wish to tell me, my love?'

She nestled closer to him. 'First I must speak of my life in Vestfold. I know I've always avoided speaking of it before.'

'I sense it was not a happy time in your life,' he said with understanding. 'I hoped that one day you might be able to bring yourself to speak of it, when the time was right.'

'I told you that my father was a warrior, a great warlord, and the Lawspeaker of Vestfold.' She sighed again, appearing uneasy, as if fearing Leon's reaction to her next words. 'What I did not tell you was that my mother was his thrall – his slave.' She paused, waiting for Leon to comment. When he did not speak she continued, 'She was not always a slave. She was travelling in a caravan with her father, a wealthy fabric merchant, when they were attacked by bandits. Most of her companions were slaughtered, but because she was young and beautiful the bandits spared her, and sold her to a northern trader. She caught my father's eye and he took her for himself.'

'Your mother could not help her fate,' Leon said with feeling.

'When his wife died, she became his new wife in all but name. I was raised in the longhouse along with my half-brothers Sven, Harald and Ragnor. Sven and Harald hated me, despised the fact that my mother was a slave, but Ragnor was my friend. He was only sixteen when my father died, and he did not have the power to stop his older brothers from presenting me as a gift to

Thorolof, a rival warlord, in an effort to bring peace to a warring land. Thorolof was a cruel brute, an evil monster . . .' She choked on her words, and her distress appeared genuine even to Rianna.

'My love,' Leon said, troubled by her pain.

'I cannot speak of my life with Thorolof,' she admitted. 'It is best forgotten. All you need to know is that I escaped and fled south.'

'How did you reach Percheron?' Leon asked.

'Percheron.' Niska sniffed and rubbed her hand across her eyes. 'I came upon a small group of silver merchants travelling south. One had just lost his wife to a fever. I was barely past childhood myself, but he still employed me to care for his two young offspring. He wanted me to stay with him when we reached Percheron, but by then he was casting lecherous eyes upon me, and I had no wish to warm his bed, so I sought employment elsewhere.' She picked up a goblet of wine and sipped it contemplatively while Leon waited patiently for her to continue.

Rianna was becoming stiff crouched on her hands and knees, so she sat down and also waited, convinced that, regardless of whether all she had heard so far was a lie, from now on Niska would certainly not be telling the truth.

'I gained employment as a maid in the house of a minor nobleman – a scholar who was often called upon to advise Lord Sarin.' Niska smiled as though these memories were far happier ones. 'Mellos was a good man, who had lost his entire family to the plague. He taught me to read, educated me, and began to look upon me as his daughter. Eventually he took me with him to court, and Lord Sarin laid eyes upon me for the first time.'

'You were at Lord Sarin's court?' Leon sounded surprised.

'Yes.' Niska admitted. 'And before you ask it, I will tell you that the Lady Rianna and I know each other well.'

'Why did you not mention it?' he asked in confusion. 'Lady Rianna never admitted to me that she'd even heard of Baroness Crissana, let alone knew her.'

'She had no reason to. The truth be, she would not have known we were one and the same. She had no idea that I had wed the baron.' Niska gave a bitter laugh. 'She was most probably under the impression I was dead, or had been sold in the slave market of Aguilar.'

Rianna tensed, waiting for the twisted lies that were about to follow. She wanted to burst in and tell Leon not to believe a word Niska said. Yet she was forced to remain hidden and say nothing. She might well put Leon's life in danger as well as her own if she carried out such a foolhardy act.

'Lord Sarin made it very clear to my benefactor that he was attracted to me, and Mellos, wanting to gain his sovereign's approval, presented me to him as a gift. I was forced to enter his seraglio. Sarin was a charmingly compelling man. I soon fell in love with him. He was so taken with me he promised that he would marry me and make me queen, despite the fact that he expected to choose a princess or a lady of royal blood at the very least. Then, in order to prevent the forces of Percheron invading Harn, the Protector offered Sarin the hand of his daughter, Rianna, in marriage. It is not unusual for the ruler of Percheron to take more than one wife, so Sarin agreed. But when Lady Rianna arrived she made it clear that she was not prepared to share Sarin. She embroiled him in her seductive spell, and just to please her vanity, Sarin set me aside. I was foolish and loved him enough to believe that one day he would see her for what she really was and return to my side. Mark my words, Leon, Rianna is a manipulative creature, and not the sweet innocent lady she pretends to be.'

Leon made an exclamation of disbelief, which Niska ignored. Rianna shook with anger, certain that Niska's attempt to destroy her reputation was far from at an end.

'Rianna appeared happy to become Queen of

Percheron. She eagerly embraced the sexually promiscuous ways of Sarin's court, while showing no concern for the fate of the man she now professes to love. Tarn was incarcerated in the dungeons and she . . .' Niska looked straight at Leon to give extra emphasis to her words. 'You must believe me, Leon. She took an integral part in all Sarin's hedonistic games. In order to ensure the purity of his line, Sarin did not allow any other man to couple with her, but he watched her being pleasured, in any number of ways, by his male and female slaves. Rianna had a constant need for satisfaction and, when he did not send for her, she gained her pleasure with other members of his seraglio. She was in a position of power, she had everything she wanted, yet she still loathed the sight of me, perhaps fearing that eventually Sarin might tire of her and turn to me again. She had me punished for the slightest offence, watching with glee as I was beaten and abused. Then she hatched a plot to be rid of me completely. She planted evidence, making it appear I was embroiled in the subversive activities of Sarin's enemies, and planned to help them overthrow him completely.'

'I cannot believe Lady Rianna would do such a thing,' Leon faltered. 'It does not seem possible.'

'I was lucky to escape with my life. Fortunately, because of our previous association, Sarin could not bring himself to order my execution. He planned to auction me in the public slave market, until the baron pleaded for me to be given to him.' She shuddered. 'I should have been grateful that he saved me from such humiliation – female slaves are sold naked and can be inspected by even the most casual of buyers. Unfortunately, the baron was a loathsome creature, riddled with disease.'

'My poor love.' Leon held her close. 'You were fortunate that the old man died so soon after your marriage.'

'I was,' Niska replied, glancing straight at the curtain behind which Rianna was hiding, almost as if she knew she was listening. 'Just remember that Rianna is skilled.

84

She weaves her spell, and entraps men in her web of deception. Look how she has deceived Prince Tarn!'

'She loves him, I'm certain of that,' Leon insisted. 'And he adores her. Did she not help him escape from Percheron?'

'Only because Sarin discovered that she betrayed him and had not been the virgin she professed to be when they wed. Not only had she copulated with Tarn during her journey to Percheron, she had most likely slept with any number of men before that.'

'Evil bitch,' Rianna muttered to herself, clenching her hands as she fought the urge to reveal herself and to hell with the consequences.

'Rianna was forced to flee, so she arranged for Tarn to go with her – exchanged one prince for another. She took her revenge on Sarin by escaping with his mortal enemy. Knowing that Sarin would set off in pursuit of them, she persuaded Tarn to help her lead him into Freygard. It was not bandits that slew Lord Sarin, it was Rianna's kin. Her mother Kitara is from Freygard, she is a cousin of the ruler, Queen Danara.'

'It is still so difficult to believe this of such a noble lady,' Leon admitted with a troubled frown.

'She is very clever.' Niska began to caress Leon, playing idly with his nipples, running her fingers through his pubic hair. 'I was afraid to tell you this, because I knew you would not want to believe me. Rianna devours men, even those who care for her. It is like a sickness. She cannot help it, Leon, it is in her blood. All the women of Freygard are the same. They are raised to despise men, to enslave them and abuse them. She uses them for her own ends, then casts them aside. Sarin was captivated by her aura of sweet innocence, and soon fell under her spell, but she destroyed him, just as she will eventually destroy Prince Tarn.'

Leon shook his head, still unwilling to believe Niska, and Rianna blessed him for it. She prayed that soon he would come to see Niska as she truly was.

'Niska, I don't know . . .' he mumbled uneasily. 'I should speak to her perhaps.'

'Best you do not. Her lies are too convincing,' Niska replied. She gently trailed her fingers over his cock, smiling as it twitched in response.

'I saw her, the other day in one of the castle corridors, with Prince Tarn,' Leon admitted almost reluctantly. 'He couldn't keep his hands off her, and she was rutting with him like a bitch in heat.'

'No man could resist her seductive ways,' Niska replied. 'Have you never coveted her yourself?'

'In my daydreams,' he muttered. 'She's beautiful, what man would not?'

Rianna shivered and wrapped her arms around herself. How easily Niska was managing to manipulate this man.

'A beauty she uses to her advantage,' Niska whispered seductively. 'Now you must consider the future, Leon. Prince Tarn's fate and the fate of Kabra may well lie in your hands.'

'I do not understand.' He groaned as Niska curved her hands round his cock.

'You will, Leon, all too soon,' she promised, sliding down his body to fasten her lips on his gradually burgeoning shaft.

Sarin threw a little more of the meagre supply of dry twigs he'd gathered on to the small fire. He didn't feel at all comfortable alone in the depths of this huge forest now that night had fallen. Zene should have been back ages ago, and he feared some ill had befallen her. They needed food for themselves as well as the horses, so she had gone to a small isolated community they had come upon by chance a few hours ago. It was only a small cluster of cottages in a clearing by a lake, but it should at least have some of the supplies they needed. He had wanted to go with her, but the suspicions of the occupants would have been aroused if Zene were seen to be travelling with just one unchained slave as her companion.

The trees grew thickly around the clearing, separated by clumps of almost impenetrable undergrowth. The place had a strange unsettling aura. As darkness had fallen the musty odour of rotting vegetation and its sweet sickly undertone had grown stronger, overpowering the clean scent of the tall pine trees. Sarin likened it to the smell of death and he wondered if this was some ancient burial ground. There were a number of small, smoothly shaped stones sticking out of the grass close to the edges of the clearing. He regretted the decision to camp here and feared the place might be cursed.

Somewhere in the distance Sarin heard the chilling howl of a wolf, but closer and far more troubling were the soft snuffling noises, and the sound of vegetation being pushed aside. His horse whinnied, putting back its ears as it shifted nervously, pulling against its tether. Sarin peered anxiously into the darkness, one hand tightly clutching the leather-bound hilt of his sword, always on the lookout for predatory eyes gleaming redly in the surrounding blackness.

Fortunately Zene had at last deemed it reasonably safe to light a fire – it was the first time they had chanced doing so on their journey north. So far the weather had been easy to contend with and winter appeared to be retreating fast. There had been only one light fall of snow on the night they had left, but it had melted in the weak morning sunshine, leaving no visible trail for their pursuers to follow. Since then the days had been cold but bright.

Sarin tensed as he heard a louder sound, made by a much larger animal – Zene's mount, he hoped. Sarin had always been brave, but the many months he had spent as Danara's prisoner had somehow sapped his strength and he occasionally felt fear, terror even. He hated and despised this unwanted weakness, and the fearful apparitions of doom that sometimes invaded his thoughts.

Gathering himself together, he rose to his feet, his sword at the ready. Then, to his infinite relief, Zene rode into the clearing, carrying a large leather bag across the front of her saddle. 'You've got the provisions?' Sarin asked, trying to hide the fact that he'd been afraid.

'Yes,' she confirmed rather curtly as she dismounted and tossed the bag down by the fire. She began to unsaddle her horse, impatiently fumbling with the fastenings as if she expected Sarin to step forwards and help her. Zene was having a difficult time adjusting to the fact that Sarin no longer considered himself a slave. As she heaved the leather saddle from her mount, and placed it close to the fire to act as a pillow, Sarin opened the bag and inspected the contents: a couple of fresh loaves; a few fabric-wrapped parcels, perhaps meat or cheese; some fruit, which had been preserved to survive the winter months; a flagon of beer or wine; feed for the horses and two tightly rolled, brightly coloured blankets. The blankets would make life more comfortable. He'd spent the last couple of nights lying on the blanket that was placed beneath his stallion's saddle, with only his cloak to cover himself. The horse blanket was grubby and covered in hairs. He constantly felt itchy now, as if insects were crawling over his skin.

'You did well.' He straightened and looked at Zene as she removed the horse's bridle and hobbled its legs together, tethering it next to Sarin's black stallion.

She glanced over at the fire, which was now spitting loudly, as globs of fat from the rabbit roasting on a stick, dripped into the flames. It was a small, scrawny creature, barely big enough for a meal for two, but it was all the game Sarin had managed to find.

'That smells good.' She smiled appreciatively, her head tilted, her hazel eyes oddly uncertain as she looked at him, still unsure quite how to treat Sarin.

'At least our stomachs will be full tonight,' Sarin commented, taking a fresh loaf from the bag and putting it on a flat stone by the fire, ready to cut up when the rabbit was cooked.

'The villagers were generous: they refused payment for the supplies.' Zene smiled, still seeming uneasy as she stared at the tall, muscular, dark-haired man, who could be so stubborn and self-willed when he chose to.

Male slaves were not allowed facial hair of any kind, so during her life Zene had only seen clean-shaven men. Sarin now had a growth of dark stubble on his cheeks and chin, which made him look even more overtly masculine.

Idly he scratched at the rough bristles. 'It is a pity we couldn't make camp closer to the lake. It's cold enough to freeze the bollocks off a bull, but I'd still have chanced bathing. I long to wash the sweat and grime from my body.'

'We're no longer short of fresh water,' Zene replied, unrolling one of the new blankets and laying it out by her saddle. 'Not far from here there is a spring. We can refill the water skins in the morning. Use some to wash if you so wish,' she added, sitting down on the blanket and idly running her fingers through her tangled copper curls.

Sarin picked up a half-empty water skin and walked a few paces away from the fire. As he slipped off his doublet he noticed that Zene was watching him out of the corner of her eye, while pretending to be intent on rummaging through her saddlebag. She produced a small bone comb and began tending to her long hair as Sarin filled his cupped hand with water and splashed it over his chest. He rubbed some under his arms, wishing he had soap and a cloth. He slopped even more water under his arms, hoping it would be enough to cleanse the odour of perspiration from the dark tuft of hair in his armpits.

Sarin knew full well that Zene was still watching him as he turned his back to her and eased down his breeches to wash his cock. The flickering firelight bathed his olive skin in a golden glow, the dim light making him appear leaner, his muscles even more pronounced. Pulling his breeches up, but not bothering to fasten them securely, he turned and caught Zene staring dreamily at him. She winced as if her comb had caught a knot, and looked away, hiding her embarrassment, while Sarin wet his dark hair, smoothing it away from the lean contours of his face.

The water dried quickly in the chill night air, making his skin icy cold, although he felt as hot as Hades itself as he looked at Zene, sitting there legs akimbo in front of the fire. She was dressed as any other warrior of Freygard in a tight-fitting leather jerkin, which cupped and cradled her breasts. Usually that was covered by a metal breast-plate, but she'd not been wearing hers when they'd left. Her leather skirt was short, and her long kid boots reached her knees, leaving most of her upper leg bare, with only a thin strip of fabric threaded between her legs to cover her sex. Sarin stared at the dark valley between her shapely thighs, growing hotter and hotter by the moment. There had been no physical contact between them since they'd left the castle and he was beginning to feel very horny.

'Are you going to wash?' he asked Zene.

'No.' She tied her newly combed curls at the nape of her neck with a strip of leather. 'I availed myself of the bathhouse in the village.' A smug smile played around her lips as she added. 'The water was very warm, and it proved to be a most pleasant experience.'

Zene had told him how eager village maidens were to gain the attention of one of the Queen's warriors – how free they were with their charms.

'How pleasant?' he snapped, a tight knot of anger forming in his stomach.

'That's none of your concern,' she said coldly, her eyes glittering angrily because he'd had the gall to question her.

'How many did you have, Zene?' he grated, stepping towards her.

'Why should I tell you?' she flared, then grinned. 'Only two. They were very eager to please. Does that satisfy you, sla – ' she faltered awkwardly.

'Why not finish,' he growled, striding forwards until he was looming over her. 'Slave was the word you were about to use.'

A flush of scarlet flooded her cheeks. 'Only because you irritated me,' she pointed out, staring at him rather warily. He had already demonstrated on other occasions how much stronger he was than her.

Sarin drew back his lips in a menacing grin, certain that she was fearful now, and unsure of him. Power filled his thoughts, and it was a good feeling, a satisfying feeling. Sarin knew without a doubt that in no time at all he would be able to put his time as a slave behind him and regain his proud masculinity and fearless nature. 'Only two of the village maidens attended you in the bathhouse,' he sneered. 'Why did you not have three or four?'

Zene looked away, her fingers plucking agitatedly at the corner of the blanket on which she sat – an unusually feminine gesture for her. 'Because there were only two maidens who were not spoken for. By my standards they were clumsy and unskilled, but good enough to temporarily satisfy my needs,' she countered. 'Now let's see if the rabbit's cooked. I'm very hungry.'

'So am I,' Sarin growled as he pounced on Zene, pushing her down on to the blanket as he leaped astride her waist. 'Famished.' His dark eyes were full of lust as he stared down at her.

'Don't you dare!' she squeaked in fury.

'I dare!' he retorted, pushing his hand under her short skirt and ripping away the thin strip of fabric that protected her modesty.

Sarin held her writhing body down as he fondled Zene intimately, his fingers exploring her sex, where the flesh was soft and warm but still relatively dry. Zene gasped in fury, yet she could do nothing to stop him, as his

91

heavy weight pinned her to the blanket. Her nails were short, but she still managed to rake an angry red line down his chest. Sarin laughed at the discomfort and moved, trapping her flailing arms beneath his knees, rocking back a little so that he did not crush her completely.

As he caressed her, easing his fingers gently inside her, the flesh gradually grew slippery with moisture. She wanted him, Sarin was sure of that. The soft pleasures of female lovemaking were nothing in contrast to the hot, hard flesh of a man. Zene would learn that soon enough, it was a lesson long overdue.

'Soon we will be well away from Freygard,' he told her, moving his fingers in a slow seductive rhythm, until she gave a muffled moan and ceased her struggling. 'You must learn to behave like a lady.'

'I'm no lady, you spawn of Mabon. May the gods smite you down, and worms devour you while you're still alive.' A string of even viler curses sprang from her lips, in a voice so loud it would have woken the dead if they'd not been buried deep below the grass of the clearing.

She struggled harder, still cursing, so Sarin leaned forwards and stopped the spew of foul language with his lips. His kiss was powerfully passionate, smothering Zene's attempts to fight him further. Her body grew limp and acquiescent as he employed all his considerable seductive powers to quell her resistance.

He sat back, leaving Zene flushed and panting, opened his breeches and drew out his cock. It was already hard, but he still slid his hand up and down the shaft, caressing it lovingly, each movement of his fingers emphasising its girth and length. Zene moaned, whether from fear or desire, Sarin did not care.

Her eyes were wide open in an expression of awesome surprise as she stared transfixed at Sarin's cock. It was smooth, the skin stretched taut, bowing slightly towards the tip, just enough to increase her pleasure as he thrust it back and forth inside her.

First, however, Sarin wanted to plunge it between her full lips and bury it in the warm cave of her mouth. In fact, in all their encounters he was the one who had done the pleasuring, not her. Now that was about to change.

'You're disgusting,' Zene gasped as she found herself up close to a man's sexual organs for the very first time. 'Women are so much prettier and neater,' she muttered, her eyes glazing as they fastened on the bulbous purplish head.

'You are going to learn how to satisfy me with your mouth,' Sarin said grimly.

Zene grimaced in disbelief. 'Take that thing in my mouth?' she exclaimed in horror. All of a sudden her expression changed and a sly smile flashed across her features for just a moment. 'If you wish it,' she agreed, far too meekly.

'You'll not bite me, or even graze me with your teeth,' he warned. 'If you do I'll kill you, Zene. I have no wish to do so, but the pain will force me to do it. I'll not be able to help myself.'

For once she appeared to believe his warning and when he eased his cock between her half-open lips she did not protest or resist, just shuddered in disgust.

Sarin leaned further forwards, taking his weight fully off her arms. But she made no attempt to fight as he meshed his fingers in her hair and gradually eased his cock further inside her mouth. When his rod was half sheathed in the hot moist velvet, he gave a deep groan of pleasure.

'Suck it, lick it,' he commanded. 'Give yourself time to get used to the sensation, it's not like eating a woman. You may be called upon to do this again. Often,' he added warningly, 'if you do not please me fully this time around.'

Zene did as he commanded, cautiously sliding her pursed lips up and down the long member, gradually taking more and more into her mouth. When the head nudged the back of her throat she almost choked, tears filling her eyes. Immediately Sarin pulled back; she would learn to accommodate the entire length given time, but he was more than willing to wait until she had honed her skills.

Zene sucked on his cock, running her tongue round the rim of the head. Sarin shuddered; it felt wonderful, and his lust grew. It had been many months since he'd been sucked off. With every sensuous movement of Zene's lips, his will and determination grew stronger. The psyche of a slave, which he'd been forced to assume, would be thrust aside and gradually become extinguished completely.

'That's good,' he crooned, tensing in delighted surprise as the tip of her tongue dug into the tender slit on the head of his glans. Hot shivers radiated through his groin, and he felt his balls tighten in readiness as the sensations expanded.

Knowing that he was moving far too close to orgasm, he hurriedly withdrew and slid down Zene's body until he kneeled between her thighs. She lay there not moving at all now as he eased open her thighs and entered her. She was warm and drippingly moist, and he heard her faint whimper of submission as her grabbed hold of her arse cheeks and thrust deeper.

'Sarin,' she mumbled, half in anger, half in passion, as she lifted her legs and hooked them around his hips. Sarin increased his smooth powerful rhythm, holding back on his own pleasure so that he could bring Zene to orgasm before he allowed himself to claim his own release. His prick seemed to grow larger, filling Zene's tight hole as he ground into her with even more vigour. Then he pulled out and rubbed his cock-head vigorously over her clit, watching her pleasure climbing to the point of no return. As he sensed her orgasm about to erupt, he plunged back inside her. Then he felt her limbs grow rigid, and her internal muscles tighten around his cock, urging it to release its load. Zene's entire body trembled at the strength of her orgasm as Sarin welcomed his own climax with a loud grunt of pleasure.

The pain, anguish and suffering of the last few months drained from his body and were flushed away, sliding deep into the ground. As he withdrew from Zene he felt free as he shed the last remnants of his bondage. Zene had never allowed him to hold her in a comforting way before, but she made no sound of protest as he pulled her into his arms and held her close.

'Why?' she asked, her breath coming in short panting gasps.

'Why not?' he said in a gentle tone. 'I wanted you, Zene. And you wanted me. Is it so hard to admit that?'

'I don't understand myself,' she replied, her voice wavering. 'The girls in the village. They were so eager, just as all the maidens are when one of the Queen's warriors comes to their village. They did their best to pleasure me and yet . . .'

'We are all different; just because you were born in Freygard it does not mean you should not enjoy bedding men as well as women.' Sarin suddenly realised how small and slight she felt in his arms, and her hair smelled of spring flowers. 'You were raised to believe it was only right to enjoy being pleasured by a woman.'

'That is how things are in Freygard,' she insisted.

'Do your farm animals only seek out their own kind?' he asked her. 'Of course they do not. Nature created men and women so that they could procreate, but nature also ensures that each enjoyed the experience otherwise they were unlikely to do it again.'

'This is silly,' she complained, but still did not try to pull away from him.

'Coupling between men and women is an enjoyable experience Zene, the sooner you accept that the better. When you venture further afield you are bound to discover that satisfaction can be achieved in many different ways with either sex. You have a new life ahead of you, and I will be by your side as you set out on this journey of discovery.'

Rianna waved the maid away, irritated by the fact that she suddenly felt so heavy eyed and muzzy headed again. She had woken early feeling quite refreshed until she had realised where she was and remembered the conversation she'd overheard between Niska and Leon. Despite her misgivings she still felt well and ready to face the trials fate had thrown at her; she was even hungry enough to tackle the substantial breakfast Niska's maid brought her a few moments later. It was only a short time after she'd eaten that she had begun to feel strange.

Rianna looked suspiciously at Tanith, who was busy packing up the bedding ready for it to be loaded into the baggage wagon. Could her food have been drugged, just like the potion she had drunk soon after leaving the castle of Dane?

A sudden chill enveloped Rianna as all the fear and apprehension she'd suppressed overtook her again. Was Niska intending to slowly poison her? Did her former enemy intend to be rid of her completely, or was there some other nefarious reason for her behaviour? In future she must be consistently on alert. Niska's mind was so twisted she could be planning anything.

'Are you sure you don't want me to help you with your hair, my lady?' Tanith asked, sounding a little breathless after her brief exertion.

'No, I can manage.'

Rianna began to fashion her long, newly brushed hair into a loose plait. She tied the ends with a silver ribbon as Tanith picked up a couple of bundles and vanished through the curtain. Rianna scrambled to her feet, doing her best to ignore the swimming sensation in her head, and followed Tanith. Relieved to find no sign of Niska in the main body of the tent, she paused at the entrance and watched the plump maidservant hurry towards the baggage wagon.

The morning was icy cold. The soft grass of the clearing was now rock hard and a layer of frost covered the trees in a thick dusting of white. Each time she exhaled her breath hung in the air like thin plumes of smoke. The chill freshness was reviving, but Rianna still felt weak and not quite in full control of her limbs – as if she'd drunk far too much strong wine.

From now on she would watch everything she consumed, only eating foods that could not easily be tampered with, and only drinking water – the most finely powdered herbs would be easily visible in that. She would starve if necessary in order to keep her mind focused and her wits fully intact. Rianna fought her fear, still uncertain of Niska's plans or motives, wishing she could discover what they were. Tarn had left her in Leon's care, certain she was safe, but he had unknowingly left her in peril. She took a few unsteady steps forwards, looking around the campsite for any sign of Leon, and it felt as if the ground was undulating slowly beneath her feet.

Steadying herself on a pile of sacks and other baggage, she looked again for Leon, determined to find a way to speak to him in private. Unfortunately, she could see no trace of him, or any of his men, just an uncomfortably large amount of Niska's mercenaries milling about the camp.

Some of them stopped what they were doing to stare at Rianna, exchanging lewd comments about the beautiful, but pale-looking noblewoman. There was no respect in their demeanour, just a lustful curiosity about the shapely body that was hidden beneath her long dark cloak. Rianna tried to ignore their crude comments and the disgustingly obscene gestures they exchanged one to another.

In the distance she noticed a man who towered over the others, his head shaven, his skin like polished ebony.

97

A flicker of remembrance turned into amazement as she recognised one of the Nubian slaves from Sarin's palace in Aguilar. There had been a number of these unusually dark-skinned men serving Sarin, each had his tongue cut out so that he could not disclose any of Sarin's secrets to the outside world.

There were chambers in the palace that only Sarin and the Nubians were allowed to enter. It was said that there Sarin had carried out his more bizarre sexual excesses, practices that he kept hidden from his wife and most of the members of his seraglio. Rianna knew that Tarn had seen the inside of these chambers many times. Yet he had never spoken of his experiences to Rianna, never allowed her to share the memories of the pain and indignity he had endured at Sarin's hands.

More memories came flooding back of Sarin, Niska and, most especially, Tarn. How she wished her beloved would appear right now – gallop into the camp, snatch her up and take her far away from Niska.

Rianna was so caught up in these thoughts that she failed to notice the two men moving closer to her. One was a lean, dark man, with a bushy black beard, and a curved sword thrust into the grubby red sash round his waist. His companion was the man with frizzy, carrot-coloured hair who had been staring at Rianna in the carriage the previous morning.

Blackbeard stepped in front of Rianna and grinned to reveal teeth like blackened stumps, which made him look doubly threatening. He stank of stale perspiration and Rianna's stomach churned with revulsion as she went to back away from him, but she was brought short by the carrot-haired man who had positioned himself behind her to prevent her retreat. She found herself trapped between the two evil-smelling creatures as Blackbeard thrust his face closer to hers. Strangely enough his breath smelled surprisingly sweet, but it was overwhelmed by the fetid odour coming from his body. He spoke to her in a language she could not understand, rolling his eyes, and lewdly licking his thick lips while Rianna's revulsion increased as she saw the specks of uneaten food lodged in his beard.

She shivered. 'Don't touch me,' she said shakily, thinking him the foulest creature she'd ever laid eyes on.

His grubby hand reached for her, but all of a sudden he was grabbed and hauled away from Rianna. A fist smashed in his face; nose and teeth cracked in a spray of red, before he was flung to the ground with a loud thump. His carrot-haired accomplice moved to his aide, swiftly helping the wounded man to his feet, as Rianna's unexpected saviour looked worriedly down at her. 'Are you harmed?' he asked in a sing-song voice that was way too gentle for his hard looks.

'No,' Rianna said and gave an unconscious shudder as she saw the two men hurry away. Blackbeard was limping, blood running down his face from his broken nose. The other mercenaries displayed no sympathy for their compatriots, they just laughed and threw scurrilous taunts at the sorry pair as they disappeared from sight.

'You should not wander around the camp alone. It is not safe. Most of these men are little more than animals,' her saviour said very seriously. He was sumptuously dressed in a purple silk cloak, and unfamiliar garments, which included full black trousers gathered in tight at the top of his high leather boots. He was quite handsome in an exotically bizarre fashion, although Rianna found the deep scars on each cheek, which appeared to have been made deliberately, rather off-putting.

'I did not realise . . .' He made her feel a little uneasy. His slanted eyes were dark, a strange flat black, as if someone had sucked out his soul, leaving just the husk of a man.

He smiled politely as he took hold of her arm. 'Let me escort you to the carriage,' he said, gently but firmly turning her in the direction of Niska's coach, which was just behind the baggage wagon. 'The baroness would never forgive me if you came to any harm, Lady Rianna,' he said as he glanced around the camp. 'I am Chang, the leader of these men,' he added in a tone that made Rianna think he did not hold them in high regard.

'I must thank you for your timely assistance,' Rianna said her head still swimming a little. 'I will be far more careful in future. However, before we depart I need to speak to the leader of my own soldiers.'

'That would not be wise at present,' Chang interrupted, keeping a firm hold on her arm as if fearing she might fall if he let go of her.

'Why not?' she asked as he led her around the rear of the baggage wagon, and she spied Leon standing by one of the tents. He was frowning and deep in conversation with one of his men.

'Two of his soldiers disappeared sometime last night. He is somewhat troubled by their untimely departure,' Chang added casually, as if the matter should be of little concern to her captain.

'Disappeared?'

'Yes.' Chang deliberately steered her away from Leon and towards the carriage. 'Doubtless they have deserted. Now that the war is over all Kabrans will be eager to return to their home and families.'

'Even so, to a soldier desertion is a crime,' she pointed out.

'One your captain will be willing to overlook in the circumstances,' Chang said. 'Our group is in no real peril, is it? The war is finished, there are no dangers to contend with now that the bandits have been driven back into the mountains. Our journey will proceed just as smoothly without the presence of two extra soldiers.'

'Perhaps some harm has befallen them?'

'What harm, pray?' Chang enquired, turning to look at her, as if challenging her to suggest his mercenaries may have had a hand in the men's disappearance.

'I suppose they must have deserted,' she conceded awkwardly, hoping such suspicions were incorrect.

'You were fortunate that I happened to come by when

100

I did,' Chang told her. 'My men hold the baroness in high regard because she pays them well for their loyalty. They have had little or no contact with ladies of breeding. To them most women are whores and they treat them accordingly. Keep your distance, and you will remain safe.'

'Your warning will be heeded,' Rianna replied as he helped her into the carriage. Chang behaved like a gentleman but she suspected that at times he could be just as savage as his men.

She had hoped the carriage would be empty, but to her consternation Niska was sitting inside, wrapped in a blue velvet cloak edge with snow-white fur. It would have been a beautiful garment if Niska hadn't been wearing it.

'Rianna,' Niska threw back her hood and smiled in her usual chilling fashion. 'You look a little pale, did you not pass a restful night?'

'Quite restful, considering,' Rianna retorted.

'Considering what?' Niska enquired, raising her pale eyebrows.

'Considering I had to spend it in your tent.' The effects of whatever she'd been given were becoming even more pronounced. Her limbs were heavy and she felt that she no longer had the strength to resist anything, even Niska.

'Ungrateful bitch,' Niska said coldly. 'Perhaps I should have let you sleep outside on the hard ground?'

'I've done so before,' Rianna replied as the carriage door opened and Tanith started to climb in.

'I'm sorry, my lady,' she said breathlessly.

'Get out,' Niska savagely interjected.

'My lady?' Tanith queried nervously, staring at her in surprise.

'Ride in the baggage wagon,' Niska commanded. 'If there's no room there, you'll have to walk. Just leave us. Lady Rianna and I wish to be alone.'

Looking upset, Tanith backed agitatedly out of the carriage, and shut the door, as Rianna looked curiously back at Niska. 'What could we possibly have to say to each other that shouldn't be overheard by your maidservant?'

'Who says I have anything to *say* to you?' Niska's lips twisted in a cruelly perverted smile as the coach started to move.

'Why else would you wish us to be alone?'

'Why else indeed.' Niska stared at her in a very penetrating way.

'Perhaps you are planning to kill me and push my body from the carriage in the darkest depth of this damnable forest,' she said, semi-jokingly, trying to hide her continued apprehension from Niska.

'Very droll.' Niska gave a false tinkling laugh. 'Be assured that if I planned to kill you I'd find a far less public way to dispose of you, Rianna. However, that is not my intention at all . . .' She leaned forwards, across the narrow space of the gently rocking carriage. 'I've no wish to be rid if you.' She brushed her finger across Rianna's pale cheek. 'Mayhap my plans are of a more intimate nature?' she purred.

'Intimate?' Rianna shrank back, feeling trapped.

'You had a female lover in the seraglio. Sarin encouraged you to enjoy the sensual pleasures of your own sex,' Niska teased. 'I recall one incident only too well. We were in the palace gardens, and Sarin ordered you to wear the harness . . .'

'And I refused,' Rianna pointed out. 'And endured a beating for my disobedience.'

'You were braver and stronger then. The fire has left you now . . .' Niska caressed Rianna's other cheek, then cupped her chin in her hands. 'You do not have the strength to refuse me anything,' she cooed, moving closer until Rianna felt the warmth of Niska's cinnamon-scented breath on her face. 'Why should we not share more than just my tent on this journey?'

'You jest,' Rianna muttered. 'I'd as soon bed a snake as you, Niska.'

Niska sat back, smiling wickedly. 'I've tried that, and it was a most stimulating experience. 'Twas not a large snake, but when it slithered inside me, its body undulating, the sensation was like nothing I've ever known. I climaxed any number of times.'

'You disgust me,' Rianna said, unsure whether to believe her.

'Come now.' Niska laughed again. 'Can you find no better words to describe your feelings for me?

'I'm too much of a lady to say them aloud,' Rianna responded. 'I'll keep such opinions to myself and try to remain civil in your presence until this journey is finished.' She looked out of the window. The trees seemed even thicker than before. 'Strange, I do not recognise any of this, yet I must have passed by here on the way to the castle of Dane.'

'Leon decided it would be wiser to take the northern route, we pass fewer towns and villages this way. He wished to avoid any sort of confrontations with the retreating troops. Some may be slow to leave, and unhappy to give up this land. A few may choose to fight to the bitter end.'

'So we are still on our way to Ruberoc?' Rianna asked without thinking.

'That is a strange question.' Niska looked at her oddly. 'What makes you think we would not be?'

Rianna shrugged her shoulders, deciding it would not be wise to voice any of her many suspicions. 'I don't know,' she muttered awkwardly.

'Perhaps the posset Tanith mistakenly gave you at the start of our journey still clouds your mind a little,' Niska said, sliding fine black leather gloves on her hands, even though the carriage was warmed by the copper stove. 'It was meant for me if I needed it, not you. If you are unused to those herbs the after-effects can linger.'

'Maybe so,' Rianna replied as she tried to sort out the confused thoughts that still filled her head, and fight the increasing languor that overtook her body.

Niska fell silent for a long time, while Rianna's mind drifted. She closed her eyes, she might even have slept for a while, she wasn't sure if she was asleep or awake. Then suddenly she was disturbed by the sound of Niska yawning loudly. 'I find travelling so tedious, perhaps we could find some stimulating occupation to pass the time?'

Rianna looked blearily at Niska. 'Whatever you wish,' she replied, fighting the need to close her eyes again.

'It is strange to think that by now Tarn may well be king,' Niska mused.

'Yes.' Rianna's expression softened. 'He will be a good king, and Kabra will grow prosperous again under his rule.'

'Your relationship will also change. Tarn will have the choice of any maiden at his court.' Niska smiled slyly.

Rianna stiffened, forcing herself fully awake. 'Tarn is as loyal to me as I am to him.'

'Really?' Niska looked surprised. 'Then indeed you must fear what the future holds,' she taunted. 'I don't recall you being at all loyal to Tarn while you were in Percheron. However, we all know that it is not the nature of any man to remain loyal to one woman. Just as we know which part of their anatomy rules their thoughts.'

'Tarn is not like that. He would never betray my trust,' Rianna insisted.

'He has done so before, why should he not do so again?'

'You lie,' Rianna retorted. 'He has never betrayed me willingly.'

'I do not lie, I tell the truth,' Niska said smugly. 'I speak from personal experience. 'Twas when Sarin had sent Tarn to the dungeons, a day or so after the incident with Cador. Anger clouded Sarin's judgement at that time and I felt sorry for Tarn. So I went to him, offered him my aide.'

'You went to gloat you mean,' Rianna snapped.

'I went purely to assure myself that he was not being mistreated by the gaoler. Sarin did not care if the gaolers

104

beat the prisoners or even took their pleasure with the more desirable ones,' Niska explained coolly. 'Tarn was strong enough to keep them at bay, but he was feeling very morose, and was happy to see me. He was heartened by the fact that at least one person had shown concern for his fate.'

'You lie,' Rianna hissed. 'I could not go to him, you know that, so you tell me things that are not true. If you had tried to be his friend, why would he appear to dislike you so much now?'

'Guilt perhaps?' Niska suggested. 'Tarn is a good man, perhaps his actions weigh heavily on his mind now that he is betrothed to you. He may regret making love to me so eagerly, then doubling my bliss by pleasuring me with his mouth.' Niska's eyes glittered as she stared challengingly at Rianna.

'I don't believe one word,' Rianna faltered.

'You always were a fool, Rianna.' Niska relaxed back in her seat, a sly smile still hovering on her lips. 'I assure you, I'm telling the truth. Tarn fucked me in the dungeon. When he slid his tongue . . .'

'Shut up,' Rianna interrupted, holding her hands over her ears, as a pink flush of anger covered her cheeks. 'You're lying.'

'If you think I'm lying, so be it.' Niska gave a soft chuckle. 'When we reach Ruberoc I suggest you ask Tarn yourself. He is too noble to lie to the woman he plans to make his wife. Then at last you'll know I was telling the truth.'

# Chapter Five

'Y ou've not eaten much, my lady,' Tanith said as she picked up the tray of food. The bowl of thick delicious-smelling stew was congealed and untouched. Rianna had even left the sweetmeats. All she had consumed was a small hunk of bread and some cheese.

'I wasn't very hungry.' Rianna was relieved to be away from Niska at last. They'd spent the whole day together confined in the small carriage and that was enough to destroy her appetite, even if she hadn't been carefully examining everything she put in her mouth.

'Or thirsty.' Tanith frowned as she looked at the goblet still full to the brim with red wine. 'You need to eat and drink to keep up your strength.'

'I drank some of the water in the carafe.' Rianna had thought that much safer than wine.

'I can bring more,' Tanith replied. 'The baroness is most particular from whence the water comes. She always insists it is boiled and cooled before she will drink one drop. She thinks boiling rids it of any harmful properties.'

Rianna nodded. Most people drank beer or wine in preference to water mainly because if it was from a tainted well or stream it could make one very sick. 'Just leave the carafe, I'll finish it later.' She had no wish to be disturbed again, and she was eager for Tanith to leave before she realised that the small sharp knife was missing from the tray.

'Sleep well then.' Tanith smiled awkwardly and then departed.

Rianna waited for a few minutes then crept to the rear of the tent. The fabric sides were held down by loops of rope that were fixed around wooden pegs hammered into the ground. She slid her hand under the taut canvas and felt around for the peg. It was difficult to ease off the stiff loop of rope, and she broke a couple of fingernails in the attempt before she freed it. From then on her task became easier, as the base of the fabric was not stretched so tightly, and she released the next two ropes quite quickly, leaving her with a narrow gap under which she could crawl.

She removed her dress. Beneath she was wearing her leather riding breeches and a thin, woollen shirt. She would not be very warm but the light clothing gave her freedom of movement. Lying flat on her belly, Rianna wriggled forwards, just managing to get under the canvas.

Fortunately she was facing away from the main body of the camp and no one saw her as she scrambled to her feet and hurried into the forest. She paused behind a tree, pushed back the stray strands of hair that had escaped from her loose plait and removed the small knife from her belt, holding it hidden in her right hand.

As far as Rianna could ascertain, Leon and his men were camped apart from the others, on the far side of the clearing. She would have to skirt around near half the camp to reach them. She crept along, her booted feet making no noise on the soft grass, careful to avoid any twigs or vegetation, as the slightest sound might alert the sentries. Cautiously she darted from one tree-trunk to another, hiding behind one, making sure it was safe before she moved to the next.

107

The fires blazed brightly, and most of the mercenaries were gathered round them, talking, laughing and drinking. Rianna heard smatters of conversations about torturing prisoners with hot coals and burning splinters. Amused laughter rang out from one group as a mercenary described how an enemy's skin might be removed and preserved to make garments of the softest hide. Rianna shuddered; these men were barbarians of the worst sort. How could Niska even think to place her trust in them?

She knew she was close to her objective when far to her right she saw two soldiers standing by a tent dressed in chain-mail shirts and tabards bearing the Kabran Royal coat of arms. She would find Leon's tent, slit open the canvas and enter it from the rear – that way Niska would never know that they had spoken in secret together. She just hoped that she could convince Leon to believe her. He was infatuated with Niska and she had already filled his head with terrible lies. However, Leon was still loyal to Tarn and that alone should at least make him listen to what she had to say.

Still keeping to the cover of the trees she crept towards the largest tent. The hairs on the back of her neck prickled as she heard the sharp sound of a twig snapping underfoot just behind her. Before she could turn and try to defend herself, an arm as strong as an iron band encircled her waist and a meaty hand was clamped across her mouth.

'What have we here?' A gruff voice whispered in her ear as she was pulled back against a hard, sweaty smelling body.

The metal studs decorating the man's leather doublet dug into Rianna's back as she struggled, flailing her arms and kicking vainly at her captor's booted shins. He lifted her and began skirting the camp, moving away from her own soldiers and any chance of imminent rescue. Rianna struggled helplessly, still clutching grimly on to the small knife. His hold on her tightened until his arm was almost crushing her ribs and that, coupled with his hand across her mouth, made it doubly difficult to draw breath.

They approached a small group of men crowded around a campfire, talking and laughing loudly. They fell silent as she was borne into their tight circle; their eyes fixed greedily on Rianna as her captor spoke to them in a rough guttural language that she did not understand. For a moment his hold on her loosened a little and Rianna twisted, kicked and wriggled from his grasp. She backed away from him, fearfully gasping for breath, trapped in the tight circle of wild-looking warriors, who stared at her as if they'd not been near a woman for years.

As she turned to face her attacker, the flickering firelight emphasised his menacing looks. His long, dirty brown hair was held back by a leather band across his forehead, and there was a jagged scar down his cheek that distorted his lip, giving him a permanent leering sneer.

Her throat had almost closed with terror, and she couldn't speak, let alone scream for help. Trying to remain steadfast and in control of her fear, she forced out her words. 'A pox on you, son of a whore,' she hissed, eyeing him warily. 'Keep away from me, you filthy swine. Touch me and my soldiers will slit your throat from ear to ear.'

'I thought you were creeping round the camp because you were looking for a man to warm your bed tonight?' he taunted. 'Why else would you be out here alone, princess?' He laughed and crudely rubbed his groin. 'I've always wanted to shag a woman of royal blood. But I'm generous, I'll give you a choice: him or me?' He pointed at the oldest and ugliest of the group, who had only one eye and a hook instead of a left hand. 'He claims to be able to do wonders with that hook when he fucks a woman.'

'Help me,' Rianna screamed, desperately searching for a way to escape as the hungry eyes of the mercenaries stripped her naked. She could almost feel their filthy hands touching every inch of her body. 'Help,' she yelled, even louder.

'No one's coming,' her captor growled. 'I'll kill anyone who interferes with my pleasure,' he added, grabbing hold of her shirt and ripping the fabric from neck to hem. As Rianna gave another terrified scream, he grabbed hold of her hair, almost ripping it from her scalp as he heaved her towards him. Tears of pain filled her eyes as he twined his arms round her neck and stilled her screams with his grubby hand. Pressing his palm hard across her mouth, he swung Rianna around and her shirt fell open to display her high full breasts to his fellow mercenaries' lustful gaze. 'Scream again, pretty one, and I'll slit *your* throat,' her captor growled. 'I'd as soon shag dead meat as a live one.'

Rianna ground her teeth into his palm, biting down hard until the metallic taste of his blood filled her mouth. With an angry grunt he let go of her and she turned and plunged the knife she'd kept hidden in her hand deep into his flesh. The man gave a shrill scream of pain as he looked down in disbelief at the knife embedded to the wooden hilt, only inches from his burgeoning prick.

She turned and ran, darting between two of the seated men, nimbly evading them when they reached out to catch her. She had barely run a few paces before she was grabbed by many hands pawing at her, pulling her back. She fought hard, squirming and screaming, but her cries for help were stifled by a wad of foul-tasting rags, which were thrust into her mouth. Before she could spit them out, she was gagged by a roll of fabric, which was pulled so tight it dug into the corners of her lips.

She lost all sense of time and space as she was man-handled into the centre of the group and flung down on to a blanket. Countless fingers clawed at her, pulling her arms and legs apart like a starfish stranded on a desolate beach. Rianna was too caught up in her terror to hear the sounds of running feet, the furious shouts of Leon's men

110

coming to her rescue, followed by the clash of weapons as they fought the mercenaries who were equally determined to stop them.

Her attackers tore her shirt to shreds, ripping the tattered remnants from her body, then tried to pull off her breeches, which proved to be far more difficult to remove. She fought, squirming and wriggling, using every ounce of strength she possessed until fire filled her lungs and scorched her throat. Naked and helpless, tears sliding down her face, she felt hands touch her intimately in a multitude of places. They roughly caressed her breasts, pulling at her nipples, while callused fingers stroked her belly and explored between her thighs. Despite her fear and disgust, she became aroused. Terror made the blood course through her veins as a wild, strangely invigorating need consumed her senses. She loathed what they were doing to her, yet she welcomed it. Rianna had no chance to question her body's strange response as fingers were thrust inside her, her violator grunting with pleasure when he found how moist and slippery she already was.

He thrust deeper into the wet opening and Rianna whimpered into her gag as she unconsciously lifted her hips. Feverish with the lustful fire that ripped through her flesh, she felt arousal increase as a multitude of hands stimulated her basest senses. The cruel pleasure expanded until, to her chagrin and relief, her vaginal muscles contracted in a violent climax.

Tears of self-recrimination and disgust stained her flushed cheeks as she stared wide-eyed at the men crowded about her. Rianna shivered in apprehension as they parted and a man stepped between her splayed legs. His breeches were round his ankles and his stubby red cock stood proudly out from a nest of black hair. Bile rose in her throat, yet her body trembled at the thought of something so crudely substantial invading her most intimate parts. The smell of sweat, leather and sour wine filled her nostrils; panic consumed her and yet she still had the overwhelming need to climax again and again.

Nothing made any sense any more and she moaned, wishing she could lose herself in the dark depths of unconsciousness. She squeezed her eyes shut tight, as she felt the hot head of the man's penis pressing against the aching opening of her empty pussy. Yet there was no brutal thrust, no cock sliding deep inside her, just a dull grunt before something extraordinarily heavy fell across her, almost crushing her with its weight. The cruel hands released her, no longer clutching at her ankles and wrists as the weight was lifted from her body and she heard a gentle, sing-song voice ask, 'Are you hurt, my lady?'

Rianna glanced down at the crimson smears of blood on her stomach and legs. 'No,' she murmured, as she saw the man who'd been about to violate her lying on the ground, the hilt of a dagger protruding from his back. 'Thank you,' she said weakly as Chang wrapped her in a blanket and lifted her into his arms.

'Is she hurt?' Niska asked, her pale eyes alight with anger, as she met Chang by the entrance to her tent.

'I do not think so,' Chang replied quite unemotionally as he carried his burden into Rianna's portion of Niska's tent. 'I reached the lady just in time,' he added, laying Rianna down on to her mattress.

'Before they fucked her senseless.' Niska's face was a mask of frustrated fury. 'You should have let them do it. What was she thinking?'

Rianna had her eyes closed and she was shivering uncontrollably. Tanith kneeled down beside her and pulled back the blanket, biting her lip with concern as she saw the blood smeared over Rianna's stomach and thighs.

'It's not hers,' Chang said flatly as Tanith wrung out a cloth in warm water and began to dab nervously at the crimson stains. He looked at Niska. 'I doubt you would have wanted them to violate her. She's delicately bred.

They would have ripped her to pieces. Then she would have been no use to us.'

'I suppose you are right,' Niska agreed. 'But how could she have been stupid enough to leave the safety of my tent?'

'Why would she have been wandering around the camp in the middle of the night?' Chang added, with a troubled frown. 'I warned Lady Rianna only this morning to keep well away from my men.' He shook his head. 'I confess I do not understand women.'

'Rianna will have to be kept confined in future,' Niska said thoughtfully. 'I cannot allow this to happen again. Did we lose any men?'

'I've yet to count the full cost. Horod is checking now.' Chang watched Tanith gently cleanse between Rianna's bruised thighs. 'A number of Captain Leon's soldiers heard her screams and rushed to her rescue. At least two were mortally wounded in the resulting fracas,' Chang said in a low voice. 'Come let us leave your maid to her task,' he added, escorting Niska out of Rianna's earshot.

'The loss of any of Leon's men is of little concern,' Niska said curtly. 'It leaves us less to turn to our cause, or be rid of. Yet I fear some of our men may have been wounded or even died, which will deplete our forces.'

'We've more than enough to reach Vestfold in perfect safety,' Chang assured her. 'You just need to ensure that nothing like this happens again. I presume I have your permission to punish those involved?' he asked, pausing at the entrance to Niska's tent.

'Notwithstanding Lady Rianna, of course.' Niska pursed her lips. 'I'll deal with her myself.'

'I expected you to do so.' There was just the faintest glimmer of Chang's inscrutable smile as he added, 'A dozen lashes will suffice for the men who dared attack the noble lady.' He touched the ornate hilt of the dagger stuck in his belt. 'Although I'd as soon slit their throats. My authority needs to be impressed on all the men, not one of them must be seen to disobey my commands. I issued a number of specific orders before we set out. They included instructions to stay away from all women – even those we came across on our journey north.'

'I will take pleasure in witnessing the punishments,' Niska said with a cruel smile. 'I find whippings so stimulating. Speak to me later, Chang. Let me know when they will take place.'

'As you wish.' Chang bowed very formally, then strode off.

Niska was still angered by Rianna's stupid behaviour, but she did pause to wonder if she could find a way to use it to her advantage. She had been in the forest leaning against a tree, fornicating with Leon, when Rianna's first distant scream had punctuated the still night air. Leon had been so caught up in his imminent climax that he hadn't heard the sounds and Niska had believed it to be Tanith screaming. She had thought that a good fucking by a few of the men would teach Tanith to be more cautious about wandering around the camp in future.

Leon had heard the screams that followed, and he'd flung on his breeches and gone to investigate, while Niska had returned to her tent and found Rianna missing. By then a pitched battle was in progress between the members of Leon's troop, who had gone to Rianna's aid, and the mercenaries trying to stop the soldiers interfering with their compatriots' pleasures. Only Chang's timely intervention had stopped the slaughter.

Niska sighed with relief when she spotted Leon, apparently unhurt, striding towards her clad in nothing but his breeches. His expression was tense and his features tight with cold. Oddly enough she had grown quite fond of him of late, but she would still toss him aside without a second thought once his usefulness was at an end.

'Is Lady Rianna harmed?' Leon asked.

'Be assured she is not.' Niska took hold of his icy cold arm and led him inside her tent and over to a brazier, which glowed redly in the dim interior. 'She's upset, but apart from that unharmed,' Niska said as she draped a fur-lined cloak around his shoulders.

'Did they . . .'

'No,' she interjected. 'Chang and his men reached her in time. They'd stripped her, but as far as I know none had yet violated her.'

'Prince Tarn would never have forgiven me,' Leon said shakily.

'It is not your fault.' Niska could understand the guilt he was feeling. Leon still remained loyal to Prince Tarn. Not for long, however, she thought, as she gently touched his tense cheek. 'This only happened because Rianna stupidly chose to wander around the camp in the middle of the night.'

'Why would she do such a thing?' Leon asked. 'I don't understand.'

'Neither do I,' Niska agreed. 'Chang warned her only this morning to keep well away from his men.'

'I have to see her.' Leon swivelled around agitatedly. 'I must see for myself that she is unhurt.'

'Of course you must.' By now Tanith would have given Rianna something to calm her and make her sleep, Niska thought. Even if she were awake she would be too confused for her words to make any sense. 'First dress yourself. I had your garments brought back to the camp.'

Niska watched Leon pull on his boots and thrust his arms into his doublet, not even bothering to wait to fasten it as he strode into Rianna's portion of the tent where Tanith had just finished tending to her. Tanith rose to her feet and carried away the soiled cloths and a basin of bloodstained water as Leon looked down at his charge. Rianna's eyes were closed and she appeared to be asleep. There were no scratches or scars on her face and neck; the damage was hidden by her blankets, well out of Leon's sight.

'She looks well enough,' Leon exclaimed with relief as he kneeled down beside Rianna.

'Leon, is that you?' Rianna murmured sleepily as she

opened her eyes. 'You came,' she added in a low, breathy voice.

'Of course I came, my lady,' Leon said gently, then glanced up to Niska for reassurance.

'You see she is unharmed,' Niska said.

'Leon,' Rianna called out agitatedly, then mumbled something else but her words were near incomprehensible.

'Speak slower, my lady,' Leon urged, while Niska tensed nervously, digging her nails in the palm of her hand, hoping Rianna didn't say anything untoward. 'I did not hear what you said,' he added, leaning closer to Rianna.

'I wanted you,' Rianna said in a faint, very slurred voice as she reached out for him, twining her arms around his neck, pulling him even closer. 'I had to tell you . . .'

'Tell me what?' Leon asked in confusion, so close to her now that their lips were almost touching.

'I needed to speak to you.' Rianna agitatedly ran her hand over his bare chest where his doublet gaped open. 'Tell you that I needed you,' she muttered shakily. 'So much . . . it's not Niska, it's me you should . . .' Rianna faltered, clutching agitatedly at Leon. 'Promise me, my lo . . .' Her voice trailed off as her eyes fluttered then closed.

Leon unwrapped her limp arm from his neck. 'I don't understand.' He stared down at Rianna for a moment, then rose awkwardly to his feet.

'It is perfectly clear to me.' Niska took hold of his arm and led him into the main body of her tent. 'Jealousy prompted Rianna to seek you out. She was coming to your tent, intent on seducing you and trapping you in her web of deception. Can you not see that?'

'She intended to try and seduce me?'

'Yes. It is obvious, is it not? Why else would she be creeping about the camp in the middle of the night?'

'It is beyond belief.' He shook his head. 'She is betrothed to Tarn.'

'I warned you about her, Leon.' Niska was certain that Rianna had played right into her hands. 'She is not to be trusted. You have to see her true perfidy for yourself.'

Sarin's horse slowly picked its way down the steep, stone-strewn slope until it at last reached fairly level ground. The trek across the mountains had been hard. The narrow, icy path had been difficult to navigate and had even fallen away in a number of places. Ahead was a ribbon of flat land edged with a thin line of pines where the last wisps of a morning mist lingered. Behind the pines he could see a thick forest, where stark leafless branches reached up towards the clear blue sky.

'We are in Kabra,' Sarin announced with a triumphant smile as Zene reined in her horse beside him.

'We are indeed,' she agreed. 'And we will have to seek out a village soon. Our supplies are running low, we barely have enough food, and no feed for the horses.'

'Here in Kabra we can take anything we want,' Sarin said confidently. 'No peasant would dare deny the needs of a Percheron nobleman.' He shaded his eyes from the bright sunshine and stared ahead. 'See that thick plume of smoke in the distance. It is probably a charcoal burner. There's bound to be a village close by.'

Zene frowned. Her relationship with Sarin had altered dramatically ever since the incident when he had more or less forced himself upon her. She'd reluctantly accepted that he was the leader now, and she had already been obliged to defer to him on a number of occasions. 'It will be strange,' she said. 'To be in a land where women have little or no control.'

'That is as it should be.' Sarin chuckled cheerfully. 'You'll soon learn to accept it, Zene. Who knows, you may even come to enjoy being cherished and protected by a man.'

'I doubt that,' she replied. 'Let's go.' She dug her heels

into her chestnut's flanks. It surged forwards and settled into a fast canter, easily navigating the gently undulating ground. Sarin followed, his huge black stallion leaping forwards, enjoying the prospect of a fast canter after hours of picking its way down the treacherous slopes. The stallion easily overtook Zene's mount and galloped ahead towards the forest.

Leaves were beginning to sprout and some of the trees were already festooned with cascades of pink and white blossom. Carpets of bluebells covered the ground and as they moved deeper into the forest the blooms were crushed beneath the horses' hooves, scenting the cool morning air with the strong smell of spring.

Sarin had been right about the charcoal burner. They skirted his smoky clearing and entered a village of houses with low thatched roofs. Most were made of wattle, but a few of the wealthy villagers had houses built of stone. The inhabitants paused to stare curiously at the two riders, with Zene's unusual appearance causing the most interest. The village women wore long gowns of blue or grey, covered by shapeless tunics in a profusion of different colours. Unlike Zene, who wore her long copper curls unbound, theirs were tightly plaited and fixed close to their heads.

'Is that how women dress here?' Zene wrinkled her nose. 'They look most unattractive.'

Sarin found it amusing that a warrior such as Zene should even care. 'Don't worry,' he said out of the corner of his mouth. 'I would never expect you to dress like that,' he added, repelled by the women's work-weary faces and shapeless garments.

'Thank the gods,' Zene muttered.

All of a sudden they found their way barred by a small group of men armed with long wooden staves.

'Why do you enter our village, strangers?' the man leading them asked. He wore dung-coloured garments like the other men, but his were of a far better quality.

118

Judging by his wrinkled face and the white streaks in his dark hair, he was a village elder.

'Strangers?' Sarin repeated in confusion. They did not sound at all welcoming. He drew himself erect in his saddle. 'Do you not recognise a nobleman of Percheron?'

'Percheron.' The leader spat on the ground. 'You'll get nothing from us. Most of you scum have already fled.'

'Fled?' Zene asked, then stiffened as they all turned to stare at her.

'Yes, fled.' The man grinned as his eyes fastened on Zene's shapely legs and the generous amount of bosom that was revealed by her low-cut top. 'Did you not know that Prince Tarn drove the Percheron army from our land?'

'My army is in retreat?' Sarin exclaimed.

'Apart from a few stragglers,' the young man standing by the leader's side said. 'You should have left with them.'

'Stragglers? How long ago did the last ones depart?' Sarin asked.

'The last soldiers to travel through here were not stragglers,' the leader said and shrugged his bony shoulders. 'They were a small troop of soldiers who'd been given a promise of safe passage by our king.' Pausing he stepped closer to Sarin, his strong body odour became very apparent, as he stared insolently up at him. You seem unduly interested in them, stranger?'

'If my country's army is in retreat, I would perhaps be safer travelling with them,' Sarin pointed out. 'Tell me what you know of them, and which way they went.'

'For a price.' The man held out his hand, which shook slightly. His knuckles were red and swollen. 'Pay me for the information, and we'll allow you to continue on your way. Otherwise . . .' he said and grinned evilly at Zene, whose hand now rested very pointedly on the pommel of her sword.

'Zene.' Sarin glanced at her. 'Pay him.'

Reluctantly she removed a coin from the pouch at her

waist and tossed it to the man, who caught it neatly despite the shakiness of his hands. 'I do not know what good it will do you,' she muttered. 'It's the coin of Freygard.'

The man examined the silver piece. 'I care not what design is upon it. It is silver and that's all that matters,' he said curtly, then looked expectantly at Zene. 'It is not enough, however.'

She sighed, and tossed him two more silver coins. 'That's all I have.'

He seemed content, clutching the coins in his greedy grasp as he looked back at Sarin. 'If you intend to return directly to Percheron, then the soldiers you seek will be of little help,' he said grinning. 'They are travelling north – in pursuit of a thief. That is why they have the letter of safe passage.'

'What could be of such importance that it requires an entire contingent of soldiers to track down one thief?' Sarin asked curiously.

'They would not say. A great treasure perhaps,' the leader said slyly. 'All I know is that the thief was a woman. A lady of quality they said.'

'How long ago did they pass through here?' Sarin asked, glancing at Zene.

'Just after dawn. No doubt if you and your friend ride fast you will catch up with them in a day or so.' The leader pointed north. 'They took the trail through the forest. It's narrow but on horseback you'll move quite swiftly.'

'I'm obliged to you,' Sarin said politely. 'Come, let us depart, Zene.' He turned his horse in the direction the man had pointed.

The track through the forest was gradually getting narrower as if it were little used and that concerned Leon. He frowned and looked up at the sky, which was covered by a thick layer of grey cloud, just as it had been for the last three days and nights. It was easy enough to know

120

in which direction you were travelling when the sun or stars were visible, but there wasn't even a glimmer to betray the position of the sun today. Chang insisted they were now travelling due east and should reach Ruberoc tomorrow at the latest. Leon doubted that was true; he didn't trust Chang, nor any of his mercenaries. They should have reached Ruberoc days ago and his gut instinct told him they were still moving north.

Leon's men were as unsettled as he was, which was not surprising as they had lost so many of their companions of late. The day before yesterday a small joint contingent had gone on ahead to scout out the route and had been set upon by bandits. All three of Leon's men, and two mercenaries, had been slaughtered. However, not one of the men who'd returned had been wounded and the bandits had disappeared back into the forest again like shadows in the night. It was almost as if they'd never existed at all.

Early this morning he had discovered that two more of his remaining soldiers had deserted. They had been two of Leon's most trusted men and he found it difficult to believe they'd departed willingly. He had only five men left now out of the original troop of sixteen. Only one of them, Gavid, did he trust implicitly. The others had been surly and resentful when taking orders of late. When he walked through the camp, Leon felt the eyes of the mercenaries upon him, as if they would as soon shove a dagger in his back as allow him to pass by, and Gavid had admitted this morning that he felt as uneasy as Leon did.

Digging his heels into the side of his horse, Leon spurred it into a trot until he reached Gavid, who was riding at the rear of his very depleted group of men. 'I need you to take my mount,' Leon said, as the two men stopped by the side of the track. 'I'll travel in the baroness's carriage for a while.'

Gavid smiled tightly. 'Did you not have enough of the

noble lady's attention last night? You did not return to our tent.'

'Maybe not.' Leon swung out of his saddle and threw his horse's reins to Gavid. 'I need to have a serious talk with her. There are matters to discuss.'

'There are indeed.' Gavid glanced at the mercenaries, two columns strong, as they rode past in a double line. Shields hung low on their saddles, and their well-worn swords hung at their sides or were strapped across their backs. Some wore armour stolen from slaughtered soldiers from many different lands, others wore garments that displayed their heritage. Yet even with their motley collection of multicoloured finery, and their mismatched armour, they looked far more threatening than a well-turned out troop of soldiers. 'We should never have travelled with these men. I've told you before, Leon, it was a terrible mistake,' he said in a low whisper.

'It seemed the best decision at the time.' Leon resented the way Gavid had begun to voice his own opinions. It was not his place to do so, he was not captain of the troop.

'To be honest, I don't blame the others for running off,' Gavid continued. 'I would also leave as long as you and Lady Rianna would agree to come with me.'

Leon had not seen Rianna since the attack on her, although he had tried to a number of times. He had been told she was indisposed and didn't want to speak to him. She was keeping herself hidden, perhaps out of embarrassment or shame.

'All will be well, Gavid,' Leon said as he watched Niska's coach trundle past them.

He darted forwards and jumped on to the step, opening the door and swinging deftly inside the carriage in one smooth movement, hoping to see Lady Rianna as well, but to his consternation the only occupants were Niska and her maid.

'Baroness,' he acknowledged very formally. 'Forgive the intrusion.' He sat down before being invited to do so.

'Captain Leon?'

'I wish to speak to you in private.'

Niska glanced over at her maid. 'You may leave, Tanith.'

The maid looked anxiously out of the window. 'Leave . . .?' She wasn't a very agile person, and it would doubtless be quite hazardous for her to try and leap from the carriage while it was moving.

'Don't question my orders,' Niska said curtly. 'Go now!'

Niska smiled with cruel amusement as the maid nervously opened the door and left the carriage with an awkward jump. Leon winced as he heard Tanith give a loud, anguished squeal as she landed clumsily in a pile of rotting vegetation.

Showing no concern for her maid's fate, Niska looked back at Leon. 'This is a surprise,' she said coolly.

'My lady.' Leon kissed her gloved hand. 'Where is Lady Rianna, may I ask?'

'Travelling in the baggage wagon.' Niska shrugged her elegant shoulders. 'She chose to, after expressing a strong desire not to travel with me. She had no wish to be seen, so the baggage wagon is the only other conveyance.'

'Why should she wish to travel alone?' Leon asked worriedly.

Niska sighed. 'I tried to make friends with her, Leon. I have done everything I can for her, yet she still continues to reject my attempts at friendship. Rianna has been even more difficult to contend with since the attack on her person. At least before that she travelled somewhat resentfully in my coach, but now . . .' Niska sighed again. 'She is behaving most strangely.'

'I have tried to see her a number of times, but your maid always gives me some excuse or other,' Leon pointed out.

'Tanith merely does as Rianna instructs.' Niska pulled down the window blinds to give them more privacy. 'The noble lady shares my tent, orders my maid about as if *she* owned her, yet barely bothers to speak to me. She spends most of her time reading books I have lent her, or sitting alone staring into the distance. I have tried to persuade her to speak to you, but she constantly rejects my advice. Mayhap she is too embarrassed or upset to face you, Leon. After all, her foolish behaviour brought about the death of two of your men.'

'I fear she needs to see a physician.' He frowned anxiously.

'The physicians in Kabra are backward fools who would just bleed her or fill her with purgatives – neither would do her any good,' she said curtly, stripping off her leather gloves. 'Rianna is not an easy woman to understand. She has a complex nature. Her mood changes by the moment.'

'I've yet to see that side of her,' Leon admitted. 'On the journey to the castle of Dane she was sweet tempered and patient with not a bad word for anyone.'

'You barely knew the lady before Prince Tarn charged you with escorting her to Harn, so how are you to know her true nature?' Niska said bluntly. 'She doubtless appeared sweet tempered because she was in the presence of a handsome young captain who was trying vainly to hide his attraction to her. She hungers for a man's adoration, and without Prince Tarn to satisfy her needs, she turned to you instead. Now, at last, she has been forced to face the consequences of her insane behaviour.' Niska paused and looked sympathetically at Leon. 'I forgot – I have yet to express my regret at the loss of more of your fine soldiers.' She unfastened her cloak and shrugged it off. 'I only wish we could have found the bandits that slaughtered them. I fear they have fled north. Most of these criminals seem to take refuge in the mountains of Vestfold.'

'More's the pity,' Leon said. 'They have their strongholds in those mountains and venture forth to attack small settlements in the north of Kabra. They decimate small villages, plundering, killing, or enslaving. Prince

Tarn has sworn to stop it, but I doubt he has enough men to carry out his promise. Even during the occupation the invading army was powerless to prevent such attacks.'

'I should speak to my brother when I see him. After all, he is Lawspeaker of Vestfold.'

'Indeed you should,' Leon agreed, unable to stop staring hungrily at Niska. The neckline of her tight-fitting bodice was cut low across her breasts and he could see the rise and fall of the pale, tempting globes. He wanted her now more than ever. When they were apart she filled his thoughts day and night. Often he paused to wonder if he was losing his sanity, he was so hopelessly captivated by her charms. A wee voice did occasionally intrude on his thoughts, which begged him to question her motives and goals, but all she had to do was smile at him and his doubts and fears disappeared in an instant.

'Prince Tarn would doubtless be grateful to anyone who could persuade Ragnor and the other warlords to stop giving the bandits refuge in Vestfold,' she said as she played with the laces of her bodice, then slowly and very pointedly undid the bow at the top.

'Very grateful.' Leon fought the urge to rip open her bodice and bury his face in her breasts, as he moved awkwardly on his seat, all too conscious of his burgeoning arousal.

'What is wrong, my love?' Niska teased, easing the laces further apart, until a tempting portion of her bosom began to show. 'Was there something you wanted?'

'This,' Leon leaned forwards and jerked the bodice open by snapping the rest of the fragile lacing. He stroked and kissed Niska's bosom. Urged on by her throaty laugh of pleasure he fastened his lips on her diamond-pierced nipple, and pulled it into his mouth. He sucked on it, stretched and twisted it until she gave a soft whimper of discomfort.

'I adore you,' she purred pulling up her satin skirts

with a seductive rustle and parting her thighs to reveal her naked, innocent-looking pussy.

'And I worship you,' Leon groaned. 'Let me taste you,' he begged, falling to his knees between her open thighs.

'No,' she said harshly, grabbing hold of his chin before his lips could taste the sweet liquor of her arousal. 'I want to feel your cock thrusting inside me.'

Leon slid two fingers into her moist cunt while his other hand fumbled urgently at his breeches. His cock was already hard and weeping salty tears from the tip as he freed it. Excitedly he pressed its length against the edge of the seat, feeling the soft fur rub tantalisingly against his tightly stretched skin, setting each nerve ending alight with pleasure.

Sweet joy filled his chest and he could barely breathe as his fingers slid deeper into Niska's wet slippery flesh. It felt as if she was devouring him inch by inch. Groaning softly, she spread her legs wider. 'More,' she gasped, shivering as he eased two more fingers inside her, twisting and thrusting until her eyes glazed with bliss.

All the while he ministered to her, she rubbed herself gently but deliberately, fixing him with a foxy expression of lust. Frightened that he might climax before he'd even entered her, Leon replaced his fingers with his aching cock, forcing it inside her until his belly was pressed hard against her open quim. He clutched on to Niska's buttocks, digging his fingers into her taut flesh, while his index finger eased its way downwards, sliding into the deliciously tight hole of her anus. He began to move his hips; his thrusts gaining further power from the rocking motion of the carriage as it trundled over the rough track.

The vehicle swayed from side to side as Leon's hips moved in a wild dance of pleasure, pounding vigorously into her. Her small breasts jiggled enticingly in front of his face, the diamond sparkling as it swung hypnotically. But Leon did not even have the strength to pull it into his mouth as Niska's cunt closed tightly around his hard flesh, her juices silkily coating his shaft, dribbling down through his pubic hair to tickle teasingly at his balls as they slapped loosely against the fur-covered seat. One sweet sensation piled on another as Leon continued thrusting, his finger digging deep in her tight little arse-hole in an effort to fill her completely.

He felt her muscles convulse around his cock and the blazing fire erupted, spearing through his belly in power-ful waves. He spent his seed, pumping it into her until his body was drained and his limbs trembled from the strength of his climax.

Leon leaned against Niska, feeling spent and exhausted, but she seemed invigorated, almost as if she had gained power from his violent release. 'I want you to promise me something, Leon,' she said as she stroked his hair.

'Of course,' he mumbled. At this moment in time he'd give her anything she wanted, even his soul if she asked for it.

'I want you to promise that in future you will do exactly as I ask, without question.

'Yes . . . anything,' he said shakily.

'Let me move, my love,' she said, waiting while he eased himself away from her and perched on the opposite seat. The warm smell of sex assailed his nostrils, filling the interior of the carriage, as he watched Niska dab delicately between her legs with a lace kerchief. Her pussy was pink and swollen, gleaming wetly with their combined leavings. It looked so delicious that Leon would have given anything to fuck her again. He had the will but not the energy, he was so exhausted he barely had the strength to move.

'My lips would do that for you,' he said with a hungry groan, watching intently as she delicately wiped herself.

'Are you never satisfied? she said with a teasing smile, as she tossed the kerchief to him and watched him raise it to his nostrils to savour the strong fragrance of the soiled linen.

'I can't get enough of you, my love. You know that.'

He tucked the kerchief in his doublet and eased his cock back into his breeches.

'Why not move your things into my tent tomorrow evening?' Niska suggested. 'It will be some days yet before we reach our destination.'

'Ruberoc is not that far,' he said haltingly.

'Be honest with yourself, Leon. If we'd really been travelling to Ruberoc we would have been there days ago.'

'Then where are we going?' he asked, very aware that he'd been trying to hide the painful truth from himself.

'I think you know that already.' She slid her skirt over her knees and began to refasten her bodice.

'Vestfold?' he asked falteringly. 'But I cannot . . .'

'You promised you would do what I asked without question,' she reminded him.

'I know,' he admitted awkwardly.

'Then you will come to Vestfold with me,' she demanded.

'Niska . . .' His mind was in turmoil. Leon knew without a doubt that he would lose Niska if he didn't do as she asked.

'You have a deep loyalty for Prince Tarn, and I find that loyalty commendable, but you promised me, did you not?' she challenged, and as Leon stared at her beautiful face he couldn't bear the thought of never possessing her again.

'Yes,' he reluctantly admitted.

'Think of it, my love. We could persuade Ragnor to form a treaty between Vestfold and Kabra. This would allow the bandits that plague your land to be hunted down and destroyed. Your new king would grant you riches and power if you could achieve that!'

'Maybe so,' he agreed, swallowing awkwardly. 'But I was charged by Prince Tarn to escort Lady Rianna safely back to Ruberoc.'

'That can be easily settled,' Niska smiled persuasively. 'Her company palls on me, she is nothing but trouble.

128

We could determine a way to return her safely to her betrothed.'

Leon was confused. He trusted Niska and couldn't quite understand why she had been lying about their destination all this time. Did she ever plan to go to Ruberoc, he asked himself, as Niska moved across the carriage and sat on his lap.

'Poor Leon.' Niska twined her arms around his neck. 'So loyal, so loving.' She kissed his cheek, and smoothed his furrowed brow. 'We will discuss my plans later. There are so many other more pleasant ways to pass the time,' she murmured, fastening her lips on his.

# Chapter Six

The royal castle at Ruberoc had changed little during the intervening years. It looked almost the same now to Tarn as it had the morning he'd watched his father surrender to the invading army of Percheron. The following day he'd been sent to Aguilar as a royal hostage. Tarn had arrived expecting to be imprisoned, but he had received a welcome befitting his royal status. Lord Sarin had been kind and had treated Tarn like a well-loved, younger brother. However, in time Sarin's affections had begun to extend way beyond friendship.

Tarn had managed to persuade Sarin to allow him to return to Kabra to see his ailing father, and once there he had tried to raise an army to free his people. He might well have succeeded if he had not been betrayed by a comrade in arms, one he trusted implicitly. The rebellion had failed and Tarn had been captured and returned to Percheron in chains.

Now Brion was dead and Tarn was king. Dressed in royal robes of satin and velvet, he paced the great hall, pausing to stare up at the domed ceiling and the stone walls hung with elaborate tapestries from a bygone age. Sighing, his heart heavy with concern, he sat down on his gilded throne and stared thoughtfully into the distance.

'My liege.' A page approached and kneeled before Tarn, holding out a goblet filled to the brim with wine from a Kabran vineyard in the far south. It was one of the best vintages in the extensive cellars laid down by Tarn's grandfather, Erlich. There were few bottles left as the cellars had been all but depleted by the greedy officials Sarin had sent there to ensure King Brion always did as he was told.

The scavengers were gone now, but what they couldn't take with them they had made every attempt to destroy. Few had tried to stop them, as a large number of the Kabran nobility had sided with Percheron; they had betrayed their own people in order to retain their wealth and power. Tarn loathed these men, and had banished them all from his court as soon as Brion had died. He wanted no traitors or toadying sycophants to serve him. He would govern alone if he had to until he had gathered around him those advisors he knew he could trust.

Morosely he drained the goblet of wine, then glanced down at the finely wrought silver goblet. It was one of the few royal treasures that had survived. Most had been looted by Sarin's retreating forces. The rest he had broken up and used to pay the army that had helped him to free Kabra. However, that was the least of his concerns. Rianna should have arrived in Ruberoc days ago. He had sent out troops to seek her out, but so far they had found no sign of Rianna, or Leon and his men.

He was just about to send for the page and drown his sorrows in more wine, when a man-at-arms rushed into the large chamber. 'My liege,' he said agitatedly, as he hurried towards the throne.

'Yes?' Tarn prayed that it was news of Rianna.

'A merchant has arrived in the city,' the soldier said breathlessly, coming to a halt and bowing in one awkward movement. 'He has come straight to the palace to tell you that he has in his care a wounded man, a member of Captain Leon's troop. He found the soldier in the woods only ten leagues from the castle of Dane.'

131

Tarn's heart missed a beat. 'Bring the merchant to me, now.'

He waited impatiently until the merchant – a portly well-dressed man – was escorted into the great hall. He hurried forwards and was well out of breath by the time he reached Tarn.

'Your Majesty, this is an honour,' the man gabbled, bowing low and totally forgetting that he had been instructed to wait and let the king speak first.

'You have news for me?' Tarn tried to hide his concern. 'You found one of my men?'

'Yes, Your Majesty. He was gravely hurt, and near death,' the merchant explained, clasping his hands over his portly stomach. 'It was only my wife's skill in the art of healing that saved the man,' he added proudly. 'He'd been lying in the woods for nigh on two days.'

Tarn drummed his fingers on the gilded arm of his throne. 'How came he to be wounded, was he able to tell you?'

'The soldier, Narian, was a member of Captain Leon's troop. They were assigned to protect the Lady Riann –'

'I know that,' Tarn interrupted harshly. 'Tell me what happened to him!'

'Narian tells me that Captain Leon decided to join forces with an acquaintance of his, Baroness Crissana. She was also making her way to Ruberoc, and as she had a large number of men at her disposal, Captain Leon thought it safer for them to travel together.'

'I have never heard of this baroness,' Tarn commented thoughtfully.

'She is a noble lady of untold wealth, who has an army of mercenaries in her employ.' The man awkwardly cleared his throat. 'Narian and his compatriots had no reason to doubt the baroness's men. They made camp on the first night, and Narian and a fellow soldier went into the woods to ... er ... relieve themselves.' He spoke in an embarrassed voice as if one should not mention such matters in front of a king. 'The mercenaries watched

132

them leave, then a few of them followed Narian and his friend. They were set upon in a clearing; the mercenaries were clearly intent on slaughtering them both. Badly wounded, the two soldiers were left for dead. Narian managed to drag himself into the shelter of some bushes, but by then his friend had died. Next morning, after they had all departed, he tried to drag himself back to the castle of Dane, but he was unable to make it. The gods must have guided me to him. I found him where he had fallen almost two days later.'

'And the baroness? Which direction did she and her men take?' Tarn asked. His mind was racing.

'The northern trail to Ruberoc, I believe.' The man faltered. 'But I have been told that your betrothed, Lady Rianna, has not arrived here. Even if they took another route they should be there by now.'

'Indeed they should,' Tarn interrupted impatiently as he rose to his feet. He had no idea who this baroness was, but he was convinced now that Rianna was far from safe.

Totally ignoring the merchant who stood there, most probably expecting a reward, Tarn strode from the great hall. He would question Narian himself, then he would gather his troops and set off in pursuit.


'You have your orders,' Leon said gravely as he addressed Gavid. Once his compatriot had departed there would be no one left he could rely on, except Niska, of course.

Gavid nodded. 'I'd as soon not leave alone,' he admitted. 'Once again I beg you and Lady Rianna to come with me.'

'That is impossible,' Leon said, shaking his head. 'I assure you, Gavid, as long as we both stay close to the baroness we will be quite safe. She will ensure no harm comes to either of us.' He was officially residing in Niska's tent now. While the few men he had left appeared all to happy too throw their lot in with the mercenaries. Leon still felt very uneasy about the promise he had made to Niska to go to Vestfold with her, but he had no choice, he didn't want to lose her. She was certain that her brother Ragnor would be able to persuade the other warlords of Vestfold to negotiate a peace treaty with Kabra, and no longer allow bandits safe refuge in his land. She would be able to return to Ruberoc in triumph and Tarn would then be happy to welcome her to his court.

The plan was sound enough, but Leon was concerned about breaking the promise he had made to Prince Tarn. Therefore, he had asked Gavid to carry a message to Ruberoc advising his sovereign that Rianna was safe and well. Soon he calculated they would be close to the town of Nemedia. Leon had yet to discuss it with Niska, but he had decided they could leave Lady Rianna there. She would be protected in Nemedia until Tarn's troops were able to reach her and return her to her betrothed.

'Are you sure you will both be safe?' Gavid asked worriedly. 'You tell me that you plan to leave Lady Rianna in Nemedia, but why did the baroness not tell you that she never truly intended to return to Ruberoc when we set out?'

'I have told you already,' Leon said irritably. 'She did plan to go to Ruberoc until Lady Rianna made it very clear she would not be welcome at court. We'll not discuss this any longer,' he added awkwardly. How could he convince Gavid, when he was confused about the entire matter himself? 'Advise Prince Tarn that Lady Rianna is safe. She has moved into her own tent, and is constantly guarded by Chang. Understandably she feels safe with Chang because he came to her rescue when she was attacked,' Leon said confidently, although he still hadn't spoken to Rianna himself.

'I cannot understand how anyone could place their trust in Chang.' Gavid tightened the girth of his horse's saddle. 'There is something evil lurking in that man, I feel it.'

Leon took little notice of Gavid's opinion of Chang. He always had been a little strange and claimed he could sense things other's could not. 'You worry too much, my friend,' he replied. 'He's a good leader and the baroness trusts him implicitly. You should go – it will be dark soon, and you have a long ride ahead.'

'May the winds be with you always,' Gavid said as he swung himself into the saddle and spurred his horse forwards, soon disappearing into the depths of the forest.

Neither Leon nor his friend saw the four mercenaries lurking in the cover of the trees, watching Gavid depart. They waited a few minutes then followed the lone rider, silently stalking their prey, waiting for the perfect moment to attack.

Gavid had taken the southerly route – a narrow path that wound its way between the trees then widened enough to allow him to spur his horse into a fast canter. Drawing their weapons the mercenaries followed him, making sure Gavid did not spot them until they were well out of earshot of the camp. Gavid was just beginning to feel relieved that he was well away from a difficult situation, when he heard the menacing pounding of horses' hooves. A number of riders were approaching fast. Gavid pulled his sword from its scabbard, hoping it wasn't bandits, as he urged his mount into a fast gallop in an attempt to outrun his pursuers.

When he realised he wasn't going to be able to evade the inevitable, he stopped, turned his horse and held his ground. His palm grew slick with the perspiration of fear as he tightened his hold on the leather-bound hilt of his sword, while his exhausted mount stood there, flanks heaving, foam spewing from the side of its mouth.

Gavid couldn't say he was surprised when he saw who the men were. The four mercenaries galloped towards him yelling wildly. They attacked, their horses circling Gavid. He was a good fighter and he parried and slashed, hearing the grating sound of metal scraping against metal as he fought all four of them at once. Guiding his horse round with his knees, he swung his sword in a wide arc, never knowing from which direction the next blow would come.

He felt the tip of his sword slash through sinew and bone, setting forth a bright spray of red. Barely hearing the wounded man's cry, Gavid parried another blow and felt a blade slice through his leather doublet and cold metal pierce his flesh. Almost immune to the pain, blood seeping slowly from the wound, he pulled away and turned. One of his attacker's blades hit his horse's flanks, it whinnied in agony and instinctively tried to flee but its hooves slid on the damp grass making it stumble clumsily. Gavid lost his balance and fell to the ground.

Rolling forwards, Gavid sprung agilely to his feet, slashing at the legs of an opponent's horse. It screamed and fell, just as the blade of another weapon buried itself deep in Gavid's shoulder. Swinging his sword in a shining arc Gavid managed to near sever another attacker's arm, but his blade embedded itself in solid bone and it was too late to pull his sword free to deflect the next blow. He felt only a brief moment of pain, and uttered only a faint gurgling sound as the sword ran him through, piercing his heart. The blackness overtook Gavid before he even reached the ground.

It was near dusk when Sarin and Zene first saw the flickering flames of a campfire in a narrow valley just ahead. They had travelled far and their horses were tired, so they slowed to a walking pace as they descended the slope of the hill. The day had been surprisingly warm, but it was getting colder now. Sarin longed for a hot meal and a soft bed for the night, but he could expect nothing more than the little they had to eat in their depleted saddlebags and a few hours rest on the hard ground.

Sarin and Zene made no attempt to hide their approach as they moved close to the camp. Most of the soldiers were huddled around the fire, but two guards stepped forwards, barring their way with their long spear-tipped lances. 'Who goes there?' they demanded, as a number of the other soldiers rose to their feet, swords sliding smoothly from the scabbards affixed to their belts.

'Friends,' Sarin announced. 'One of your countrymen, soldier,' he added, his spirits raised by the sight of his crest on their tabards.

'Countrymen, you say?' A young man wearing the insignia of a lieutenant stepped forwards. His sword was undrawn but his hand rested pointedly on its ornate hilt.

'I am a nobleman of Percheron,' Sarin said coolly, still thinking it wise not to announce his true identity at once. However, he hoped that someone within the camp might recognise him, but to his frustration he saw no sign of this in the eyes of the young lieutenant. 'We are low on supplies, and find ourselves in a land where we are clearly no longer welcome. My comrade and I seek your aid and protection, Lieutenant.'

The young man frowned, and glanced over at Zene who stared haughtily back at him. But she was careful to keep her hands on her reins and well away from her weapons.

'You are dressed like a common mercenary, sir. And this woman?'

'Is a warrior of Freygard,' Sarin finished sharply. 'Allow us to enter your camp and we will explain everything.' Moving slowly and very carefully, Sarin drew his sword and tossed it to the ground. It landed point down in the hard soil, swaying gently. 'Zene,' Sarin prompted, waiting while she rather resentfully relinquished her weapons, tossing her sword and dagger at the lieutenant's feet.

'Why do these men not trust you?' she asked Sarin. 'They are your countrymen.'

'We are in a land we once ruled, where we are now looked upon as mortal enemies. Would you not also be cautious?' the lieutenant addressed Zene.

137

'I would be cautious also,' she agreed, eyeing him with suspicion. 'But I would still recognise my own kind at once. Are you so stupid you cannot do the same?'

The lieutenant smiled wryly. 'Your friend sounds as if he comes from Percheron, I'll give you that,' he commented, still staring thoughtfully at Sarin.

'And your men outnumber us over five to one,' Sarin pointed out. 'What harm can come to you if you allow us into your camp?'

'You are right,' the young man agreed. 'Perhaps I am being overly cautious, sir. I should welcome a fellow countryman.' He beckoned them forwards. 'Come. Sit by the fire and share our meal. Perhaps you would care to tell us how you and your companion came to be here, so far from the border of Percheron, when our army is in retreat?'

Sarin and Zene walked their horses slowly into the centre of the camp. Surrounded by a tight circle of soldiers, they dismounted. Sarin handed his horse over to one of the men without a second thought, but when another soldier stepped forwards to take hold of the chestnut's reins Zene glared at him. 'No!' she exclaimed.

'He just wishes to see to your horse,' the lieutenant said to appease her. He had probably never seen a woman so scantily dressed in public before and his gaze slid pointedly over her bare arms and legs, before coming to rest on the low neckline of her tight-fitting leather bodice. 'Sit by the fire, lady, you must be cold.' Despite the chill of approaching night, Zene had not bothered to put on her cloak, which was still rolled up behind her saddle.

'Cold,' she derided. 'Why should I be?' she added, staring at the soldiers in their heavy chainmail shirts. 'Your men are weak,' she taunted with a sarcastic smile. 'Female warriors are far stronger.'

'The warriors of Freygard all dress that way,' Sarin explained, irritated by Zene's lack of tact; the last thing Sarin wanted to do was antagonise these men. 'They do not appear to feel the cold overmuch. Often she puts me to shame. They are a hardy race it seems.' He sat down by the fire, holding his hands out to its heat, and rubbing them together to warm them further before accepting a leather cup containing spiced wine. 'I thank you for your hospitality, Lieutenant?'

'Lieutenant Faros,' the young man said, looking expectantly at Sarin.

'My companion's name is Zene – she is, or rather she was, a member of Queen Danara's personal guard.' Sarin was still cautious enough to keep his own identity secret until he'd sized up the situation a little further. His army believed him dead; all of Percheron believed him dead. They might be unwilling to accept the truth, especially as he had no evidence to back up his claim. Few of his men had actually seen him in the flesh, apart from those who guarded his palaces in Percheron. The only likeness most of them would have encountered was his profile stamped on their coins. 'Until Zene helped me escape I'd been a prisoner in Freygard for nigh on half a year.'

Sarin's confession caught the interest of all the soldiers around the campfire as they stared even more curiously at Zene.

'We've heard stories of life in Freygard. Of the warrior women and their beautiful Queen,' Faros said with a knowing smile. 'Not one of us has ever come across a man who has been captured by them and escaped to tell the truth of his imprisonment. Would you be willing to give us an account of your adventures?'

'Of course,' Sarin agreed. 'But first I would beg some sustenance. Once we learned of your presence in the area, we made an attempt to track you down, not even pausing to rest or eat. My stomach is so empty it groans.' Even as he spoke one of the soldiers stepped forwards and placed a steaming bowl of stew in Sarin's hands. 'Thank you, my man,' he said politely, while thinking that much had come to pass since he'd left Percheron.

139

Here he was thanking a common soldier for something that was his divine right.

'Eat. Then we will talk,' Lieutenant Faros said. 'No man should be required to speak for long on an empty stomach,' he added, as he motioned for the man to pass food to Zene as well.

The bowl and the wooden spoon he was required to use were crude, but Sarin didn't care as he ladled the delicious stew into his mouth. It was only simple fare but it was the best food he'd eaten for months. 'This is very good,' he said, greedily wolfing it down, while Zene, also ravenous, followed suit. Yet all the time she ate she warily watched the soldiers.

A soldier, carrying a couple of bulging water-skins, staggered into the camp after having just filled them at a nearby stream. 'Lieutenant . . .' he faltered and grinned wolfishly as he noticed the scantily dressed woman. 'Should I . . .' His mouth dropped open as his caught sight of Sarin. The skins fell from his hand, spilling water all over the ground. 'You're dead,' he gasped as the steadily spreading puddle of water made a loud hiss when it hit the glowing embers of the fire. 'My lord,' he muttered, falling to his knees.

'What is wrong with you, man?' the lieutenant snapped as the soldier shuffled on his knees towards Sarin.

'I thought for a moment I'd seen a ghost, my lord,' he mumbled. 'But you are flesh and blood,' he added excitedly as he grabbed hold of Sarin's hand.

Sarin endured the soldier slobbering deferentially over his hand with good grace – thanking the fates that at last someone had recognised him.

'What is wrong with you, Bathen?' Lieutenant Faros said irritably. 'Have you no shame?'

'The shame is yours, Lieutenant,' Zene said with an arrogant and very condescending smile. 'Do you not recognise my companion. His head is on all your coin, is it not?'

'Our coin?' Faros frowned. 'Lord Sarin's head is still upon . . . Freygard,' he mumbled weakly. 'You mean?'

'I do indeed,' Zene confirmed, watching the lieutenant's jaw grow slacker and slacker with disbelief.

'It is Lord Sarin, come back to life,' Bathen gabbled, at last letting go of Sarin's hand.

'*You* are Lord Sarin?' The lieutenant rose awkwardly to his feet.

'I am he,' Sarin said coolly as he wiped his hand over the side of his doublet to remove the unpleasant remains of the soldier's saliva. 'I admit I do look a little different; the facial hair is not my choice,' he agreed, touching his beard. 'How did you recognise me, Bathen?'

'I served you, my lord. I was a guard in your palace at Aguilar. That is why I was sent on this mission,' Bathen explained nervously.

Sarin frowned, not recognising Bathen at all, but he'd rarely taken any notice of the many guards in his palaces. 'You will be rewarded when we return to Percheron,' he told Bathen. 'As will you, Lieutenant Faros,' he added, knowing the promise of a reward would always increase a soldier's loyalty – greed was at the centre of most men's hearts.

'We were told you had perished in Freygard, Majesty,' Faros gabbled, still overcome by the revelation. Most of his men, meanwhile, were staring at Sarin, not knowing quite what to do. 'Forgive my disrespect.' Faros went down on one knee. 'I'd never seen you. We believed you dead, and I never thought . . .'

'The matter is settled,' Sarin said calmly, relieved they'd accepted him without question. 'You are forgiven. It was an honest mistake, one I might have made myself in a similar situation. All I ask is that you swear allegiance to me and agree to follow all my orders from now on.'

Faros looked uneasy. 'I already have my orders, Lord Sarin, from Chancellor Lesand.'

'Lesand now rules in my place?'

'He rules as first minister, he will take no higher honour,' Faros explained. 'He has only recently managed to wrest power from a small group of your former generals. It was the chancellor who decided on a peaceful settlement with Kabra, and agreed to withdraw our troops.'

'So Tarn did not drive them out?' Sarin said pensively. 'Sit, Faros, my days of insisting on due deference are long past.'

'I fear he would have eventually,' Faros admitted, cautiously squatting back on the ground. 'The Kabrans fought long and hard, and morale among our troops was running low. The chancellor decided that it was not worth the loss of even more men for the battle to continue when Prince Tarn of Kabra was so determined to succeed.'

'He always was stubborn.' Sarin smiled as he held out his cup. 'More wine?' As his cup was quickly refilled by a nervous soldier he added, 'And what are your orders, Lieutenant?'

'We are tracking a thief.'

Sarin looked around him. 'All these men for one paltry thief?'

'Far from paltry, my lord,' Faros said very seriously. 'The thief gained entrance to the treasury and stole most of the royal jewels – a king's ransom, Chancellor Lesand said.'

'My jewels,' Sarin muttered angrily. 'Who could do such a thing?'

'Baroness Crissana. Her late husband was part of the staff of the treasury. She had his keys copied, entered the palace soon after his death and stole most of the jewels.'

'Security in the royal palace must have grown slack of late,' Sarin commented curtly. 'Did the guards not raise the alarm? Who is this woman? If I recall correctly the baron's wife was dead.'

'She was his second wife. They'd not been married long.' Faros sounded uneasy. 'The lady's presence was

142

not questioned because the guards thought she had a right to be there. It was said that she used secret passages known only to the chancellor and of course you, my lord.'

'I know of only one other,' Sarin mused, then gave a harsh barking laugh. 'Niska married that old lecher Baron Crissana?'

'As I understand it the generals gave her little choice.' Faros shrugged his shoulders.

'So she repaid them by stealing my jewels?' Sarin chuckled, angered yet also highly amused. 'The greedy bitch! I would have expected no less.' He paused and drank his wine slowly and reflectively. 'She's no doubt travelling to Vestfold, where she thinks she'll be safe.'

'We have been following her for some time. We tracked her to Ruberoc, but then the order to withdraw came,' Faros explained.

'So Lesand asked the king for a letter of safe passage for you and your men?'

'Signed by King Tarn himself.' Faros patted his doublet. 'I keep it on me at all times.'

'Tarn is king at last. I'm surprised Brion lasted as long as he did.' Sarin's emotions concerning Tarn were confused, even now, even after all this time. 'In that case, Zene and I will accompany you. We will track down Niska, and I will take possession of my jewels,' Sarin added, thinking that this had not turned out badly after all. He'd pay back Niska for her betrayal, and he'd regain what he thought he had lost. The jewels would give him the resources to hire men. With a large army backing him, he could easily wrest control of his kingdom from Lesand.

Rianna watched Chang move silently around the tent totally ignoring her presence. He'd been guarding her for two days now, in a small red-striped tent pitched only a short distance from Niska's equally temporary abode. At first Rianna had been nervous and fearful of him, but

Chang had been surprisingly kind and considerate of her welfare. In a strange way she now felt she could place her trust in the obsidian-eyed man with the inscrutable expression that revealed none of his true thoughts.

Since the near rape, Niska had insisted that Rianna be kept permanently confined. By day she travelled alone in the baggage wagon, tethered inside the small space by a heavy chain which fastened around her ankle and was bolted to the side of the wagon.

At night she was chained to a thick peg that had been hammered into the ground. Rianna was under no illusion, she was and always had been Niska's prisoner, but she had no idea what fate had in store for her. She didn't know why Leon had allowed this or made no attempt to see her. She'd even begun to wonder if he and his men were still alive. The need to escape consumed her thoughts but so far no opportunity had presented itself.

'Have you finished eating?' Chang enquired.

He had not bothered to change his ways because of Rianna's presence. Every evening he removed his garments and sat for hours meditating. His only concession to Rianna's modesty was a small loincloth draped around his lean hips.

'I've finished. It was delicious as usual,' Rianna said and handed him her empty dish.

Chang cooked for himself, as he didn't appear to eat meat, which was the staple diet of the other men. After Chang had watched Rianna refuse most of the food Tanith brought her, he had suggested she might like to try some of his. In order to show her it wasn't tampered with in any way he had served her food from the same bowl as his. Rianna had taken a liking to the highly spiced stew of vegetables and grains that they ate every evening.

As Chang bent to take her bowl Rianna watched the way the tattooed creatures on his body seemed to come alive when he moved. They both fascinated and repelled her. She had asked him about the scars on his face and

144

he had told her they were his badges of manhood. On reaching a certain age the members of his race were required to take part in a ritual scarring of great religious significance, where they inflicted the wounds on themselves. Most men had a scar on either cheek, and Rianna could imagine how painful it would be to deliberately cut oneself. It was only those courageous enough to inflict more cuts, like Chang, who were considered the bravest and most revered members of his tribe.

'I regret this, my lady,' Chang said as he gently took hold of Rianna's wrists and tied them together with a silken cord. It was the first time he had done this. 'The baroness's orders,' he explained.

'Does she fear me that much?' Rianna was forced to lie back on the thin mattress as Chang tethered her wrists to a peg hammered in the ground above her head.

'The baroness fears nothing,' Chang replied as he solicitously slipped a pillow under her head, then covered her with a soft blanket. 'Sleep well. I will be outside. If you need me you have but to call.'

Rianna did not answer as Chang departed, she was wondering why Niska had ordered this extra confinement. After all, she was chained by her ankle and couldn't leave the tent even if she'd wanted to. Her questions were answered as she heard the rustle of silk skirts and Niska walked into the tent.

Niska paused and looked down at Rianna. 'I trust you have recovered?'

'What concern is it of yours?' Rianna snapped, turning her face away from Niska.

'It concerns me greatly. I would not like to think you had been scarred or permanently damaged in any way. It detracts from your worth,' Niska sneered.

'Is it your intention to ransom me?' Rianna asked, determined not to give up hope though staying steadfast in the face of adversity was far from easy.

'Ransom?' Niska pursed her lips and sat down by Rianna's side, pulling off her blanket. 'I wonder what

145

price Tarn would be willing to pay?' She took a small jewelled dagger from her belt and tested the sharpness of the blade with her thumb. It brought forth a bright bead of blood, which she daintily licked from her fingertip. 'Almost all he has, I'd wager,' she continued, holding the dagger in front of Rianna's face.

'I thought you said that damage detracted from my worth.' Rianna tried not to show her fear as she stared at the small razor-sharp blade.

'Sadly it does.' Niska replied regretfully. 'I would dearly love to see you screaming in pain. I could destroy your beauty in an instant,' she purred. 'I'd enjoy that, but I must resist the temptation.' She used the blade to slice through Rianna's bodice and the thin shift beneath, peeling the garment back to stare down at Rianna's breasts. 'The bruises are all but gone I see,' she commented thoughtfully. 'A few days more and they'll barely be visible at all.'

The pain of what had occurred that terrible night would stay with Rianna long after all the visible signs had faded, but she was not about to admit that to Niska. Just as she couldn't admit how she really felt as Niska's cool fingers reached down to circle her breasts, trailing teasingly over the soft curves of her bosom. Ever since she had arrived in Niska's camp Rianna had been having strange erotic dreams, constant lustful thoughts and sexual desires she couldn't explain.

Despite her loathing of Niska, her skin welcomed the gentle caresses, her body cried out for them, aching with need. Rianna shivered as Niska's fingers stroked and rubbed her nipples. She tried not to show how much Niska's touch aroused her, but her body betrayed her conscious thought and her nipples hardened into firm peaks. 'What a greedy little whore you are,' Niska taunted, amused by Rianna's unsuccessful attempt to stem her instinctive response.

Niska used the blade to slit Rianna's skirt from waist to hem, pulling it open leaving Rianna naked with only the remains of her tattered garments clinging to her arms. She did not have the luxury of a brazier to warm her tent and the chill air hit Rianna's flesh, raising goosepimples on her pale skin.

Smiling cruelly, Niska played with Rianna, running her hands over the soft swell of her belly and through red-gold curls at her pubis. A carnal shudder coursed through Rianna as Niska's hand slid between her thighs. Suddenly there seemed no point in resistance and she relaxed and opened her legs as Niska explored the moist cleft of her sex.

Filled with guilt, Rianna suddenly realised this was what she wanted, she had been aching with unfulfilled desire ever since the mercenaries had stripped her and cruelly violated her. She'd hated every moment of the experience, yet even as she had loathed and despised those disgusting men she had longed to feel a cock penetrate her, spearing her vitals with its thrusting strength. Her cunt was an aching void that needed to be filled. It was as if something dark and sensual had taken over her body and was driving it mad with lust.

'Why not admit that you're a whore,' Niska taunted, leaning closer to Rianna, the strong scent of her perfume seeping into every pore of her helpless victim. 'See how greedily your body welcomes me.'

'No.' Rianna clenched her teeth together. 'I will not,' she managed to gasp, denying her basest needs.

'You will soon enough.' Niska withdrew her fingers, now wet and shiny with Rianna's dew, and smiled slyly. 'I know you've avoided the wine, so I had Tanith put a tiny drop of a special potion in the water she gave you. It's a very sophisticated aphrodisiac. By the time you reach Vestfold you'll be so sexually frustrated you'll not care who or what fucks you.'

The name Vestfold penetrated Rianna's confused thoughts. 'Vestfold?' she repeated.

'Yes.' Niska placed her soiled fingers, still wet with Rianna's secretions, in her mouth. 'Musky, surprisingly sweet. I've always wondered what you tasted like. Now I know,' she said. 'I am taking you to Vestfold as a gift for my half-brother, Ragnor. He'll be delighted to have such a special prize as his slave.'

'No!' Rianna exclaimed in horror. 'You cannot,' she pleaded, as she recalled the terrible tales she'd heard about the brutality of the northern warlords.

'This has always been my intention ever since I persuaded Leon to travel with me,' Niska told her. 'And don't think he will try and stop me, he does everything I tell him to.' She pulled the blanket back over Rianna. 'If you refuse the water Chang will force you to drink.' She patted Rianna's cheek, but was forced to snatch her hand away quickly as Rianna tried to bite it. 'Shame on you.' She laughed. 'Ragnor despises mawkish women, so he'll like you Rianna, especially with your blood fired by the potion. However, I should warn you that he quickly tires of women if they resist too much, and beats them when they do not do as they are told. You'd better learn to behave if you want to survive long in Ragnor's stronghold.'

'Tarn will come after me,' Rianna hissed. 'He'll kill you, Niska, and I'll enjoy watching while he does it.'

'I look forward to that.' Niska's eyes glittered with excitement. 'Ragnor has many men under his command. Once he has defeated Tarn I'll get Ragnor to give him to me as my own personal thrall. Tarn is already well skilled in the duties of a pleasure slave, is he not, Rianna?' she said with a harsh laugh. 'And if his lovemaking is anywhere near as satisfying as the one time I fucked him, then I'll be content.'

Leon yawned, suddenly feeling very weary as the man sitting next to him round the campfire silently passed him another flagon of wine. This was even rougher than the last and the sourness caught the back of his throat as he gulped it down. Fighting the urge to cough, a sign of weakness, Leon passed the flagon to the next man.

The sky was clear tonight. It was almost as if the weather was in cahoots with Niska and no longer needed to hide the fact that they were travelling due north. Leon was obsessed with Niska. She was a witch who had cast a spell over his heart; he adored her and could deny her nothing. Yet he lived with a constant nagging feeling of guilt that he had betrayed the trust Prince Tarn had placed in him. Rianna shouldn't be here – she should be safe in Ruberoc with her betrothed.

So far Niska hadn't told him how she intended to return Rianna to Prince Tarn, but Leon planned to escort the noble lady to Nemedia tomorrow whether Niska approved or not. Perhaps he should go and tell Niska now, he thought, as he rose to his feet, not feeling even slightly inebriated from the copious amounts of wine he'd drunk. Leon bade goodnight to his drinking companions, then walked just a shade unsteadily through the camp. He yawned again as he plodded towards Niska's tent, looking forward to climbing into bed next to her soft warm body.

He smiled at the thought as he entered the tent, but his expression changed as he paused in amazement at the sight that confronted him. The two huge Nubian mercenaries were naked, their oiled skin gleaming in the soft lamplight. A thin sliver of pale flesh and silver-gilt hair was sandwiched between their polished ebony forms in a tableau of obscene intimacy.

Leon could hardly believe what he was seeing as the woman who professed to love only him lifted her head and smiled, unconcerned by his intrusion. 'Why, Leon. Come join us,' she said with a soft husky laugh, followed by a groan of pleasure that made the bile rise in his throat.

'No,' he spat in disgust. Yet he was weak and even as he spoke he was pulling off his clothes. Overcome with the combined effects of wine and lust, Leon staggered forwards and collapsed on the huge mattress. The smell of sex surrounded him, seeping from their sweat-soiled bodies, and enveloping him in its seductive embrace.

Leon had been fascinated by the two Nubians ever since he had first laid eyes on them. Even though they were both mute he had still learned what he could about them from their fellow soldiers. He recognised the one lying on his back beneath Niska. He was Osa, the younger and bigger of the two men. Leon wanted to fasten his hand around Osa's neck and squeeze the life out of him for having his cock embedded in Niska. He hated the thought, yet the sight of her pale body draped across Osa's dark flesh was highly arousing. The other man, Yeo, kneeled behind her, his superbly muscular body taut with concentration as he caressed her buttocks, running his huge thumbs slowly down her crack.

Leon's cock hardened at the sight of these two impressive creatures pleasuring the woman he loved. Jealousy and excitement consumed him as he saw Yeo slide his index finger into Niska's arsehole. She shuddered and gave a soft feral growl, pressing her buttocks back against his hand.

Leon had always been proud of the length and girth of his erect penis, but the size of Yeo's black, shining cock put it to shame. It stood out from Yeo's muscular groin, oiled and stiffly erect. The skin on the shaft was coal black, but it grew redder towards the tip and Leon couldn't tear his gaze from the sight, the organ was so huge. He watched, fascinated as Yeo twisted and turned his finger inside Niska, while reverently wanking his cock with the other hand until the skin on the polished rod looked taut and ready to burst.

Hungrily Leon reached for his own penis, rubbing the aching shaft. Niska smiled, her pale eyes glittering as she watched him pumping. 'Poor Leon,' she taunted. 'Do you want to join us? Yeo's cock is magnificent, isn't it? Think what it would feel like inside you.'

'No!' he gasped, slowing his pace as he felt his balls

start to tighten. He had no wish to come yet; he needed to spill his seed inside Niska.

'Haven't you ever wondered what it would feel like to be penetrated by a man?' She wriggled her bottom as Yeo pulled out his finger and leaned forwards to lick and kiss her buttocks.

'The thought is obscene,' Leon mumbled as the man beneath Niska began to jerk his hips in wild rapid movements.

Niska groaned with pleasure, her belly trembling at the strength of the powerful thrusts. 'He's huge, it feels so good,' she purred, never taking her eyes off Leon.

Jealousy gnawed at his innards, as a strange excitement crawled over his skin. Leon cupped his balls, massaging them gently, while his hand set to work again on his aching shaft. He slid his fingers up and down the burgeoning length, hating Osa and hating Niska. He stared resentfully at Niska, wanting to be the one lying there with her pale flesh embracing his hungry cock.

'Stop moving,' Niska told Osa, putting a hand on his chest. 'Yeo likes to fuck men,' she told Leon as she ground her open quim against Osa's flat belly. Yeo meanwhile was pressing his tongue teasingly against Niska's arsehole and it looked extraordinarily pink in contrast to the darkness of his skin. 'When Yeo was Sarin's body slave his master always promised him that one day he could fuck Tarn.' She gave a soft laugh. 'Of course he never let Yeo do it. Sarin was too possessive; he kept that delicious pleasure all to himself.'

'You lie,' Leon groaned as he stopped pumping his cock, squeezing the tip between his finger and thumb to prevent himself exploding.

'Has Tarn never spoken of the hours he was forced to spend in Sarin's pleasure vault, being subjected to every erotic indignity his master could think of?' She looked back at Yeo. 'Push your tongue deeper, I want to feel it wriggling inside me.' Yeo obeyed, pushing the tip of his

151

tongue deep into her, until she gave a soft sigh. 'That feels delicious.'

'Tarn is no pervert,' Leon spat. 'He is a man. He beds women, not men,' he added, squeezing his throbbing balls harder, wanting the discomfort to blot out Niska's words. 'He was a prisoner in Sarin's dungeons not a pleasure slave,' he said almost choking on his words.

Leon had heard of men who liked fucking other men, but he'd never known such a creature – apart from Yeo of course. He looked derisively at Yeo, whose tongue was still working on Niska's arse. Even his sex-crazed soldiers would have balked at penetrating a man, and Tarn would never have endured such an indignity, Leon told himself.

'You deceive yourself, Leon.' Niska eyed him with amusement as he crawled towards her. 'You should ask Tarn.'

'I would never presume,' he growled, leaning across the prone Nubian to kiss Niska. Spurred on by the thought of Osa's cock inside her, he thrust his tongue deep into her mouth. His engorged cock pressed against Osa's hip as Niska grabbed hold of his head, kissing him harder.

'Fuck me now, Leon.' She pulled her lips from his. 'In my tight little nether hole.'

The thought of penetrating her so crudely, while Osa's cock was still lodged in her pussy, was impossible to resist. Leon pushed Yeo aside, and the Nubian backed away and crouched on his haunches, his engorged penis swaying gently.

'I know that you've always wanted to do this,' Niska teased with a husky laugh. 'But you've never dared to ask.'

A lustful heat filled his loins and his knees trembled as he kneeled behind Niska, wishing he knew what it would feel like to be impaled on two cocks at the same time. Wild excitement coursed through his veins as he went to grab hold of her buttock cheeks and pull them apart.

152

Before Leon could press his cock to the tight little hole, a hand shot around his waist and held him motionless as Yeo's fingers, dripping with fragrant oil, reverently greased his shaft from root to tip. The seductive movements of Yeo's hands were arousing and despite his instinctive disgust Leon found the sensations highly pleasurable.

'Do it!' Niska commanded, lifting her hips back towards Leon, and allowing Osa's huge, shiny penis to slide half out of her cunt.

Leon's heart raced, pumping so hard it felt as if it might explode as he eased his way inside the rosy ring of muscle. His cock slid smoothly into the tight opening, burrowing deep into the narrow channel. The muscles were so tight and tautly contracted that it was far better than bedding the most reluctant virgin.

With a soft groan, Leon forced his cock deeper and the pressure became so intense that he had to breathe deeply and try to hold back – fearing he would come too quickly. By now Niska was making a faint keening whimper, and Leon was beyond caring if it was from pain or pleasure as he jammed his pelvis hard against her buttock cheeks.

He grabbed hold of her hips, thrusting her down hard on Osa's cock and the penetration was so complete that Niska gave a loud, wailing scream. Leon could feel the hardness of Osa's cock-shaft pressing against his penis. Gently he began to thrust, timing his movements to match Osa's, so that they fucked Niska in a smooth mutual rhythm.

Leon was so caught up in his own lustful excitement, that he barely felt Yeo's hands on his hips, but he felt the fierce agony as the Nubians' cock was suddenly thrust deep into his anus. Yeo's pungent-smelling body pressed hard against Leon's buttocks, as he was pierced to the hilt by the massive organ. The painful pleasure was exquisitely exciting and decadent beyond belief.

Trapped by bodies both front and rear, Leon was

forced to endure the cock thrusting back and forth in his vitals, filling him with a sweet dark pleasure he'd never tasted before. The four of them moved in perfect unison, one mass of rutting humanity as Leon endured the hedonistic experience of both penetrating and being penetrated at the same time. A red mist of blood grew behind his eyes as the powerful sensations grew and expanded, thrusting Leon into the dark side of bliss and beyond.

# Chapter Seven

*T*arn's keen blue eyes swept the hills and valleys ahead, looking for the slightest sign of movement. A cold grey mist hid the tops of the hills, filling the air with a chill dampness, which deposited sparkling droplets of dew on his heavy velvet cloak.

Tarn's horse was near exhaustion, as were the mounts of his men. He had made them travel at an unrelenting pace since leaving Ruberoc – his overwhelming fear for Rianna's safety driving him onwards. They had easily picked up the baroness's trail in the forest north of the castle of Dane, and judging by the many tracks, she was accompanied by a large body of men.

As time passed there had been more terrible signs of her recent presence. They'd found stiff corpses of slaughtered soldiers, their eyes pecked out by crows and their bodies half-consumed by scavengers. They were all Leon's men and no attempt had been made to hide their corpses. Tarn was convinced they had all been murdered. For all he knew Leon and every one of his soldiers might be dead by now, and he couldn't even allow himself to consider his beloved's fate.

'We'll have to stop soon, sire, and allow the horses to rest,' Tarn's aide cautiously pointed out. Jentius was a promising young captain and a friend of Leon's. That was why Tarn had chosen Jentius to accompany him.

'I know.' Tarn narrowed his eyes, peering into a valley half shrouded in mist, still unsure how close they were to catching up with the baroness. Tarn and his men were travelling much faster, but she had over a week's head start.

'Is that smoke?' Jentius asked, pointing towards the far end of the misty valley.

'It could be.' Tarn frowned. During the night they had traversed some rocky ground, and the tracks had been barely visible even to the keenest eyes. Horsemen coming from another direction had passed this way as well and Tarn wasn't even certain that they were following the right tracks any more. But he'd travel to the ends of the earth to find Rianna. 'If it is smoke, it's coming from only one fire.'

This part of Kabra was sparsely populated, mainly because of the attacks by bandits who sheltered in the mountains to the north. Most of the smaller settlements in this area had been raided and burned to the ground. The survivors had fled to the few large walled towns where they were better protected.

'Should we take a look?' Jentius asked.

'Yes, come.' Tarn spurred his horse forwards, down the damp, grass-covered slope, beckoning his men to follow him.

As they moved closer they saw that the thin pillar of smoke came from the fire of a small group of men camped in the shelter of a thicket of trees. Judging by the uniforms they were Percheron soldiers. Tarn wondered if they had failed to receive the order to retreat. He glanced back at Jentius. 'I'll go in first, the men are to follow me. Tell them to remain alert and ready to defend themselves, but they are not to draw their weapons. I wish to show the soldiers that we mean no harm, and I've no desire to fight them unless we are forced to.'

156

'Why would they still be here, this far north?' Jentius asked.

'I don't know, unless . . .' Tarn recalled the document of safe passage he had issued to a small troop at Lesand's request. Could it be them, he asked himself, as they approached the camp.

There were a couple of small tents, a group of hobbled horses and about a dozen men. Most were taken by surprise at the appearance of so many Kabran soldiers. A number reached for their weapons. One, who'd been stirring something over the fire, dropped his ladle in surprise and shouted out a warning, while two soldiers holding long spears moved to bar Tarn's way.

'Who's in charge?' Tarn's icy gaze surveyed the camp, while he half-slid his sword from its gilded scabbard.

The two soldiers stepped threateningly towards Tarn, but suddenly a voice shouted, 'Hold there.' A lieutenant strode forwards and waved back the men. 'Sir, we have a letter of safe passage . . .' he faltered as he stared at Tarn, recognition dawning in his eyes. 'I am in charge of these men, your highness,' he stuttered.

'No, I am.' The cold familiarity of Sarin's voice hit Tarn like a hard blow to the stomach.

'You?' Tarn could not hide his amazement.

'A surprising change of circumstance is it not?' Sarin commented, his dark hawk-like features radiating supreme self-assurance. 'The last time –' Sarin stepped closer to Tarn, waving Lieutenant Faros and his men back. Lowering his voice so that only Tarn could hear he continued, ' – the last time we were together you were my slave, confined in a cell, bound and helpless, forced to submit to my every whim. I recall that I enjoyed taking my pleasure . . .'

'Why dwell on the past?' Tarn harshly interrupted, unable to think of the painful intimacy of their last encounter. He straightened in his saddle, staring coldly down at Sarin, looking every inch the monarch he now was. 'It bears no relation to the present. I am the King of

Kabra while you are merely an escaped prisoner seeking refuge in my kingdom.'

Sarin smiled sarcastically. 'The past is not so easy to forget, King Tarn.' He bowed, making the deferential gesture seem overexaggerated and condescending. 'However much we like to think it does not, the past bears every relation to what is happening now.' He grinned, his teeth looking startlingly white against his dark beard. The facial hair made Sarin look even more rakishly handsome but doubly threatening. 'I may only be an escaped prisoner in your eyes, but I'll soon regain my rightful position as monarch of Percheron.'

'If I care to let you,' Tarn coolly pointed out, swinging his leg over his horse and dismounting. 'Why should I allow you to return to Percheron? You are my enemy, why should I not imprison you? I have made peace with the new leader of Percheron, Chancellor Lesand. If I allowed you to return to your kingdom, and you regained your throne, you might not stand by the treaty.'

'We can reach an agreement that satisfies us both, Sarin said confidently. 'Kabra is no longer of interest to me. If I regain control of Percheron and assume my rightful place on the throne again, I'll be content.' He took a few swaggering steps back. 'As you see, I am travelling under the protection of Lieutenant Faros and his men. You've not forgotten the letter of safe passage you gave him?'

'No, I've not forgotten.' Tarn glared at Sarin. 'However much I may loathe to do so, I'll stand by the document and allow it to extend to you as well,' he added in a harsh tone.

'Still the noble barbarian?' Sarin taunted. 'Even though your magnanimity chokes your throat.' He glanced over at Tarn's men. 'We are outnumbered. You could easily overpower my small troop and take me captive.'

'Only *you* would carry out such an ignoble act.' Tarn's lips twisted into a sarcastic smile. 'The King of Kabra stands by his word.'

'Then let us offer you our simple hospitality.' Sarin

pointed towards the campfire. 'Warm yourself for a while. Have a cup of spiced wine.'

Tarn regally inclined his head. His men would appreciate a few moments rest. It was possible that Sarin's soldiers may have seen the baroness and her men pass by and the information would give them some idea of how far behind her they were. Tarn followed Sarin over to the fire. Even after all this time he still found it difficult to face this man. Memories of the sexual intimacies they'd shared plagued his thoughts. He recalled the cruel ways Sarin had used to subjugate and humiliate him, and the thoughts aroused feelings and emotions he had tried so hard to suppress.

'I'm surprised you managed to escape from Freygard,' Tarn commented as he accepted a cup of spiced wine from one of the soldiers.

'I expect you are,' Sarin agreed with a cutting smile. 'No doubt you thought I was out of your way forever. Zene helped me to escape Danara's clutches,' he said in a surprisingly calm voice as he pointed to one of the small tents. An attractive young woman stood there staring thoughtfully at the two of them.

Tarn glanced at her for a moment, then grinned as he recognised Zene. 'I remember her. She and I . . .' he paused. 'It is best forgotten.'

Sarin looked questioningly at Zene, but she looked calmly back at him as if Tarn's words meant nothing to her. 'If it were not for Zene, I would never have got out of Freygard alive.'

Tarn gulped down the wine, feeling the warmth hit his parched throat. 'So now you plan to return to Percheron?'

'No.' Sarin shook his head. 'Lieutenant Faros has orders to hunt down a fugitive. I will accompany him, recover what is mine, then return to Percheron.'

'Ah, yes.' Tarn realised he had no idea of the fugitive's identity. He wondered if the person they sought could be the baroness. Surely that would be too much of a coincidence? 'Tell me more about this fugitive.'

'Her name is Baroness Crissana, she stole jewels from the royal treasury.' Sarin grinned wryly. 'You may know her better, of course, as my former wife, Niska.'

'Niska!' Tarn gasped. His surprise at seeing Sarin was nothing to the fear that gripped his heart when he heard Niska's name. 'Niska has Rianna?'

'What has Rianna to do with this?' Sarin asked.

'It appears that my betrothed is in the company of your fugitive,' Tarn said, his voice tight with concern. He was unable to conceive how Rianna could ever have agreed to travel with Niska.

'*My wife*, you mean,' Sarin reminded him. 'Rianna and I are still wed,' he added cuttingly. 'You should not forget that.'

'I've no intention of discussing such matters now,' Tarn cut him off.

'How did Rianna come to be travelling with Niska?' Sarin appeared as confused as Tarn was.

'I wish I knew the truth of it,' Tarn replied, finding it very difficult to accept that he was standing here talking to Sarin as if they were old acquaintances, not mortal enemies. 'It is not easy to comprehend. Nevertheless, I fear that Rianna is in great danger. I need to reach Niska even more urgently than you do.'

'Niska must have her reasons for taking Rianna with her,' Sarin said, showing no concern for his former bride. 'If Niska has not killed her already, then she is safe for the present. I know Niska well enough to deduce that she must have some use for Rianna – a use you have yet to ascertain.'

'I care not for Niska's reasons,' Tarn said agitatedly. 'I just have to rescue Rianna.' He turned to look for Jentius, who was deep in conversation with Faros. 'We must leave now, Jentius.'

'I'm more than certain Niska is headed for Vestfold,' Sarin told him. 'She often used to speak fondly of her half-brother, Ragnor. They were close when they were young.'

160

'Vestfold?' Tarn repeated. 'May the gods protect Rianna.'

'May the gods protect us all,' Sarin added as Tarn swung round, intending to depart. 'Wait, Tarn.'

Tarn flinched as Sarin put a hand on his arm. 'Why should I wait?'

'Let us put our enmities aside,' Sarin suggested. 'We both seek Niska, so it makes sense for us to do so together.'

'No,' Tarn replied, shaking his head. 'That is impossible.'

'Niska has a large band of mercenaries in her employ. They will be difficult enough to contend with. If we are forced, as I fear, to pursue her into Vestfold we will be in even greater danger. We will need a goodly force even to survive. The more men we have, the better our chances.'

'It is impossible for us to work together,' Tarn replied. 'We are enemies, Sarin. Too much has occurred for us to ever be anything but that!'

It seemed to Rianna that dawn had come hours ago, yet she was still lying in her tent, bound hand and foot, just as Niska had left her the night before. There was little of the usual sounds of movement in the camp, none of the normal bustle and noise she associated with preparations for their departure. She had not slept well trussed up like that. She was hungry and thirsty, physically frustrated, and her bladder was feeling uncomfortably full. She heard a faint noise and turned her head towards the entrance, expecting to see Chang, but it was only Tanith carrying a goblet and a hunk of freshly baked unleavened bread.

'My lady.' There was little trace of deference in Tanith's tone, as if Rianna no longer deserved her respect.

'It's late. Why have we not departed?' Rianna said, licking her dry lips.

'The baroness thought the men were growing tired of

161

constant travel. Some of them have gone hunting for fresh game in order to replenish our supplies before we take the mountain pass to Vestfold.' Tanith kneeled by Rianna and raised her head. 'Drink,' she said, putting the goblet to Rianna's lips.

Rianna wanted to refuse, fearing the water might contain the potion Niska had spoken of, but her throat was so parched she couldn't resist taking a few sips. 'Free my hands and I can feed myself.' She looked pleadingly up at the plump maidservant.

'I have no orders to free you.' Tanith broke off a small piece of bread and put it in Rianna's mouth. 'I made this myself this morning. It is good.'

Rianna chewed the bread and swallowed it quickly. 'I cannot escape, even if you untie my hands. My ankle is still chained,' she pointed out, staring longingly at the leather bucket Chang kept in the tent for her to relieve herself. 'Please, I need to go.'

Tanith's smile had a cruel edge to it. 'Are you feeling uncomfortable?'

'Yes,' Rianna murmured. 'You have to let me.'

'Let you what, Rianna?' Niska's cold voice interjected as she strolled leisurely into the tent and over to Rianna.

'I just asked Tanith if she could free my hands so that I can feed myself,' Rianna replied, turning her face away from Niska's penetrating gaze. She had no intention of humiliating herself in front of her enemy. She would wait and ask Tanith for the bucket again after Niska had left. Although the dull ache of fullness in the pit of her belly was becoming very uncomfortable.

'She needs to empty her bladder.' Tanith jerked back the blanket, Rianna's only covering, to reveal her belly. 'She feels full,' Tanith said as her fingers explored the lower half of Rianna's stomach, running teasingly over the taut skin.

Rianna could not repress a faint murmur as Tanith's fingers pressed a sensitive spot, and the need to urinate

162

became more urgent. Tanith smiled and eased her stubby fingers between Rianna's thighs, burrowing her way into the slit of her sex. Her ragged fingernail scraped across Rianna's aching clit and she jumped agitatedly. Tanith gave a cruel giggle and rubbed the callused pad of her fingertip across the sensitive bud. The pleasurable friction became almost painful, as Rianna's need to pee increased. Scared that something might leak out she clenched her muscles determinedly.

'Leave her be,' Niska snapped.

Tanith jerked her hand away nervously. 'Sorry, my lady.'

'I'll attend to Lady Rianna myself,' Niska added sharply.

'Yes, my lady.' Tanith scrabbled to her feet and scurried out of the tent.

Rianna's skin crawled as Niska kneeled down by her side and slowly surveyed her naked body. 'Is it too hard to bear?' she purred, brushing her fingers across Rianna's full belly.

'What do you want of me?'

'Why, to humble and humiliate,' Niska said with a soft laugh. 'It is an enjoyable way to pass the time. You've been tied up all night and half the morning. I'll wager that by now you are desperate to relieve yourself.' Niska pressed the heel of her hand gently down on the base of Rianna's stomach, above the pubic bone, and it was just enough to force out a tiny trickle of the golden liquid.

'Please, no!' Rianna begged, turning pink with embarrassment as she felt the warm liquid trickle down the crack of her sex. If Niska applied more pressure she feared it would become a torrent.

'What a naughty whore you are! I do believe you've wet yourself,' Niska taunted. She grabbed hold of one of Rianna's nipples in a clamp-like grasp and jerked it upwards, lifting the entire weight of Rianna's bosom with the tiny teat. Then she slapped the underside of the stretched breast. 'Very wicked,' she added, slapping the

163

breast again, then applying a couple of blows to Rianna's stomach.

Rianna endured the stinging discomfort without a whimper. She was reminded of the months she'd spent in Sarin's seraglio. He'd taught her that there was a fine line between pleasure and pain. He applied it to her in equal amounts, teaching her how addictive they both could be. She had almost forgotten the sweet sensations such cruelty could create, but the remembrance of it all flooded back as Niska forced open her legs and slapped the soft skin of her thighs just below the juncture of her pussy.

Niska eased open Rianna's sex with her fingers, splitting her like a ripe peach to display the soft succulent flesh. She rubbed Rianna's clit, and the pressure on the sensitive flesh merged with the aching fullness of her bladder, making her arousal increase.

'Brings back memories, does it not?' Niska teased, almost as if she could read Rianna's mind. 'Sarin schooled you well. They are lessons you'll never forget.' She rubbed and squeezed the tight nub of nerve endings, while continuing to gently stroke Rianna's full belly. The pleasurable torture was like nothing Rianna had ever known and she fought to suppress the sensations, fearing that she could not control herself much longer.

Niska smiled, her attentions becoming even more determined. She teased and stimulated Rianna until another small dribble of liquid escaped. Dabbling her fingers in the warm trickle she used it to anoint Rianna's sex, rubbing the moist liquid round and round her aching clit until the pressure on Rianna's insides became unbearable. Niska must have known how close she was to losing control. She thrust three bunched fingers into Rianna with a rough stabbing movement. Rianna climaxed at once and the orgasm ripped through her flesh. She closed her eyes as the pulsing pressure was followed by a steady stream of liquid seeping, then spurting from her body. It flowed down over her thighs and buttocks in a scalding stream until she was lying in a damp pool of embarrassment and her cheeks were scarlet with shame.

Niska gave a chilling laugh as she wiped her damp hands on Rianna's blanket. 'What a dirty girl, you are,' she sneered as she rose to her feet. 'I'll have to send Chang in to clean you up.'

'No,' Rianna begged. 'Haven't you humiliated me enough?'

'I haven't even started yet,' Niska told her with a tight smile. 'I'll instruct him to ensure you are forced to sleep on this soiled mattress until we reach Vestfold. It will remind you constantly of the further humiliations that lie in store for you there.'

Rianna kept her eyes pointedly averted from Chang as he moved around the tent, packing up the contents ready for departure. The hunters had returned with plenty of game and they had been ordered to move again. But Rianna doubted they would travel far today as it was already well past noon.

She found it difficult to face Chang after she had endured the indignity of him seeing her lying there naked in a pool of her own piss. When he'd released her arms, for a brief moment she had thought she saw a flicker of sympathy in his dark eyes but it disappeared in an instant. He had brought her warm water with which to wash herself and clean clothing, appearing unmoved now by her nudity. Rianna had never known a man like Chang. She did pause to wonder if he preferred to take his pleasure with men. Yet most of the time he was remote, almost sexless, as if he kept his physical needs permanently suppressed.

'We are almost ready to depart.' He unfastened the heavy manacle from her ankle and helped Rianna to her feet. Her arms still ached a little from the discomfort of having them tied above her head all night. She'd have given anything to move freely and unfettered for a while, but no doubt she was destined to be chained in the baggage wagon again. She walked slowly over to the entrance of the tent, conscious that Chang was carefully watching her to ensure she wouldn't try to escape. There was no point; she would be recaptured in an instant.

She surveyed the part of the camp she could see, hoping to get a glimpse of Leon. At least then she'd know he was still alive. She stepped back when she saw a middle-aged grizzled man with a patch over his left eye walk towards her tent. It was Hordo, one of Chang's most trusted men.

'My lady,' Hordo politely acknowledged as he paused at the entrance and looked at Chang. 'We are ready to depart.'

'Go with Hordo,' Chang ordered. 'He will attend to you today.'

Hordo cautiously took hold of her arm and escorted Rianna to the wagon, which as usual was parked close to her tent. As he helped her inside Rianna noticed that it stunk of slaughter. Bloody hunks of meat wrapped in cloths were stored at the far end, while other pieces of meat had been rolled in salt to preserve them. Her stomach gave an uneasy lurch, yet she had no choice but to sit down on a pile of sacks as Hordo picked up the chain affixed to the side of the wagon.

'Make yourself as comfortable as you can,' he said gruffly, appearing not to notice the overpowering stench.

Rianna smiled shyly at him and was heartened to see that he was not immune to her charms. 'My poor ankle is so sore,' she complained. 'Could you not fasten that cruel thing around my wrist instead?'

Hordo frowned as he stared at her beautiful face. 'Of course. If you wish it, my lady, I cannot see the harm,' he said with an understanding smile.

Rianna had already prepared herself just in case. Her bodice had long pointed sleeves that extended over the back of her hand and she had tied a lace kerchief around her wrist as well to increase its bulk. 'This will ensure that the rough metal does not irritate my skin,' she told him sweetly. Her wrists were slim and her hands small. She had no wish for Hordo to realise that the manacle would be very loose.

'With a skin as soft and delicate as yours, we must be careful,' he said gruffly as she fluttered her eyelashes at him. He clamped the metal band around her wrist and fixed it firmly in place, holding her hand a shade longer than necessary. 'You remind me a little of someone I once knew . . .' he admitted awkwardly, then faltered as if unable to put his feelings into words.

'A sweetheart perhaps?' Rianna asked gently.

He nodded, then stepped out of the wagon, pulling the canvas flap back in place to afford her privacy. Rianna remained perched on the pile of sacks, listening to the sounds of the men preparing for their departure. Within minutes the wagon lurched forwards, trundling noisily over the rough track.

Once they were well underway Rianna rummaged under the sacks and took out a small bundle containing hard biscuits and strips of dried meat that she had purloined from the cook's stores in the rear of the wagon. She had spent the last couple of days searching for things that might prove useful for her escape.

Stripping off her woollen skirt she slipped on a pair of breeches she had discovered in a bundle of clothing. The only doublet she had found was fur lined and far too big, with a musty odour that was none to pleasant, but it would keep her warm. The soft kid riding boots she had on were her own, and were not designed for walking but she hoped they would prove sturdy enough.

The cook kept a large pot of fat in the wagon and she pulled it towards her. Removing the kerchief from her wrist, and pulling up her sleeve, she dipped her fingers in the greasy mass and smeared the rancid fat around her hand and wrist. Once her skin was slippery enough it didn't prove too difficult to slide the manacle off. Quickly, she wiped the smelly fat from her skin, and put on the doublet. Picking up her bundle of food, she made her way to the back of the wagon and eased back the canvas just a crack.

Fortunately the mercenaries following the wagon were some distance behind it. Rianna waited until they turned a sharp bend in the tree-lined road. Once out of their sight she climbed over the tailboard and jumped – aiming for some thick shrubs, which she hoped would break her fall. She lost control of her leap and landed awkwardly in a clump of ferns, then slid down a stony slope into a deep cleft by the side of the track. She froze, praying she wouldn't be spotted as the long column rode past her.

It was probably only a few minutes but it felt like ages to Rianna before the squeak of the wagon and the chatter of the men faded into the distance. She lay there, her hands stinging where she had grazed them in her fall, hardly daring to breathe. Eventually the forest was quiet with only the shrill sound of birdsong piercing the still air.

Rianna scrambled to her feet, not knowing how long she had before they discovered she was missing. Apart from feeling a little bruised and battered, she had suffered no ill effects from her fall. Brushing the dead leaves and grass from her hands and face she looked around her, having no idea where she was, or how far it was to Ruberoc. She picked up her bundle and turned back in the direction she had just come from. Surely by now Tarn would have sent out soldiers to look for her, and if she travelled south she might eventually come upon them. If not she would have to find a place where she could hide from Niska's men until they tired of looking for her. She set off, not daring to use the track, instead walking through the trees, just keeping the path in sight so that she would not lose her way.

Rianna was close to exhaustion when dawn came, streaking the sky with gold and red. By now she had left the forest and was traversing a gently undulating grassy plain. Anxiously she scanned the horizon, looking for a stream or river – any sign of water to drink. Her throat was parched, her lips dry. She saw a glimmer of something suspiciously like water in the distance, and she increased her pace, then she heard the distant pounding sound of horses approaching fast.

Fearful it was Niska's men coming to look for her, she glanced around for cover. Even if it wasn't the mercenaries it was safer not to be seen until she had discovered who the riders were. There were barely any places to hide on this bleak plain, but in the distance she saw a pile of boulders surrounded by thick glossy-leafed bushes. Fear made her forget her tiredness as she ran over the rough ground towards them, trying not to trip over stones and tufts of grass. She caught her foot in a hillock, just managing to regain her balance but she dropped her bundle of food on the ground. There was no time to pick it up. She left the bundle where it was as she ran towards the boulders.

Her breath burning in her throat and her limbs feeling weak she threw herself in the cover of the bushes. Pressing herself close to the cold ground, she crawled towards the centre of the cluster of stones. Her heart pounding fearfully, Rianna looked back at the track as a line of mercenaries, led by Chang, rode along it at full gallop. She was relived when they rode straight past the point where she had left the track and continued on their way. She'd almost begun to believe that she was safe when Chang suddenly pulled his mount to a halt and spoke to one of his men. The mercenary dismounted and walked back along the track looking closely at the ground and carefully examined the grass that bordered the narrow pathway.

Rianna froze in fear as the man stared thoughtfully down at a patch of soft grass then shouted and pointed in her direction. Chang and his man cantered back and followed the scout as he began to make his way slowly towards Rianna's hiding place. He stopped only once to pick up her bundle of food and show it to Chang. He nodded then stared thoughtfully at the pile of boulders almost as if he knew for certain that that was where she was hiding.

Agitatedly she slithered backwards, then turned and crawled through the long grass until the ground dipped downwards. Once out of the direct line of sight of her pursuers, she stood up and ran as fast as she could.

The ground gradually grew softer and spongier beneath her feet, hampering her speed and making running much harder. She was forced to slow to a near-walking pace when her feet hit softer, even boggier ground. One more step and the mud grabbed at her booted feet, and as she struggled to lift them she was sucked deeper into the soft morass. Frantically she struggled to free herself, but with every movement she made she was sucked deeper and deeper.

Rianna knew all was lost when she heard the soft thud of hoofbeats getting closer and closer. She turned her head to see a grim-faced Chang riding towards her.

Rianna's entire body ached and she would have been sick to her stomach if her sore belly hadn't been so empty. She was bound hand and foot with rawhide cords, which cut cruelly into her skin, and she was draped awkwardly across the front of Chang's saddle. Every step the horse took jarred her body and she developed a pounding headache from being held upside down.

Chang brought his mount to a halt, dismounted and grabbed hold of Rianna. Heaving her across his shoulder he carried her into Niska's tent and tossed her unceremoniously on to the ground. Rianna landed with a painful thump at Niska's feet.

'You've done well,' Niska said to Chang. 'Did she get far?'

'Further than I ever thought,' he replied.

'She's filthy.' Niska grimaced as she dug her toe in

Rianna's ribs. 'Her little escapade has caused an unnecessary delay and she must be punished,' she continued coldly.

'As you wish.' Chang sounded as though he did not care either way as he grabbed hold of Rianna and hauled her to her feet.

She kept her eyes lowered, not looking at Niska, feeling bruised and battered and filled with such wretched disappointment it was hard to hold back her tears of frustration.

'Tanith, help Chang strip off those filthy clothes,' Niska said coldly. 'And then tie her to the tentpost.'

Tanith cut the rawhide binding Rianna's ankles and began to strip off her mudstained garments. Tanith was enjoying what she was doing, judging by her expression, and her hands lingered on Rianna's naked flesh. When the bindings on Rianna's wrists hampered the removal of her shirt, Tanith picked up the knife again and sliced through the flapping fabric.

When Rianna was naked Chang pulled her over to the nearest gilded tentpost, fastening her hands to it, stretching her arms so tight above her head that she was barely able to keep her heels on the ground. As he stepped away from her, Niska moved forwards, holding a fine silver chain which she fastened tightly around Rianna's slim waist. There was another chain fastened to it at the front, which hung down over Rianna's belly. She tensed as Niska threaded the trailing chain between her thighs, lodging it in the narrow crack of her sex, pulling it so tight it almost split Rianna in two as it was fastened to the middle of the chain in the small of her back.

The cold links pressed tightly against Rianna's clit and dug into her nether mouth. The sensation was humiliating, yet subtly arousing as Rianna was fastened to the post by a piece of rawhide cord wrapped around her waist, close to the straining chain. The post separated Rianna's bosom, pushing her breasts lewdly out either side of the gilded pole. Her pussy and buttock cheeks closed around the chain until it was barely visible at all. It dug into the entrance of her arsehole and caused a constant chafing pressure on her clit.

'You may play with her for a minute, Tanith,' Niska said. 'While I select her instrument of punishment.'

Tanith giggled as she circled Rianna, looking her up and down like a child who'd just been presented with a new toy. She touched Rianna's breasts, stroking and squeezing them roughly. Her fingers caught hold of Rianna's nipples and rolled them between finger and thumb, rubbing and pulling at them until they hardened. She concentrated on them so intently that they soon reddened and became sore from the constant stimulation. Smiling cruelly at Rianna she dug her fingers in the abused teats, watching her victim struggle to hide her discomfort.

'My lady enjoys inflicting pain and so do I,' she confided, her hand caressing Rianna's hip. She wedged her finger under the tightly drawn chain and pulled, making it cut cruelly into Rianna, forcing from her a moan of painful pleasure. The heat in her belly increased, mingling with the constant straining pressure on her clit, and Rianna raised herself on her toes as if it would somehow relieve the cutting fire lancing through her.

'Step back, Tanith, you may play again later,' Rianna heard Niska say. Tanith's mouth drooped with disappointment, but as she stepped back she slapped Rianna's breasts hard in a last defiant gesture.

Niska came into Rianna's view, not carrying a switch or a whip, just a wide flat wooden paddle covered on one side with soft green leather. Niska slapped it against the side of her hip and it made a sharp cracking sound that turned Rianna cold with fear.

Sarin sighed in his sleep, dreaming of the past: of his palace in Aguilar, of Tarn and of Rianna. The dream was so vivid that when he awoke he did not know where he

172

was for a moment. Not until he saw Zene's body curled up in a foetal position beside him.

'It's time to wake.' He blew softly on her cheek. She sighed and rolled over to nestle lovingly against him, her small breasts pressed to his bare chest, her left leg twined around his.

'No, tis time for pleasure.' She kissed the warm skin of his chest, her lips nuzzling at his flat brown nipples. Sarin smiled as he felt her hand stroke his penis, caress his balls, then brush tantalisingly against the ultra-sensitive ridge just behind the soft sack. Zene had learned swiftly, and she was becoming an expert in the art of seduction.

Sarin held the soft fragrant-smelling woman hard against him, enjoying the feeling of closeness. His libido was always at its zenith at this time in the morning and his dreams had already half-aroused him, while Zene was doing the rest. He pressed his hips to hers, pulling her leg further up his thigh as he eased his engorged cock into the moist channel of her sex. Zene gave a soft groan as he angled his entry so that his cock-head stimulated her most sensitive spot.

'Wonderful,' she murmured, clutching hold of his shoulders as he began to thrust into her.

Sarin gave a soft groan in reply as he thrust vigorously, his hands clutching firmly at her arse. Zene's teeth nipped his neck as he pumped harder, grinding his pelvis against hers until his pleasure peaked, then erupted. As she climaxed, Zene gave a loud scream that no doubt woke any of the soldiers in the camp who were still asleep. Sarin chuckled and stilled her scream with his lips until the trembling of her limbs ceased and she lay replete and contented in his arms.

Sarin was still smiling as he cleansed himself with a damp cloth and put on his clothes. It felt good to be rid of the heavy metal cuffs around his wrists. Yesterday one of the soldiers had managed to break open the remains of the manacles he'd worn since leaving Freygard. Run-

173

ning a hand through his dishevelled hair, he stepped out of his tent and paused to fasten his doublet.

The soldiers inclined their heads deferentially, but Sarin was certain he could see jealousy in their eyes. No other man in the camp had the pleasure of a woman to warm his bed at night.

Sarin forgot their presence as he caught sight of a man standing by the campfire staring morosely into the distance, his long blond hair moving slightly in the breeze. It was a chill morning but he stood there dressed only in tight-fitting breeches and high boots. Sarin caught his breath; he'd always thought that Tarn was the handsomest man he'd ever laid eyes on, and his beauty had not diminished since they'd parted in Percheron. Despite all the enmity between them, Sarin still desired Tarn. He had lusted after the handsome youth ever since Tarn had arrived as a hostage in Aguilar. When Tarn had been returned to him as a captive, Sarin had forced him to become his pleasure slave, and had been able to slake his lust on him at last. But their union, and the satisfaction Sarin had derived from it, had always been followed by a bitter aftertaste. Sarin wanted Tarn to come to him willingly, but he doubted that was ever possible. He desired Tarn the man, yet he was far from at ease with Tarn the monarch. There was a fierce determination in Tarn now that had been far less prevalent in the past.

Tarn's eyes held just the faintest glimmer of amusement as Sarin approached him. 'You've not changed have you, Sarin?' he said with a twisted grin. 'You appear to have been keeping Zene very busy.'

'Now that she's discovered how pleasurable coupling with a man can be she is insatiable,' Sarin said with a shrug of his shoulders.

'I remember her when I was in Freygard,' Tarn commented as a soldier handed Sarin a bowl of thick, glutinous-looking oatmeal. The food wasn't to his taste but it kept the hunger at bay.

'You do?' Sarin forced down a spoonful of salty porridge. He had spoken to Zene about Tarn but she claimed she barely remembered him at all.

'I was in the stables working when Zene and her friends came upon me. They decided to try out their newest slave. They held me down in the straw and Zene . . .' Tarn paused as if he'd said too much.

'Zene what?' Sarin felt suddenly jealous that Zene had desired Tarn before him.

'Isn't that obvious?' Tarn said awkwardly as his blue eyes focused on the mountains again. 'We should be leaving. We still have a long way to travel. Every moment that passes leaves Rianna in even greater peril.' He sighed. 'I only wish I knew how she was faring.'

Leon was thinking the selfsame thing as he strode through the camp towards Niska's tent. He had just heard that Chang and his men had found Lady Rianna and brought her safely back to the camp. Leon had no idea what had possessed her to run off.

He had woken early this morning with a foul taste in his mouth and a pounding head. His body felt bruised, it ached in unmentionable places and he felt disgusted with his own behaviour. Both the Nubians had already left the tent but the smell of them and the odour of sexual depravity still clung thickly to both him and Niska.

Unable to face the woman he adored until he'd mulled over all that had occurred the night before, Leon dressed and went outside. Some of the men were preparing to go hunting for game and Leon decided to join them, thinking that the thrill of the chase would help clear his head.

When they'd eventually returned laden with fresh meat, the rest of their party was already preparing to depart. Leon had rode along behind the rest of the men deciding not even to tell Niska about his plans to take Lady Rianna to Nemedia and leave her there. The large town was less than ten leagues away by his calculations and once the deed was done it would not be easy for

Niska to take Rianna back. Why that thought should cross his mind he didn't know.

When they had stopped briefly to water the horses, Leon had made his way to the baggage wagon to acquaint Lady Rianna of his plans. He had opened the canvas flap to find no sign of the noble lady. Niska had been horrified to discover Rianna had disappeared and had sent Chang and a small group of men to find her.

During the long wait many of the men had idled away their time gambling and drinking, while others had set about cleaning and sharpening their weapons. Leon paused as he noticed one man with frizzy red hair lovingly polishing a sword with an ornate silver hilt. The weapon was so familiar to Leon that his heart missed a beat. Recovering his composure he paused and said casually, 'That's a fine sword. Where did you get it?'

'I paid twenty gold pistoles for it,' the man replied, running his grimy fingers up and down the highly polished blade. 'I purchased it from him!' he informed Leon, pointing to a tall burly-looking mercenary who was talking to Hordo. Leon recognised him as one of a small band of Chang's most trusted men. 'Spoils of war. It belonged to a nobleman that he killed with his bare hands.'

'Can I inspect the blade?' Leon asked.

His hand shook a little as he took the weapon and turned it over to examine the all too familiar crest carved in the hilt. The weapon had been a gift to Gavid from his father. Gavid treasured it so much he never let it out of his sight.

'It's a fine blade,' Leon remarked, filled with indescribable pain, as he handed the sword back to its new owner.

The man nodded and resumed polishing the weapon while Leon strolled casually over to where the horses were tethered. At the rear were a number of spare mounts and all his suspicions were confirmed when he found the roan with a white star-shaped blaze on its nose.

'Easy, Castor,' Leon muttered as he ran his hands over Gavid's mount. It appeared unhurt. Then he found the raised line on its left flank beneath its thick winter coat. It was a half-healed wound, which certainly had not been there before Gavid had left the camp. Leon now knew without a doubt that his friend was dead, butchered by Niska's men just like all his other missing soldiers.

# Chapter Eight

*F*illed with guilt, anger and immense pain, Leon stormed into Niska's tent, roughly shoving aside the mercenary who tried to bar his way.

'Niska what the . . .' he faltered in utter amazement as he saw Rianna, naked, tied to a post being beaten by Niska. 'By the gods!' he yelled, rage consuming him.

Leon pulled Niska away from Rianna, slapped her hard across the face and threw her roughly to the ground with such force that she crashed into a brass-topped table. Niska was so confounded she just lay there as Leon drew a dagger from his belt and cut Rianna's bonds. She collapsed limply in his arms. Draping his cloak around her, he lifted her and carried her from Niska's tent. Rianna was too distressed to say anything as Leon carried her into her own tent and laid her gently on her mattress.

'Forgive me,' he mumbled, filled with such a multitude of emotions he felt he might explode. His stomach contracted as he stared down at Rianna's beautiful tear-stained face. How could he ever have allowed himself to believe all the terrible things Niska had said about her?

Leon felt even more guilty when Rianna smiled and said with relief, and not a trace of enmity, 'Thank the gods you are alive.' She tenderly touched his face. 'I feared you were dead.'

'My mind was for a long time,' he admitted painfully. Niska had told him so many lies and it was difficult to sort truth from fiction. 'Forgive me, my lady. I've been such a fool.' He saw Rianna wince as she moved and added worriedly, 'How badly are you hurt?'

'My pride as much as anything else,' she said with a sad smile. 'If Niska had wanted to do me real harm she would have used a whip.'

'Let me see.' Rianna showed no false modesty as Leon unwrapped the cloak and examined her abused back and buttocks. 'The flesh is red and inflamed but unbroken.'

'I'll heal soon enough, no doubt,' she said with a faint catch in her voice. 'She'll not want me permanently damaged. She intends to present me as a gift to her brother, Ragnor.'

Leon began to feel sick to his stomach. His lust for Niska had blinded him completely. He stared down at Rianna's damaged flesh, thinking that her vulnerability made her look even more beautiful. She had a warmth and kindness that was absent in Niska. He remembered the sight of her naked and helpless, bound to the post, and the heat grew stronger, filling his loins with desire.

It was only then that he noticed the chain fastened tightly around Rianna's waist and the other chain coming from it that disappeared between her buttock cheeks and surfaced just above her slit. Rianna tried to sit up, shivering as the chain cut into her even more. Leon's lust expanded; the sight of that chain, half-hidden by her private parts, sent him wild with desire. 'Can you remove it, please,' Rianna begged. 'The cutting pressure is driving me insane.'

Leon gently unclipped it at the back, but it was clasped so tightly between her buttock cheeks that he rolled her on to her back and eased open her thighs. 'I'll be gentle,' he said as he pulled open her pussy lips to remove the metal, which was warm and moist with her secretions.

179

He saw the shape of the links imprinted on her succulent pink flesh. The need to possess her, and wipe away her pain consumed his thoughts. 'What did she do to you?' he asked, tossing the chain aside. 'Did she hurt you here as well?' He brushed his fingertips gently across one red, swollen nipple and Rianna gave a soft, breathy sigh. Leon was unable to resist leaning forwards and licking it, anointing it with his spittle before he pulled it into his mouth.

'Leon,' Rianna weakly protested, but she made no attempt to push him away.

Leon's skin tingled with excitement as he caressed Rianna, feeling her tremble as he ran his hands over her naked body. When he caressed her belly, her thighs rolled open as if she wanted him to touch her there. He told himself he was purely comforting her, while his traitorous fingers slid into the soft moistness of her pussy. His fingers brushed her tortured clit and Rianna gave a soft moan, lifting her hips up towards Leon as he stroked the aching nub.

He couldn't deny Lady Rianna what she so clearly wanted, Leon decided, as he willingly allowed lust to overtake his conscious thoughts. Continuing to stimulate her, he pulled his breeches open with the other hand. She didn't move, just lay there trembling, her eyes closed as he positioned himself between her open thighs.

Rianna drew in her breath sharply as he slid his fat cock into her slippery warmth. Supporting himself on his arms, he thrust deeper while his lips returned to her swollen teats. Rianna's hips moved in unison with his as he powered into her hard and fast. They were both fired with a wild passion that had forced them to seek solace in each other's arms.

He climaxed quickly, and Rianna followed him, desperately rubbing her clit, a soft sighing word escaping her lips. 'Tarn,' she murmured as though she'd been making love to him.

Leon was filled with so much guilt he could barely

breathe as he withdrew from her. His mind was in turmoil but one overwhelming thought was clear in his mind: they had to leave, both of them, right now.

'We must make ready to depart . . .' He faltered as Chang strode into the tent.

Chang's inscrutable expression did not change as he saw Leon agitatedly fasten his breeches and Rianna cover herself.

'The baroness wishes to speak to you, Captain Leon,' Chang said coolly. 'She appears somewhat upset,' he added.

Leon turned to look at Rianna, hoping she would know exactly what he was thinking. 'My lady?'

'Go now,' she said, staring at him with understanding. 'As quickly as you can.'

'Are you certain?' he asked, bowing. 'I've no wish to desert you at such a time. However, I will be back as soon as I can.'

'I know you will, Leon,' she said softly as her eyes glittered with the suspicion of unshed tears.

'You should not keep the baroness waiting,' Chang pointed out as he casually cleaned his nails with the point of his dagger.

Rianna silently mouthed, 'God speed,' at Leon as he gave her one last reassuring smile.

He left the tent certain that Rianna knew he intended to try and make a run for it while he still could. She was guarded closely but for the time being he was not. He had to find help, then come back and rescue Rianna. After what had occurred, Niska was most probably furious and would no longer place any trust in him. Anyway, he doubted he could stay and manage to hide from her the fact that he now knew the full truth of her perfidy. In truth he had no wish to ever lay eyes on her again – because of his foolish desire for her Gavid and most of his men were dead.

As he passed by another tent, he picked up a cloak someone had left there and made for the horses. Niska was bound to send men after him, but he had to evade them and find a way to reach Prince Tarn. Praying he would succeed, Leon mounted his horse and cantered off into the forest.

Rianna's thoughts had been with Leon for the last three days. There had been no sign of him, or the men Niska had sent after him. She was determined not to give up hope, but it was fading fast now, especially as she was sitting opposite Niska in her coach driving into Ragnor's stronghold. It had taken them most of those three days to navigate the icy mountain paths and enter Vestfold – a land ruled by barbarian warlords who had the power of life and death over all who served them.

Rianna had expected to see a castle, perhaps surrounded by a village, but the reality was far different. Ragnor's stronghold was set in a fertile valley close to the side of a massive lake. The place was huge; farms surrounded by fields and at its centre a village almost big enough to be classed as a town. High banks topped by a wooden wall surrounded the entire settlement and it was guarded by fierce-looking ruddy-complexioned warriors dressed in heavy woollen garments and skins. They looked just as threatening in their own way as Niska's mercenaries.

Niska glanced out of the carriage window. 'Look Rianna, the slaves are preparing the fields for planting. Ragnor prides himself on the number of thralls he owns,' she added with a self-satisfied smile.

Rianna did not reply. She continued staring out of the window at her new home. As they passed by the lake, she wrinkled her nose at the overpowering smell of fish. Thousands of gutted fish hung on large wooden racks drying in the weak sunshine.

The smell faded as they entered the main body of the settlement, which was contained within an even higher wall. Inside were numerous wooden houses and tall well-fed people in brightly coloured clothing. They all turned to stare curiously at Niska's coach as it trundled past. Rianna sat back, out of sight and pulled her cloak tighter around her naked body. This morning she had been washed, oiled and scented under Niska's careful instructions. Silver chains had been fastened around her wrists and ankles, allowing her just enough movement to walk unhampered, while a silver collar now circled her neck. She was frightened, terrified even, but she tried not to show it, holding her head high and staring coldly at Niska. Yet she still failed to repress an unconscious shiver as they drove through a wide gate and into a closely guarded keep.

The coach stopped beside a large wooden building decorated with ornate carvings. 'Ragnor's longhouse,' Niska announced.

Chang opened the carriage door and helped Niska out but Rianna instinctively hung back. Chang grabbed hold of her and pulled her out of the carriage, heaving her under his arm, as there was still snow on the ground and Rianna was barefoot. Carrying her inside the longhouse, as though she weighed practically nothing, Chang set her down in the anteroom and looked expectantly at Niska.

'Prepare her,' she commanded.

He jerked off Rianna's cloak and clipped a chain to her neck collar, handing the end of it to Niska. It was not overly cold in the anteroom, yet Rianna shivered as Chang pushed open the heavy doors. He stood back to allow them to enter and Rianna's feet slid slightly on the polished-wood floor as Niska roughly jerked the chain.

The raucous noise, the surprising heat and the foul smell of unwashed humanity overwhelmed Rianna as she was dragged into the huge longhouse. The walls, ceiling and support posts were covered in elaborate carvings of coiled serpents and strange beasts. Most of the walls were decorated with tapestries thickly embroidered in bright colours and silver and gold thread, depicting scenes from ancient myths and legends.

The majority of the occupants were men. Some were

dressed in silk tunics and sumptuous furs, with heavy gold bracelets encircling their wrists, and gold headbands holding back their hair. Yet with all their fine garments, in Rianna's estimation they were still barbarians as they turned to look at the pale-skinned beauty with a mass of glorious red-gold hair as she was led forwards naked and in chains.

Rianna cared not for their lascivious glances, all her attention was focused on the tall blond giant who lounged on his carved wooden throne. She was to be given to him as a slave, to do with as he wished. Rianna already knew how cruel and brutal these northmen could be.

Female slaves wearing shapeless white woollen garments walked among the men serving them food and drink. Some men openly pawed at the women, crudely fondling them as they served them ale and mead from huge jugs. Linen cloths covered the wooden tables upon which were heaped great joints of meat, dried fish, bread and cheese. A number of men drank from huge curved horns decorated in silver, gulping down the alcohol, careless of the way it streamed down their chins to soil their elaborate clothes.

They stopped in front of the throne. Ragnor was a fine-looking man with hair almost as pale as Niska's. Because he was tall, muscular and blond, in a way he bore a faint resemblance to Tarn. But his features were coarser, less refined, his complexion ruddy and roughened by exposure to the cold northern winds, while decorating his top lip was a trailing blond moustache. He smiled as he greeted his sister, but Rianna detected no warmth in his smile or his words. However, she had no idea what was being said. The lands of Kabra, Harn and Percheron had a similar language with only different dialects to contend with but here in Vestfold they spoke a rough guttural tongue unlike anything she'd ever heard.

Niska roughly jerked Rianna's chain to pull her forwards, and Ragnor smiled more warmly, appearing impressed with his new slave. Rianna was expected to fall to her knees as befitted a new thrall, but she dared to face him boldly, not even deigning to bow or curtsey.

Slowly he looked Rianna up and down, and she saw hungry desire light his blue eyes. Pieces of his long hair were plaited at the sides and held in place by tiny skulls, while the rest streamed down his back. His eyes were a deeper blue than Niska's, but still chillingly cold. He was an uncivilised barbarian, and Niska's close kin, but he did not give Rianna the impression he was an inherently cruel man. However, his hands were huge and Rianna felt sick at the thought of them exploring her most intimate parts. Yet with that thought came a surge of lust. Niska was still feeding her the aphrodisiac and her body ached with a sexual frustration that she sometimes found difficult to hide.

'So you are the daughter of the Protector of Harn? A princess?' Ragnor's accent was strong but he spoke her language well.

'I am, sir.' Rianna regally inclined her head.

'She is a virgin?' Ragnor addressed Niska, clearing expecting Rianna to have been touched by no other man. His eyes greedily returned to his prize, focusing on Rianna's high full breasts.

'No,' Niska replied and Ragnor frowned. 'She is far better than an innocent virgin,' Niska hurriedly explained. 'She was wed to Lord Sarin of Percheron. You must have heard tales of his sexual excess and of the lasciviousness of his court. Sarin schooled her well. She is more expert in matters of the flesh than the finest courtesan.'

Ragnor pursed his lips and thoughtfully stroked his moustache. 'She looks so innocent.'

'Looks can be deceiving, brother.' Niska leaned towards him. 'She's insatiable. She'll do all you ask of her and much more. She is a prize beyond all others because now that Sarin is dead she has captured the heart of Prince Tarn of Kabra. He worships her and plans

185

to make her his bride, but now she is lost to him and is your slave to do with as you wish.'

'Kabra?' Ragnor grinned. 'I've heard of this prince who dared to challenge the might of Percheron. When Sven was Lawspeaker before me he tried to convince the other jarls to join together. Sven was convinced that with our vast forces combined we could have conquered Kabra and Percheron, all the known world if we wished it. We could have been the most powerful warriors of all time, but the other jarls refused to even consider his proposition. I do not have Kabra but I do have Prince Tarn's betrothed . . .' He pulled Rianna towards him, holding her chain tightly so that she had no choice but to stand there and submit to his crude inspection. His battle-roughened fingers stroked her skin, felt and weighed her breasts, then caressed the curve of her belly and touched her pubic hair. 'Her skin is so soft.'

'Perhaps you'd like to examine my teeth as well?' Rianna spat, determinedly clamping her legs together so that his fingers could not slide intrusively between her thighs.

Ragnor frowned in annoyance, then threw back his head and laughed loudly. 'My sister warned me you had spirit, wench.'

His huge hand curved around Rianna's waist and she was hauled on to his lap. She was forced to sit there as he caressed her – all too conscious of the heat emanating from his flesh, and surprised to smell, not body odour, but the clean scent of herbs. She was so close to Ragnor she could see the lines etched round his eyes by the cold, harsh northern winds. His teeth were large and white while his breath smelled slightly of wine. Thank the gods Ragnor did not repulse her. He was an attractive man and she could feel the demanding line of his cock beneath his soft plaited leather trousers. Its hardness pressed against her buttock cheeks and it felt pleasingly large. She was filled with a sudden lust that made the blood sing though her veins. Rianna's nipples stiffened, and her pussy grew wet with anticipation as she imagined his huge cock sliding into the tight dark hole of her sex.

'Come here, girl,' Ragnor roared and a dark-haired thrall scurried forwards with a goblet of wine. Ragnor took it and held it to Rianna's lips. 'Drink,' he commanded.

Rianna obediently gulped down the wine, embarrassed by her wanton thoughts. She preferred to be drunk, even insensible, before he bedded her. Rianna was certain that she would not have to wait long judging by the size of his prick. She just prayed that he wouldn't choose to start getting intimate with her here with everyone watching. Judging by what was going on in the rest of the hall most of these men cared little for privacy. She just had to hope that Ragnor was different and bedded his women in private.

Ragnor threw the empty goblet at the nervous thrall. She just managed to catch it and scurried away, while Ragnor ran his rough fingertips over Rianna's nipples. 'Do as I wish and no harm will come to you,' he said softly. 'Your skin is so delicate it would scar easily.'

She stayed silent as he stroked her belly and pubis, fighting the urge to open her legs and allow him to touch her aching pussy. 'Please . . .' she begged, looking at him with anguished eyes.

'Later,' he said gruffly, tipping her from his lap on to the bearskin rug at his feet.

She landed in a tangle of arms and legs. Awkwardly she sat up, pressing her legs together and resting her arms across her bosom to hide them from the lecherous gaze of the other men present. However, most of the occupants of the hall were ignoring her now, as they became drunker by the moment. They appeared to have disgusting table habits, shovelling food into their mouths, spilling it on their clothes and causally spitting out anything that did not please their palate. Some were singing raucously and banging their fists on the table. A few in the corner were engaged in a reasonably

187

good-natured fight, while the rest were talking and gesturing very loudly or pawing the women.

Some had half-stripped thralls draped across their laps, lewdly fondling them. One had a red-headed girl on her knees between his legs with his cock buried in her mouth. Others were fornicating with slaves like rutting beasts. A small group had a naked girl spread-eagled on a table. A tall scar-faced man was fucking her front and rear with a doubled-headed carved wooden dildo, while the rest were slobbering over her body, and she was moaning and writhing in pleasure.

Rianna clamped her legs even tighter together, aroused and yet unsettled by such debauchery. She couldn't bear the thought of being forced to participate, although she'd seen far more erotic spectacles at Sarin's court. However, Sarin's orgies had always been well planned, with an exotic finesse that had proved highly arousing even to those who were watching. Also, with a few exceptions, the participants had always been willing, which did not appear to be the case in Ragnor's longhouse.

Ragnor pushed another goblet of wine into her hand and she gulped it down, hoping the alcohol would help blot out the sights and sounds around her. Ragnor, meanwhile, was focusing all his attention on Niska, who was fluttering her eyelashes coyly and openly flirting with her half-brother in a provocative fashion.

Suddenly Ragnor touched Rianna's arm. 'You are tired,' he told her. 'Go with the thrall, she'll find you somewhere to rest.' He grinned lewdly as he beckoned the dark-haired thrall, who'd served him earlier, forwards. 'I want no sign of weariness when I bed you for the first time, wench. Gunnar will tell you that I have a lusty appetite and expect my women to be both inventive and passionate.'

The thrall blushed and smiled coyly at Ragnor, clearly enamoured of her master, as Rianna went to clamber to her feet. Ragnor stopped her moving by clamping a heavy hand on her shoulder.

'Is something wrong?' she asked. 'I thought I was dismissed.'

'You were, but first there is a matter to attend to,' he said gruffly. 'There is no need for chains here, you cannot escape.' He held out his hand to Niska. 'The key?'

'As you wish brother,' she agreed meekly, handing the key to Ragnor without even deigning to glance at Rianna.

Ragnor unfastened the chains on Rianna's wrists and ankles. 'We can rid you of the collar later.' He frowned thoughtfully, then unfastened the red silk cloak he wore across his shoulders. 'At times modesty becomes a woman,' he said wrapping it around Rianna.

She smiled gratefully at him as she rose gracefully to her feet. Ragnor smiled back at her, the warmth softening his cold blue eyes, and she began to feel a little less fearful as she turned to walk away with the thrall. Ragnor watched in silence as Gunnar led her from the large chamber and into a smaller room set behind it.

The noise of the celebrations in the hall diminished as Gunnar shut the heavy wooden door. She picked up a pair of fur-lined slippers made of soft hide and handed them to Rianna. 'My master has a good heart,' she told Rianna. 'You've no need to fear him, he is far kinder than most jarls. Also he is very amorous. He often takes more than one wench to bed at a time.'

Nothing she could say would shock Rianna where Ragnor's sexual appetites were concerned. Compared to the crudeness of his followers his needs sounded simple enough.

'Would that he would slake his lust on you and the other thralls and leave me alone,' she replied, surprised that Gunnar spoke her language so fluently.

'You'll change your mind soon enough,' Gunnar said confidently as she led Rianna out into the cold evening air. It was getting darker and the sky was streaked with a plethora of brilliant colours. At another time Rianna might have stopped to enjoy the beauty of the sunset, but the treasures of nature were far from her mind.

'I doubt that,' she muttered. 'His followers are all barbarians. Can he be that different?'

'The men here may be rough and ill mannered at times, but they'll not harm you. It's the drink that makes them so unruly. Drunkenness is considered holy in Vestfold,' she said with a soft sigh that conveyed more than words ever could.

'You speak my tongue well,' Rianna commented as Gunnar opened the door of a large wooden hut and they were hit with a blast of hot air.

'My mother was from Kabra. She was captured in a raid and brought here as a slave.' Gunnar touched the silver chain at her neck. 'This is all I have left of her. She was forced to travel with my father when he left for Valhalla.'

Rianna knew that Valhalla was the resting place of warriors, but she didn't think it wise to question Gunnar further: the thrall's expression was tight and a little strained. By now Rianna was struggling to breathe. The air was so hot and dry, it near scalded her throat as Gunnar led her into an inner chamber. It had wooden benches round its sides, and a heap of glowing stones in the centre of the room.

'What is this place?'

'A bathhouse.' Gunnar removed Rianna's red silk cloak and placed a thin linen towel on one of the benches. 'Sit,' she urged. 'The heat and the steam will cleanse your skin.'

'Steam?' Rianna questioned.

'Yes.' Gunnar picked up a ladle and poured water over the glowing stones. In seconds steam billowed around the room and at once Rianna felt the sweat seep even more freely from her pores. The heat was overwhelming yet not unpleasant after days spent travelling across icy mountains, always feeling damp and chilled to the bone.

'How long do I stay here?' Rianna asked. Perspiration was running in thick rivulets over her hot flesh, while her hair stuck limply to the back of her neck.

'Long enough,' Gunnar said enigmatically as she left, pulling the door shut behind her.

Rianna sat down and leaned back against the warm wooden wall. She closed her eyes and let the heat seep into her weary limbs. She heard the hiss of water striking the stones and opened her eyes, thinking Gunnar had returned. From out of the white billowing steam walked a tall muscular figure, his body looking pale in contrast to the ruddiness of his face. Ragnor was naked, and she could see that his chest was covered by a thick matt of blond hair. It thinned over his stomach, then grew thickly around his cock. Pulling her eyes away from his flaccid sex, which appeared large even in repose, she noticed strange blue tattoos covering his upper arms. Rianna couldn't repress an uneasy shudder and her stomach churned in fear. She never expected to have to face him again just yet.

'I could wait no longer.' He spread a towel on the bench and sank down beside her. As he sat with his legs splayed lewdly apart, his balls and cock rested on the white linen, drawing Rianna's eyes towards them. She swallowed nervously. She had prayed this would never happen, but she was determined not to show Ragnor how afraid she was.

'If this had been left on longer it might have burned your skin,' he said, lifting her damp hair and unfastening her slave collar. It was fashioned out of silver yet he cast it on to the glowing stones as if it was of no value at all.

'It did not hurt me,' she said shyly as his huge hands stroked her body, polishing it lovingly with her perspiration until her skin gleamed in the soft lamplight. His caresses were far from unpleasant and Rianna found herself relaxing, even welcoming his touch. She did not protest even when his fingers crept between her thighs.

'You are frightened of me, are you not?' he said softly as he eased his thick fingers into the moist valley, sliding them into the opening of her cunt.

'A little.' She drew in her breath as his fingers slid

191

deeper. It felt so good after the long frustrating nights she'd spent, aroused by Niska's aphrodisiac and aching with need for Tarn.

'You've no need to be afraid. I'll not hurt you,' he growled, frigging her with his fingers while his lips took possession of her mouth. His kiss was passionate but the hairs of his moustache rubbing against her upper lips felt very strange. She wanted to close her eyes and convince herself it was Tarn. But no matter how hard she tried she could not avoid the fact that it was Ragnor thrusting his fingers deep inside her. A languorous desire overtook her senses, and she looked down at Ragnor's cock. It had grown huge, sticking out lewdly from its nest of blonde hair, rigidly erect, with beads of sweat glittering on the thick, heavily veined shaft.

He whispered something in his rough guttural tongue, then lifted her and sat her astride his muscular thighs. Trails of perspiration were running down his pale flesh and she touched the salty droplets. Gently he guided her hand to his cock, groaning as she shyly rubbed her fingers up and down its length until it was taut and shiny, the purple bulb at its end increasing even more in size.

With a hungry grunt, Ragnor pulled her forwards, spearing her on his cock, forcing it inside her until it filled her completely. Rianna clutched hold of his shoulders, threw back her head and closed her eyes. It felt good, so deliciously good, that she couldn't resist working her hips, lifting her body, then ramming it down on to his prick until he groaned with pleasure.

His hands grasped her waist, and his pelvis started to move in unison with hers. Rianna became immune to the sticky trails of sweat on her skin, the musky scent of Ragnor, and his harsh, laboured breaths. She just lost herself in the sheer joy of fucking a man again. The fire rose swiftly, her essence mingling with her sweat and drenching the folds of her sex. She gave one last thrust and the draining pleasure erupted, coming with a swift uncomplicated violence that took her breath away.

She leaned against Ragnor's hot slippery flesh, feeling the rough hairs round his nipples tickle her breasts, as he lovingly stroked her hair. Suddenly and without saying a word, he lifted her and carried her into a much colder room. Rianna shivered as he set her down on the cold floor and made her stand there as he sponged her body with warm water. Then he wrapped her in a blanket and sat her down on a bench. Feeling tired and drained, she watched Ragnor rub handfuls of snow into his skin, then rinse it off with ice-cold water. He then scoured his flesh with a rough cloth until it glowed redly.

Without bothering to dress, he lifted Rianna into his arms and walked out of the hut into the chill darkness. He made for his longhouse, taking her straight to his private chamber, where he laid her gently in his large comfortable bed.

Tarn looked down at Leon's grey drawn face as he finished another bout of coughing which left him gasping for breath.

'He'll recover,' Jentius said confidently as he covered Leon's shaking form with yet another blanket.

'Are you certain?' Tarn asked, feeling no pity for Leon, just a strange tightness in his chest as he looked down at the man who had betrayed him and placed the woman he loved in such peril.

'Only the gods can be certain,' Jentius said as he followed Tarn from the small tent.

'The gods,' Tarn said thoughtfully as he looked up at the leaden sky, 'are not on our side today.' The snow was still falling but it was lighter now. They had endured a raging blizzard for the last fifteen hours which had forced them to stop and make camp. Every moment they spent here frustrated Tarn because he felt they were moving further and further away from Rianna.

'Leon was lucky that he came upon us, alone for much

longer without supplies he would have surely perished. He was exhausted, but insisted on accompanying us and even then I feared he would not be able to keep up this relentless pace. He has fallen victim to his own determination.' Jentius shrugged his shoulders. 'Also Leon is consumed by guilt.'

'So he should be,' Tarn said with a coldness he rarely displayed. He had tried but he couldn't even begin to forgive Leon. Perhaps once Rianna was safe in his arms he could look at things differently. At present he preferred to keep as far away from Leon as possible.

'I've not seen you like this before, sire,' Jentius said. 'During the war you kept up the men's spirits with your determination to win. Now I wish I could say something to help ease your concern . . .'

'You cannot. No one can.' Tarn gave a deep sigh as he entered his tent.

He rubbed his hands together and shook the snow from his heavy cloak. It was a little warmer in the tent than it was outside, but it was still freezing. Sarin, Zene and Faros were huddled around a small table playing cards. When the weather had deteriorated Tarn had insisted that every soldier slept under cover. As there were not enough tents to go around, Sarin and Zene as well as Faros and Jentius had been obliged to share Tarn's large tent. With so many inside it was a crush.

'The snow has all but stopped,' Tarn announced. 'We should send out a man to scout ahead. We cannot be far from Ragnor's lands now. I want to know his stronghold's strengths and weaknesses and the size of the force we will be facing.'

He glanced at Zene. Even she was huddled in her cloak, and she was also wearing a spare pair of Faros's breeches.

'I'll go,' Faros offered. 'I know a little of Vestfold. My father purchased a slave who had been born in Ragnor's jarldom. Although his brother Sven had been lawspeaker then.'

194

'What would a slave know that could be of use?' Sarin said scathingly.

'More than you no doubt, my lord,' Faros said a little too boldly even for Tarn's liking.

Sarin glared at Faros. 'How dare you!'

'The cold and snow are affecting us all, making tempers short,' Tarn interjected appeasingly. 'Faros and I could both go. Jentius can remain here and organise the men.'

'Watch me you mean,' Sarin said with a cold smile. 'You still don't trust me do you, Tarn?'

'Or you me,' Tarn said. 'As I have said before, we are enemies drawn together by circumstance.'

'Then we'll be drawn even closer.' Sarin rose to his feet and pulled on a pair of gloves that Tarn had magnanimously given him. 'I will accompany you and Faros can remain here with Jentius. We are both strategists. Once we have surveyed the place, together we should be able to come up with a feasible plan to gain entry to Ragnor's stronghold.'

Tarn was in no mood for a long argument, and he knew Sarin well enough to be certain that his mind was set and he would not be dissuaded. 'If you insist,' he said curtly. 'But if Ragnor's men should find this camp in the meantime and attack . . .'

'Do you not trust Captain Jentius?' Sarin enquired cuttingly.

'You know that I do.' Tarn glanced at Jentius. 'While we are away, send a couple of the men out to try and find some game. We could do with some fresh meat. And ensure that the rest are ready to depart just as soon as we return.'

He pulled on his heavy leather gauntlets and took up his sword, sliding the blade into the gilded scabbard attached to his belt. Pulling the hood of his cloak over his head, Tarn stepped out of the tent.

'Tis a pity we have no tracks to follow,' Sarin said as he followed Tarn.

'We'll just make our way straight down the mountain. I'm more than certain we'll be headed in the right direction,' Tarn said confidently. 'We will just have to be very cautious. If we were both captured what a fine prize that would be for Ragnor.'

'Then we must ensure we are not captured,' Sarin said cheerfully as they reached their horses.

# Chapter Nine

*R*agnor smiled indulgently at Rianna as he watched her put on the white woollen gown he'd just given her, which was far more elaborately cut than the simple gowns most thralls wore. She had spent the last two nights in his bed, and his lovemaking had been surprisingly gentle. Perhaps it was because she was a noblewoman in her own right that he afforded her far more respect than the other female slaves who served him.

The gown was held in place by two heavy silver brooches decorated with intertwining leaves. A finely wrought silver filet was worn across her brow to hold back her long hair, which Ragnor insisted she always wore loose. She sat on the bed to pull on a pair of long, deerskin boots, still conscious of his pale-blue eyes watching her every move.

'This is for you.' He held out his hand. The heavy amulet covered almost his entire palm and was affixed to a heavy plaited gold chain. Shaped like a half cross with a scrolled eagle's head at its top, the amulet appeared to be made of solid gold.

'You are too kind to me,' she said awkwardly, as he lifted her hair and reverently fastened it around her neck. 'It is beautiful.'

'It is Thor's hammer – a powerful symbol,' Ragnor explained as his callused fingers stroked her cheek. 'While you wear it you are under his protection.'

'I am honoured,' she exclaimed, feeling the weight of the amulet pulling at her neck.

Rianna had arrived here expecting to live every day in fear, but she was protected by Ragnor's desire for her. She felt safe even in this enclave of barbarians, as long as she remained Ragnor's favourite, but when that would end she had no idea.

She often thought that it might have been easier to bear if he had been cruel to her. Then she wouldn't have felt such lust for him, wouldn't have found pleasure in sharing his bed, and wouldn't have been forced to endure the constant guilty feeling that she was betraying Tarn. Ragnor had a strong sexual appetite, and when he wasn't with her he was probably rutting with another willing slave. That didn't trouble Rianna. Her relationship with Ragnor was simple and uncomplicated, fuelled only by lust and self-preservation on her part.

She tried not to think of Tarn. If she were brutally honest with herself she knew it was doubtful she would ever see him again. Even if he did discover where she was, it would take an army to free her. If Tarn did attempt to attack Ragnor it would probably start a war between Kabra and Vestfold, and she couldn't expect him to do that even for her.

'Thor must be a strong god,' she said, touching the amulet.

'He protects me, my men, and now you.' Ragnor pulled her close, kissing her passionately. As he thrust his tongue into her mouth, he pulled up her skirt and cupped her pussy. One thick finger slid inside her.

'You told me that we must not be late for the celebration, my lord,' she reminded him, far preferring to remain here and have sex with him, than join Ragnor's warriors in the hall. She still didn't feel altogether comfortable in their presence and found it difficult to accept their rough uncivilised ways.

'I would stay here, with you,' Ragnor groaned. 'Yet I have to attend.' He pulled away from her. 'You've cast a spell over me, Rianna.'

She smiled. 'I know nothing of spells,' she added awkwardly, not wanting to be associated with such a dangerous thing as witchcraft.

Rianna was surprised at how superstitious these people were. Their lives revolved around the worship of the great ash tree, Yggdrasil, and their powerful gods. They cast stones, covered with strange symbols, in an effort to foretell the future. Runic symbols were carved in propitious places in their dwellings, and tattooed on their bodies. Not only did Ragnor have a number of these tattoos on his arms, he also had scars in the same strange shapes. He'd used his dagger to cut one into his flesh every time he'd been about to do battle, in the belief that the symbol would help ensure his victory.

'I know.' He smiled. 'But I would swear that Freya led you to me.'

'Perhaps she did,' Rianna replied. 'Freya protects the land of my birth as well as Vestfold.'

'We spring from the same earthforce. That is why your people are warriors like mine.' Ragnor pulled open the heavy wooden door. 'Come,' he ordered.

He strode towards the hall, his scarlet silk cloak billowing out behind him. Rianna was obliged to almost run to keep up with his massive strides. Even from a distance she was able to hear the raucous din coming from the chamber where the celebration was being held.

Judging by the spectacle that confronted them – the overpowering noise and pungent odours – the mourning feast had been going on for some time. Perhaps it had never ceased from the previous night. Ragnor's uncle, Hjor, had died before Rianna arrived here. During the ten days of mourning it was expected that the grieving

199

friends and relatives would keep drinking themselves into a near permanent stupor.

Ragnor sat down on his throne and Rianna perched beside him on a low stool, while thralls hurried to place a table in front of them. Soon it was laden with food and drink. Rianna had little appetite and nibbled at some wheaten bread, refusing the disgusting drink of fermented milk they called skyr. Ragnor, however, stuffed meat into his mouth and quaffed a large goblet of thick sweet mead.

Many of the men lay across the tables snoring loudly, others had vomited where they sat and had begun drinking again. The sour smell tainted the warm close atmosphere, making Rianna's stomach lurch in disgust. The majority of Ragnor's men were mere warriors; others were jarls or lords in their own right who had prospered under his leadership. He was respected by all of them and was fortunately a little more cultured and well educated than those who served him. Rianna glanced at Ragnor, trying to ignore his lack of good table manners as he crammed meat into his mouth and laughed at the capering antics of a jester. In a corner sat a blind lute player but his music could not be heard above the raucous din.

Suddenly two warriors dressed in fine garments brought forward a blonde-haired buxom slave. She was smiling as if she had been afforded a great honour as they bowed to Ragnor. He dropped his food, wiped his hands on a square of linen and spoke in a loud booming voice. 'Who among you will die with Hjor?'

Ragnor bent his head to whisper in Rianna's ear, translating the words as the thrall said, 'I will,' in a slurred voice.

Turning to look at her companions, the thrall unfastened the iron brooch that held her tunic together and let it drop to the floor. Her skin was pale and covered in freckles, her thighs dimpled and her breasts so large that they hung down, elongated by their weight.

She sank to the ground, pulling the taller of the two men with her. Her mound was only sparsely covered by pale-blonde hair and when she opened her thighs the red slit of her sex was easily visible. Her inner thighs were shiny as if smeared with the remains of many men, and even from a few feet away Rianna could detect the powerful odour of spent sex clinging to the woman's flesh.

'She shares herself with the warriors closest to Hjor before she accompanies her master,' Ragnor told Rianna as the man on his knees between the thrall's thighs, opened his trousers and freed his prick.

The man thrust into the slave, just as Ragnor slid his hand in the front of Rianna's gown to fondle her breasts. Rianna shivered, watching the man publicly fucking the thrall with a rough vigour that made the woman moan with pleasure, while Ragnor played with her nipples. He pulled and squeezed them roughly and she felt the familiar warmth grow between her thighs.

The man in front of her gave a loud grunt as he climaxed. He stood up, his shiny cock still exposed for all to see, and grinned as if he'd just completed a great feat. 'I will tell Lord Hjor that you have done this out of love for him,' he said to the thrall, still lying on the floor with her legs splayed open lewdly. He strode off to rejoin his friends while his companion kneeled and prepared to copulate with the slave.

'At other times I would also have publicly taken her,' Ragnor confided as he pulled Rianna on to his lap. 'But I choose you instead.' He slid his hand under her full skirt to stroke her pussy.

He pushed three bunched fingers deep into her cunt and Rianna gave a soft moan of bliss, unable to tear her gaze from the rutting figures only a few feet away from her. The ceremony was barbaric, yet crudely erotic. The smell of sweat, mingled with the stale odour of former sexual encounters, wafted towards her, exciting her even more.

The second man finished, rose to his feet and spoke the words required of him. Then, to Rianna's amazement, a third man stepped forwards to possess the thrall. The tall, rangy, brown-haired warrior was Jorvik, Ragnor's second in command. How many more men would the slave accommodate, Rianna wondered, wriggling excitedly on Ragnor's lap as he fingerfucked her in a smooth compelling rhythm. She watched Jorvik pull open his breeches, take his place between the thrall's thighs and thrust roughly into her.

Rianna was getting close to her orgasm when suddenly Ragnor withdrew his fingers and fumbled with his trousers. Gently he eased her back until he could slide his cock inside her. She coloured in embarrassment, certain that everyone could see what he was doing to her as he moved his hips, making her bounce up and down on his straining prick. But all eyes were on Jorvik and the thrall. Rianna gave a soft moan as Ragnor's callused finger stimulated her clit. She was only half aware of the thrall's shrill scream of pleasure, and Jorvik's accompanying grunt as Ragnor pumped harder. As he spilled his seed inside Rianna, her internal muscles contracted and her guilt-filled climax washed over her.

Niska pulled her fur-lined cloak tighter around her body. She had forgotten how cold it could be in Vestfold even on a clear morning such as this. It had been snowing hard for two days, but today the sun shone weakly down from an azure sky as Ragnor's followers stumbled drunkenly from the longhouse.

There were many things she had forgotten about Vestfold, she thought, as she watched the men lurch unsteadily towards their horses which the slaves held ready for them. The warriors could be uncouth and rude, even Ragnor displayed a lack of gentility at times, despite the nobility of his line. But he had grown from an attractive youth to a handsome man. He was her half-brother but she still had a mind to fuck him if the opportunity arose.

202

The sight of the thrall rutting with three of Ragnor's most loyal jarls had aroused Niska. Now she was ready for the taste of hot, hard cock herself. But first she had a ceremony to attend.

She had seen Rianna sitting on Ragnor's lap, her cheeks afire, and Niska had known exactly what her half-brother was doing under her skirts, and she envied the bitch. Rianna seemed to enjoy being fucked just as much as the thrall lying on the floor in front of her. She was a whore pure and simple, Niska decided, as she saw Rianna climb into one of the sleighs. She was far too regally clad for a thrall, and the heavy gold pendant around her neck must be a gift from Ragnor. Her brother was a fool, just like most men.

Niska had expected Rianna to be treated like a slave. To be used and abused by her half-brother, then passed down to his men to be taken by all and sundry. Yet Ragnor had become smitten just like Tarn and all the rest. She had seen the way Ragnor looked at Rianna, his tongue almost hanging out with desire for her. Things would have to change; she couldn't possibly allow Rianna to remain in the privileged position that Ragnor's affections afforded her.

She stared at her magnificent half-brother as he strode forwards and mounted his horse. The cold air was reviving his followers and they gathered behind him for the short journey down to the side of the lake.

Niska climbed into the second sleigh, having no wish to be forced to endure the smug expression on Rianna's face. The procession began to move and the sleigh, pulled by two shaggy-coated ponies, slid smoothly forwards on the snow-covered ground.

The wooden walkways that led down to the lakeside were covered in a pristine layer of white, but the jetty and its surroundings had been swept clean. A cold wind came off the water, rippling its grey, glassy surface, making the large boat move up and down on the gentle waves. It was a magnificent drekar, dragon ship, with a dark wood hull and a high-raised prow at each end. Both were carved in the shape of curved snakes. Hjor's body was already on the vessel, laid upon a silk-draped bier. Exposed to the cold winds his flesh had shrivelled and turned black. Beside him lay the butchered remains of two horses, three cows and his favourite dogs.

Niska saw Rianna's sleigh stop close to the drekar. Rianna's face turned ashen as she saw what the longship contained, and Niska found her horror amusing, because it was likely to irritate Ragnor. Northmen despised mawkish sentimentality and weakness in women.

The blonde thrall was led forwards, dressed now in a loose white linen garment. Her feet were bare and she shivered with cold. The icy breeze caressed her flesh as she walked beneath a wooden bar held atop two high posts: the symbolic doorway between this world and the next.

Fascinated by the thought of what was to come, Niska stepped forwards, her boots cracking the thin layer of ice on the wooden slats as she went to stand beside Jorvik.

'He called me; take me to him,' the thrall said in a shaky voice.

Niska saw the girl's expression change and her eyes widen with fear, as the enormity of what she was about to face pierced her alcohol-fuddled brain. The thrall was a fool to agree to this – no man was worth dying for. Ragnor was a magnanimous ruler, he would never have forced a slave to sacrifice herself. The girl had done this of her own free will and now it was too late to turn back.

Niska had not been given such a choice at the age of fourteen, when Thorolof had died. She'd been expected to sacrifice herself on his funeral pyre. Instead she had killed the two women left in charge of her and fled for her life.

A wizened old woman, dressed all in black, hobbled forwards, her arthritic joints creaking in the cold, and handed the girl a cup of sweet wine, called nabida.

'The angel of death,' Jorvik whispered in Niska's ear as if the woman truly was what she pretended to be.

The thrall gulped down the nabida, and her hand shook so much she dropped the empty goblet. Whereupon she was seized by a couple of warriors and led on to the drekar accompanied by four other warriors. She began to struggle as she was laid at the side of the blackened corpse. Two men held her feet, and another two men held her hands as the angel of death looped a thin cord around her neck. Everyone was silent, holding their breath in anticipation, as the old woman handed the crossed ends of the cord to the other two warriors.

Niska moved closer to Jorvik. He slid an arm around her waist and pulled her back against his hard body as the men surrounding them beat their shields with staves to drown out the thrall's fearful cries. The ancient rhythm pounded through Niska, adding to her arousal as Jorvik splayed his hand across her belly and forced her back against him until she could feel the hardness of his erection digging in the crack of her buttock cheeks.

As the old woman lifted a broad-bladed dagger and plunged it between the girl's ribs, the warriors jerked the cords until they cut deep into the victim's neck. Jorvik rubbed his cock sensuously against Niska's behind and pressed his fingers into her pussy, through the thick velvet of her skirts, as she watched, enthralled and excited by the sight of the thrall's limbs twitching as death claimed her. Freya was the goddess of sexuality as well as death and the two were inexorably intertwined here on the edge of this lake in her brutal homeland.

Ragnor had already shed his clothes. He stepped forwards, his naked, muscular body looking pale against the grey waters of the lake as the warriors and the old woman left the vessel. Holding a blazing torch, he stepped on to the drekar and set the kindling, placed close to the prows at each end, alight. The wind whipped the flames sending them cracking and leaping along the hull. Ragnor stepped back on to the jetty and stood watching until the entire hull was set alight, then he loosened the ropes and the blazing vessel drifted majestically towards the centre of the lake.

Primeval emotions filled the onlookers, and more than a few couples moved away to find a quiet spot. Niska saw Ragnor, still naked, his cock fully erect, grab hold of Rianna and lead her into a small hut near the edge of the jetty. The lust that had grown in Niska when she had watched the slave being pleasured in the hall, and then sacrificed for her master, grew even stronger. She loathed Rianna even more now, knowing that at this moment Ragnor was fucking her in that tiny hut.

'Come,' Jorvik said, pulling Niska towards a pile of barrels. He edged between them until they were partially out of sight, and pushed Niska roughly over a barrel as he flipped up her skirts. The icy air hit her arse as Jorvik parted her thighs and buried his cock into the moist warmth of her cunt. Niska gasped and clutched at the rough metal banding the barrel as Jorvik's rock hard prick rammed into her, taking her brutally, his balls slapping wildly against her legs in time to his powerful thrusts. She was able to sneak down between her legs, however, and rub herself lewdly. She came quickly, at the selfsame moment as Jorvik spent his load inside her.

Her hands were shaking as she pulled down her skirts, and wrapped her cloak more tightly around herself. 'My brother seems far too taken with his new thrall,' she said, glancing towards the hut where Ragnor was still servicing Rianna.

'No doubt that pleases you,' Jorvik commented, readjusting his clothing. 'She was your gift to him. Did you not want him to enjoy the slave?'

'Enjoy, yes,' she cautiously agreed, conscious of the overpowering ache in her pussy that the quick fuck with Jorvik had not cured. It had only left her wanting more, but not from Jorvik – from Ragnor. Or even Chang, she thought, as she glanced round the jetty. She had expected to see Chang at the ceremony but he was nowhere to be seen. 'But I do not feel it seemly for Ragnor to honour her as he does. He treats her more like a treasured courtesan than a slave.'

'I've never seen him so enamoured of a woman,' Jorvik said thoughtfully. 'She is of royal blood and he needs a wife . . .'

'A wife?' Niska exclaimed in horror. It was not unusual in Vestfold for a thrall to be gifted her freedom by her master. However, Niska had never believed Ragnor would come to feel this way about Rianna, especially in such a short space of time. 'My brother may well need a bride, but not Rianna. She contributed to Lord Sarin's downfall. If I'd not taken her captive she would have eventually destroyed Prince Tarn as well. I have no wish for Ragnor to allow her to influence him, and suffer a similar fate!'

Tarn and Sarin crouched behind a boulder on a cliff that overlooked the valley. Far in the distance they could see the flames of the burning longship as it glided majestically across the grey waters of the lake.

'The defences are impressive,' Tarn said, surveying the high-banked ramparts topped by a sturdy palisade. There were higher walls constructed out of whole tree-trunks protecting the village, and more internal walls to protect the inner stronghold where Ragnor's two huge long-houses were situated.

'It would not be easy to storm, even with an entire army,' Sarin added. 'Would that we'd caught up with them before they took refuge here.'

'Perhaps it would be better for just a few of us to enter in disguise?' Tarn suggested. 'If we were dressed as mercenaries they would not be able to tell us from Niska's men.'

'That may be a possibility,' Sarin agreed, frowning. 'But even if we do get inside, I doubt we would be able to just walk into Ragnor's longhouse unchallenged. He will be guarded by his own personal troop, and they may well be Berserkers.' Wolf Skins or Berserkers as these wild northern warriors were often known, believed that they were descended from the shapeshifters of ancient myth. Clad only in animal skins, they were feared by all soldiers as they fought more like mad beasts than men.

'No matter what I *have* to rescue, Rianna,' Tarn insisted, as he turned his piercing blue eyes on Sarin. 'You've come this far to wreak your revenge on Niska. Are you prepared to give up when your goal is in sight?'

'I do not allow emotion to over-rule logic as you do, Tarn,' Sarin said coolly. 'I'll weigh up the odds before I decide to do anything. Taking my revenge on Niska is important but it is not worth losing my life for.' He glanced back at the valley. A thin line of mounted men were leaving through the main gate. 'A patrol. We had better move.'

They turned and walked back through the thick snow to their horses. If the patrol passed close by they'd see their tracks and know that someone was spying on the settlement, but they had no time to cut down a fir branch and sweep the snow clean of their presence.

Tarn and Sarin mounted their horses and rode back up the mountainside, just as a light dusting of snow began to fall again. Soon the breeze became stronger and the snowfall thicker. The thick white flakes wiped out all sign of the tracks of their descent, making it difficult to remember exactly which way they had come.

They reached a narrow valley cut into the slope of the mountain that had a small river meandering along its length. Tarn was relieved, recognising the valley, it was the same frozen river they'd crossed earlier that day. The thick ice had easily supported the weight of both men and their horses. Tarn dismounted and Sarin followed suit. Holding his mount's reins, Tarn stepped cautiously on to the ice, which was now covered by a thin layer of snow. Frozen flakes stung his eyes, forcing him to squint as he led his horse safely across to the flat bank on the other side.

As he turned to check on Sarin, a low chilling rumble filled the air, followed by a short, sharp cracking sound. To his horror he saw the ice open up in zigzags beneath Sarin's feet. The black stallion gave a shrill whinny and leaped forwards, just making it to the snowy bank. As the horse's reins were torn from Sarin's grasp, he stumbled and lost his footing, falling into the icy water.

The ominous splashing sound still filled Tarn's ears as he fell to his knees and lay flat on the remains of the ice. He edged forwards across the cold surface praying it would hold his weight. Dipping his gauntleted hand in the icy water, he made a grab for Sarin's flailing hand, knowing Sarin would die within minutes if he didn't get him out.

Tarn managed to grab hold of Sarin's wrist, then shuffled backwards, pulling the near impossibly sodden weight with him. Once Sarin was half out of the water, Tarn managed to grasp his other hand as well and heave him to the safety of the bank. Panting with exertion, Tarn scrambled to his feet, knowing he had to try and find shelter. Drenched through in such cold conditions, Sarin would never make it back to their own camp alive.

Sarin's face was ashen, his exposed skin beginning to turn an unhealthy blue. His teeth were chattering so hard he could not speak and he was shivering uncontrollably. Tarn lifted him on to his horse, laying Sarin across the saddle, as he was too weak to sit up. Then he led both mounts up the snowy slope, aiming for a splodge of black in the whiteness, which he hoped might be the entrance to a cave. Fortunately his presumptions were correct, and as they got closer the size of the gaping black hole increased. The cave looked deep enough to shelter in but the strong smell of wild animals made the horses reluctant to venture inside.

Tarn looped their reins over a boulder, then drew his sword and crept into the cave. It stunk of bear and wolf, but neither was in residence and, judging by the remains of a fire, humans had used it at some time in the past. They had even left a pile of twigs and brushwood in a corner that would keep a fire burning for a good few hours.

Stepping back outside, Tarn found that the snow was falling even more heavily. He led his horses under the overhang of the cliff at the entrance to the cave, where they would be protected from the force of the blizzard, then he lifted Sarin from his horse. Sarin's sopping garments increased his considerable weight as Tarn carried his semi-conscious burden inside the cave. He laid Sarin down, then gathered the twigs and brushwood together, got out his tinderbox and lit a fire. As it flared into life, Tarn began to methodically strip Sarin, placing his sodden clothing by the fire to dry. He laid the barely alive man on a blanket and looked uneasily around. They only had one other blanket, which would not be enough to keep Sarin warm. There was no other choice but to use his own body heat – it was that or let Sarin die.

Trying to forget all the enmities of the past, Tarn stripped off his clothes. He lay down, pulled Sarin's ice-cold form into his arms and heaped his clothes, cloak, and blanket atop them. The fire was banked high, and would burn for at least a couple of hours, he decided, as he felt the cold clammy flesh draw heat from his own skin.

Tarn could hear the wailing sounds of the blizzard and the crackling of the fire as the flames cast eerie shadows on the dark walls of the caves, which were covered with strange red hieroglyphics. Gradually Sarin's unconscious shivers ceased, and his body relaxed as it slowly grew warmer. Tarn closed his eyes and tried not to think of the man who lay naked in his embrace.

The fire was still burning when Tarn awoke, but judging by the warmth of Sarin's skin and his steady breathing at least an hour or more had passed. Tarn's arms were becoming a little stiff from holding Sarin so close.

As he went to move, Sarin surprised him by speaking. 'Don't leave me yet, please,' he begged in a low husky voice.

'I have to tend the fire,' Tarn replied.

'A few minutes more,' Sarin pleaded. 'There's something I need to say. I have to tell you that I owe you my life, Tarn.'

'I would have done the same for anyone,' Tarn said gruffly. After all this time it was strange to feel Sarin's naked body pressed against his again. Tarn was reminded of his days in Aguilar as Sarin's slave. Forced by circumstance, he had reluctantly shared Sarin's bed on many occasions. They were times he didn't like to think of, even now. Yet they flooded back like they were only yesterday: the sensation of total submission and the pleasure Sarin had given him despite all his struggles to resist. He had found a sexual satisfaction in Sarin's embrace that he couldn't understand, couldn't explain. The complexities of it would most likely puzzle him for as long as he lived.

'Would you truly have done *this* for anyone else?' Sarin rolled over, leaning his head against Tarn's inner arm as he stared into his eyes. Their faces were so close that Tarn could feel Sarin's cinnamon scented breath on his cheek.

'I don't know.' He shivered as Sarin touched his chest, teasingly circling his nipples with the tips of his fingers.

'You feel it too, don't you?' Sarin said hoarsely.

'Feel what?' Tarn's voice shook, his muscles tensing. He wanted to pull away, but something held him motionless as Sarin edged closer. Tarn felt a rigid cock touch his thigh, and he knew that Sarin desired him even now. Strangely enough the thought didn't make him sick to the stomach as he'd expected. It aroused a strange primeval excitement in the pit of his belly, forcing thoughts and feelings he'd struggled so long to suppress to come to the surface again.

'The needs, the desires.' By accident or design Sarin's fingers brushed Tarn's belly.

'No needs, no desires,' Tarn said harshly, fighting the wild emotions that threatened to overwhelm him. He was certain he was going insane, his mind was addled by the cold, there was no way he could want Sarin.

'Is that so?' Sarin's fingers teasingly touched Tarn's cock and it twitched excitedly, blood pumping into the organ, making it grow hard and rigid. 'Why lie?' he whispered as his hand took hold of the aching shaft. Tarn wanted to protest but it felt so good, and he no longer had the strength or will to pull away.

Sarin began to stroke Tarn's cock in a smooth seductive rhythm that aroused his senses. Lust flooded Tarn's veins and for a brief moment he was able to stand back and view what was happening as though he was not involved. He saw two men, fuelled by a primeval passion, cocooned in a white, frozen wilderness far from signs of civilisation, and he knew that he was trapped in this world of magic and mystery, where light and dark intertwined. 'This place must be cursed,' Tarn gasped, helplessly enduring the delicious pleasure of Sarin wanking his cock.

'Or perhaps blessed,' Sarin said, still keeping up the compelling movements of his hand. 'So many times in the past I took my pleasure with you whether you were willing or not. I forced you into slavery, tortured you into submission. Now I want you to use me as you will, Tarn. Take your pleasure, slake your lust. I'm yours to command.'

'No,' Tarn protested, pushing Sarin's questing hand away, trying vainly to fight his rising excitement. The struggle seemed hopeless as the blood pounded in his ears, and the need to fuck grew stronger.

'You must.' Sarin slid under the heaped covers and pressed his face close to Tarn's belly. Sarin's hot breath brushed Tarn's stomach. Then his lips fastened around Tarn's cock, drawing it deep into the warm wetness of his mouth. He forced an anguished groan from Tarn's lips as he sucked and licked the organ, anointing it with his saliva until the shaft grew iron hard, the taut skin moist and slippery.

'You cannot,' Tarn pleaded, feeling the pleasure build as Sarin's lips worked his cock, while his fingers teasingly caressed Tarn's balls.

Sarin surfaced and turned, pressing his firm buttocks back against Tarn's muscular belly. He pulled his cheeks apart, offering his body up to Tarn. 'Do it, please.'

Tarn's fingers brushed the tempting ring and the muscles trembled as if begging his fingers to slide inside the dark hole. Tarn swallowed anxiously and filled with an overpowering urge to take what Sarin offered so freely. His revenge would be sweet. But when Sarin had taken him, he'd always liberally oiled his prick before thrusting it inside Tarn. There were no such luxuries as scented oil in the barren cave. 'It will hurt,' he muttered.

'A hurt I both need and desire.' Sarin gave a soft laugh. 'The pain will be but a passing phase, making the pleasure that follows even sweeter. I feel this is so right. This one act could shatter the boundaries that have grown between us: make us the friends we once were in the past.'

'I doubt that,' Tarn grunted as he slid his cock between the pert cheeks and pressed the head against Sarin's taut opening. Immediately he was filled with an all consuming need to thrust.

'Despite everything I've always loved you, Tarn,' Sarin whispered.

Nothing made sense any more to Tarn. Caught up in his primeval desires, he thrust his cock into Sarin's tight arsehole. Spurred on by Sarin's groan of pain he thrust harder and deeper until he was fully embedded and his balls slapped against Sarin's backside. The sensation of tightness was exquisite, like nothing he'd ever known, as Sarin's flesh embraced his engorged prick.

'This is so right,' Sarin gasped, pressing his buttocks

back against the invasive cock. 'You feel so huge. So many times in the past, when I've had my shaft buried deep inside you, Tarn, I've wondered what it would feel like to be penetrated so completely.'

'Now you know.' Staying buried inside, Tarn flipped Sarin over on his stomach, pressing him down against the rough blanket. Sarin gave a submissive moan, enduring Tarn's heavy weight atop him.

'Thrust hard, hurt me,' he begged, as Tarn lifted himself on his arms and began to move his hips. The covering had fallen off them both and the chill air caressed their skin, but they were both so caught up in their sexual excitement that they were immune to the cold. The fire was burning lower now, the flickering flames casting huge shadowy pictures of them copulating on the dark walls of the cave, like two prehistoric creatures from times long past.

Tarn's climax was building too quickly, so he withdrew and rimmed Sarin's anus with the head of his cock, until Sarin begged him to fuck him again. Rising to his knees, he pulled Sarin with him. Once again Tarn invaded the tight dark hole, holding Sarin close, twining his arms around his waist. Tarn grabbed hold of Sarin's cock, wanking it in time to his violent pounding thrusts, losing himself in the pleasure of possessing the man who had used and abused him so cruelly in the past.

As his climax came and the wrenching pleasure consumed him, Tarn's fingers tightened around Sarin's cock. Spunk spurted from the tip, coating Tarn's hand, dribbling over Sarin's stomach and thighs.

Roughly he pushed Sarin down on to the blanket, rolled him over and sat aside his trembling form. 'Lick it clean,' Tarn ordered, shoving his hand close to Sarin's face.

Niska pulled the neckline of her dress lower so that it showed the generous curves of her breasts and her nipples, which were almost on display, then she left the

214

refuge of her bedchamber. For the first time she felt a little uneasy in Ragnor's domain. Her renewed relationship with her half-brother had not turned out to be quite as she had anticipated as both had changed greatly from the children they were in the past. Matters had not been helped, of course, by the indulgent way he treated his new thrall.

Less than an hour ago Chang had said goodbye to Niska and set off on a quest to find a valley he'd been told of. It was said to be a magical place set close to the borders of Asgard. It was never cold, snow never fell, flowers bloomed eternally, and the trees were always festooned with blossom. A beautiful sorceress lived in the valley, one powerful enough to lift the curse on Chang. Niska had wished him well on his quest, although she'd doubted he'd ever find this magical place, which probably only existed in the stories men told round the campfires at night.

Chang had left Hordo in charge of the mercenaries. He was strong but Niska didn't trust Hordo like she did Chang. With Hordo in control of them, she no longer felt she could fully rely on her men. She'd begun to feel uncomfortably alone, here in a place that had once been her home. Vestfold was almost alien to her, she had changed so much in the intervening years. Also she was certain that many of the jarls secretly despised her because she was the bastard child of a slave, despite the fact that she was Ragnor's half-sister. Women were considered of little consequence in Vestfold and without her brother's affection and visible support she had little more influence here than the lowest slave.

After the ceremony by the lake the men had spent the entire night feasting. Rianna had retired early: Niska had seen her leave. But Ragnor, as custom decreed, had stayed up carousing with his men. She had decided to see him now, before Rianna's influence over him became even stronger, and settle matters between them once and for all.

She was about to ask one of the warriors, who was wandering drunkenly around the longhouse, to take a message to Ragnor, when the door of the hall was flung open and her half-brother strode out. He was walking a shade unsteadily as if he were intoxicated, although during his youth Niska had seen him consume vast quantities without appearing drunk.

'Brother, can I talk to you?' Niska asked.

'Talk?' Ragnor stopped and looked quizzically at Niska.

'Talk alone,' she said, glancing around the empty passageway. 'In the privacy of your chamber?'

He grinned and draped a heavy arm around her shoulder. 'If you wish it, sister.'

Ragnor stank of wine, overlaid with a strong masculine scent of musk and sweat that made her senses spin. She found it highly arousing and was already beginning to feel lightheaded by the time they entered his chamber. Fortunately Rianna was nowhere to be seen as Ragnor guided Niska to a padded settle placed close to the hearth, where a huge fire blazed.

Ragnor sat and pulled Niska down beside him. She looked at his huge hands resting on his muscular thighs, seeing the way his breeches stretched tautly over the large mound of his sex. The bulge looked extraordinarily tempting, and she longed to touch it, recalling how magnificent he'd looked naked when he'd set the drakar alight.

'I wish to talk of the future,' Niska said.

'You mean your future, Niska,' Ragnor replied, staring at her intently, suddenly appearing far less intoxicated. He grinned. 'I hear you arranged to deposit a large chest of money and plate in my stronghouse. You never mentioned what a wealthy woman you had become.'

'I intended to tell you brother, when the time was right,' she said. Ragnor did not know about the chest of jewels hidden in her room – only Chang and Tanith knew of them. She took hold of his hand. 'If I thought

216

you needed it you would be welcome to share my wealth. Have I told you how much I missed you, Ragnor? We were so close once.'

'We can be again, sister,' he replied, but she sensed no true depth of feeling in his reply.

'Did you not miss me, also?'

'Of course,' he said gruffly. 'You are my kin.'

She pressed his hand to her bosom. 'Feel my love for you, brother. It fills my heart.'

His fingers briefly closed over her breast and her nipples tightened in anticipation, but then to her disappointment he pulled his hand away. 'Your heart beats like any other. Only women know of such matters as love,' he mumbled awkwardly.

'I know of many things other than love, far more than you give me credit for. I have had my mind opened by my travels, my sojourns in other lands,' she said. 'Do you know much of other lands far beyond the borders of Vestfold, Ragnor?'

He chuckled. 'Have you forgotten the many times father beat me because I would not listen to my tutors and wanted to pass my time in more manly pursuits?'

'While I envied your right to an education,' she added. 'Father thought it wasteful to educate women.'

'He often failed to understand your complexities, Niska.' Ragnor kissed her cheek in a surprisingly affectionate gesture. 'But why do you talk of other lands?'

'Because there is a land in the south, far across the seas. A fertile land of great riches where the monarch has wealth and power beyond your dreams. The monarchy survives and flourishes because it is the custom for brother and sister to wed and rule together.'

'Brother and sister?' Ragnor muttered uneasily.

'Tis not wrong,' Niska insisted. Is it not told in the saga of Kveldeg that he married his sister, Berthega, and had many fine sons? It was they who drove the phantoms from Vestfold and will return to protect us from the wrath of the gods.'

217

'A fine story,' Ragnor agreed. 'But merely a legend.'

'You are the one who believes in our heritage and keeps our legends and customs alive.' She touched the rune scars on his arms. 'That is why you are such a great leader, Ragnor. If you have my riches and the knowledge of other lands I posses you could be even greater. We could hire mercenaries, build an army so massive, that you could easily control all of Vestfold. We could conquer Kabra, Percheron, any land you wish. Think of the power . . .' She placed her palm on his bulge, feeling the heat and the hardness. When Ragnor made no move to pull away or protest, she dug her fingers into the plaited leather and gently began rubbing the shaft.

'Niska!' Ragnor exclaimed as she pulled open the laces and freed his cock. 'You forget yourself,' he muttered as she stroked the shaft until it stiffened and grew hard.

'I want you, Ragnor. Together we could be so strong, so powerful.' Niska leaned forwards and pulled his cock into her mouth, rimming the head with her tongue, trying to swallow as much of its massive length as she could.

Ragnor gave a soft groan as Niska slid her lips smoothly up and down his shaft, pulling it halfway down her throat, then sliding her mouth up to the head again. 'Feel my love, experience its strength.' She pulled his hand under her skirts and pressed it to her naked pussy. Ragnor's thick fingers instinctively stroked her denuded flesh, sliding into the hot moistness of her cunt, while she continued sucking his cock, digging the tip of her tongue teasingly into the narrow slit on its bulging head.

Niska had almost begun to believe she had won him over when he gave an angry growl and shoved her away from him. She landed in an undignified heap on the floor at his feet. 'Niska,' he hissed, his face contorted in anger. It had turned the same purplish red shade as his cock. 'You almost made me forget myself. Have you no honour?'

'Honour?' She rose to her feet, feeling frustrated and almost as angry as he was. 'You're a fool, Ragnor, if you don't take what I have to offer.' Niska pulled up her skirts and she saw his eyes focus hungrily at her naked mons. He'd probably never seen a hairless woman before – most men found the sight intoxicating. 'Look harder,' she taunted, pushing her pelvis towards him, opening her thighs and parting her sex lips with her fingers. 'See how wet I am, my sex weeps for your stupidity, brother. With my untold wealth at your disposal and me at your side you could become the strongest, most powerful warrior Vestfold has ever known. Almost as strong as Thor himself.'

'Get away from me,' he yelled, stuffing his rigid cock back into his breeches. Ragnor's hand was trembling and Niska knew that he was far from immune to her charms and the offer she'd just made him. 'You are my sister. It's not seemly.'

'Seemly,' she screamed. 'Neither is it seemly to slobber over a mere thrall in public.' She dropped her skirts. 'You demean yourself, Ragnor, you demean me. Rianna is a slave yet you treat her more like a wife.'

'How I treat my thrall is *my* concern not yours,' he blazed, standing up and looming menacingly over her. 'You forget your place, woman. Now begone before I forget myself completely and take a whip to you.'

'Perhaps I would enjoy that almost as much as fucking you.' She smirked sarcastically. 'You are a fool Ragnor, just like all men,' she sneered, walking out of the room and pulling the door shut behind her with a resounding bang.

# Chapter Ten

$T$arn could barely bring himself to look at Sarin as they rode back to the camp. He didn't even want to think of the many sexual excesses they'd shared during the long dark night in the cave. He'd been like a man possessed, indulging in a wild frenzy of lust he'd never believed he was capable of. It was as if they'd been transported back to the past, but this time he'd played the part of the master and Sarin the slave.

Sarin had claimed that the sexual acts would exorcise Tarn's demons but they had not. The encounter had left him confused and troubled by dark thoughts.

As they rode into camp, Tarn chanced a glance at Sarin, who had also been surprisingly quiet. He seemed disappointed by Tarn's response as if he'd expected their relationship to have changed dramatically in the last few hours.

'Last night . . .' Tarn awkwardly cleared his throat.

'You prefer not to speak of it. I understand,' Sarin said quietly. 'I'd hoped it would demolish the barriers between us. But you are far from ready to do that just yet.'

'My liege, we were so troubled.' Jentius strode towards them smiling in relief. 'I'm pleased to see you are safe and unharmed. We feared your capture, or worse.'

'We are both well,' Tarn told him. 'The blizzard forced us to take refuge in a cave for the night.'

'You saw Ragnor's stronghold?'

'It will not be easy to get inside.' Tarn glanced at Sarin who nodded his agreement.

'Far from easy, Captain Jentius,' Sarin confirmed.

'A few of us may be able to enter disguised as Niska's mercenaries,' Tarn said and jumped from his horse. He drew his sword. Using the point he drew a rough map in the snow. 'See this overhanging cliff, close by the lake and the outer wall. We'll move the men to that spot. There's plenty of cover, so we can watch the place as we make our plans. Order the men to pack up and make ready to depart.'

'I will, sire. But first you must eat. You and Lord Sarin must be famished.'

'I'll change first,' Sarin announced. 'My clothes are still damp.'

'Damp?' Jentius questioned, then looked rather uneasy, fearing that he may have spoken out of turn.

'It is a long story.' Sarin smiled. 'Ask your king. He may be prepared to tell you how he saved my life.'

As Sarin strode away, Tarn moved to the fire, sniffing appreciatively at the bubbling pot of rabbit stew. 'That smells good,' he told the man who was stirring the pot.

Tarn ate two bowls of the stew in quick succession, knowing that Jentius was eager to hear what had occurred, but dare not be so bold as to question his king. Tarn was relieved, as he had no wish to even think about what had happened in the last twenty-four hours.

Once he was finished he dismissed Jentius, ordering him to personally oversee preparations for their departure and sat staring morosely into the flames of the campfire. When all was ready Tarn mounted his horse and moved to the front of the troop accompanied by Jentius, rather relieved Sarin had not bothered to rejoin him. He decided it would be wiser to keep his distance from Sarin in future. He rode from the clearing. He looked down noticing more than one set of tracks in the freshly fallen snow. Not only were there Tarn's and Sarin's tracks leading into the camp, but the tracks of two horses leaving before them and heading in a northerly direction down the mountainside.

'Have you sent out scouts?' Tarn asked Jentius.

'No, my lord,' Jentius replied, frowning.

'Then whose tracks are these?' Tarn asked.

'I saw no one leave, but I'll check to see if anyone is missing,' Jentius said. He turned his mount and rode back along the line of men.

He returned moments later looking confused.

'Who? 'Tarn asked.

'I don't understand,' Jentius muttered awkwardly. 'The only two missing are Lord Sarin and Zene. Why should they ride off alone and unprotected?'

'Why indeed,' agreed Tarn. He recalled what Sarin had said, and could appreciate that he had decided not to risk his life to capture Niska, but that still didn't explain why he'd left without telling even his own men. Why hadn't he taken his escort with him, and why was he travelling north, not south? Tarn stiffened, not even wanting to consider the reasons for Sarin's unexpected departure.

Niska ran her fingers through her tangled white-blonde hair as she stared thoughtfully at Jorvik lying naked on his bed, his hands clasped behind his head. His lean chest was hairless but there were thick dark tufts in his armpits that had a pungent masculine odour she found very sexy. This was the first time she'd taken any interest in Jorvik since their encounter by the lake, and the experience had been surprisingly pleasurable. Jorvik's lovemaking lacked finesse and he'd displayed a rough brutality that excited her. If she couldn't have Ragnor beside her then she'd have his second-in-command instead.

'Have you spoken to Ragnor about his relationship with his new thrall?' she asked.

'It is not my place to do so,' he said curtly.

222

'Do the other jarls not think it strange that he's so taken with Rianna?' she pressed.

'They keep their opinions to themselves,' he growled. 'You've been away from Vestfold far too long, my lady. It's not acceptable here to question the behaviour of one's betters, not if you value your life.'

'Do you not find it frustrating?' She played idly with his small flat nipples. 'Always having to obey Ragnor's commands.'

'I never think about it.' He gave a soft growl as she touched his cock, sliding her hands teasingly up and down the shaft, stroking the velvety pouch of his balls.

'You should,' she said, leaning forwards to kiss his belly. 'What if a dispute were to arise between Ragnor and an opposing warlord? The man might kidnap Rianna, and my brother would be forced to do battle to recover what was his.'

'Such action might well start a war,' Jorvik said, seeming more interested in what she was doing with her hands than their conversation.

'And if Ragnor were killed in the battle, you would be forced to take command of his forces, perhaps eventually become lawspeaker yourself?'

'Surely you do not wish your brother dead?' he asked, twisting his lips in disgust.

'Of course I do not, Jorvik,' she insisted. 'I just wondered what would happen if such a terrible tragedy should occur. I love my brother in ways you'll never know.'

'And he deserves your full loyalty,' Jorvik replied as she climbed astride his chest, wriggling her pert buttocks teasingly.

'Pleasure me,' she demanded. 'How I showed you before.' She inched her hips backwards until her pussy was poised temptingly over his face.

'I told you, I find this demeaning,' he grumbled. Yet earlier, when she'd first introduced him to pleasuring a

223

woman with his mouth, Niska was certain that despite his complaints he had enjoyed the experience.

'Don't deny me what I want,' she purred, pressing her sodden quim against his lips. 'For I'll deny you also,' she teased.

His tongue wriggled between her swollen lips and probed her sensitive channel. Niska sighed. Jorvik's first attempt had been clumsy and unskilled but still arousing. She kissed his cock, wrapping her lips around it and sucking hard, encouraging it to grow. She toyed with the sensitive organ while her fingers stroked and teased the soft sack of his balls. Gradually she pulled his long member into her mouth, until it hit the back of her throat. Fighting the urge to wretch, she continued sucking and licking the shaft, while Jorvik's mouth roughly worked her pussy.

As he pushed his questing tongue into her cunt, and flicked it over her clit, Niska could feel her orgasm beginning to build inside her. It crested and broke like a huge wave when Jorvik unexpectedly thrust a finger deep into her anus. As she came, Jorvik climaxed, his creamy spunk spurting deep into her throat. Then, before she'd even recovered, there was a loud knocking on Jorvik's door.

'Yes,' he growled, pushing Niska roughly aside as if she were no better than the lowest slave.

'Lord Ragnor commands your presence, sir, in the great hall,' a man's voice shouted through the thick wood.

'One moment.' Jorvik leaped from the bed and began to fling on his clothes.

Totally ignoring Niska he finished dressing and left the room. Jorvik was a boorish oaf who needed to be taught some manners, Niska thought irritably, as she dressed and dragged a bone comb through her pale locks. It was not often that the jarls were summoned so unexpectedly; something of great importance had obviously occurred.

Filled with curiosity, she hurried towards the gathering

place, surprised to find that there was a warrior on guard at the door, which led from the private family quarters into the great hall. 'What is happening?' she asked.

'A stranger arrived at our gates boldly demanding to see Lord Ragnor. He insists he has something of great importance to offer us, yet he is a foreigner, who cannot even speak our tongue. They are bringing him here at once. Lord Ragnor will decide the fool's fate.'

As the warrior opened the door for her Niska caught sight of Ragnor, not lounging on his throne as usual but sitting bolt upright as befitting the ruler he was. Jorvik stood to his right, and Rianna stood just behind the throne to Ragnor's left. To Niska's consternation Rianna was no longer wearing white, as a thrall should, instead she had on a magnificent green velvet gown that matched the colour of her eyes. However, her face was pale and her expression tense, as if something momentous was about to occur.

Few foreigners ventured into Vestfold, and they were mainly mercenaries seeking employment. No man in his right mind would dare come here and demand to speak to Ragnor, not unless he was mad, foolish, or very brave, Niska thought as she moved into the room. There was a small group of jarls clustered behind Ragnor. She edged between them, ignoring their irritated glances, until she was standing only a few feet away from her brother and could see all that was happening.

She caught her breath as she saw two guards leading a tall dark man forwards. He didn't appear at all fearful or nervous as he shook off their hands and bowed to the throne. 'Greetings, Lord Ragnor.'

His voice sent shivers down Niska's spine, and she could hardly believe her eyes. She could understand now why Rianna had looked so strained. Either it was a ghost that had assumed corporeal form or Sarin was far from dead!

'Who are you? What gives you the right to demand

entrance to my stronghold?' Ragnor said in the loud booming voice he employed on such auspicious occasions.

'Lord Sarin of Percheron at your service,' Sarin boldly announced, staring Ragnor in the eye as only one who considered himself equal could.

'Sarin?' Ragnor repeated in amazement. 'I thought you were dead.' He looked questioningly at Rianna.

'Tis he,' she confirmed in an unsteady voice, never tearing her gaze from Sarin.

Niska heard the warriors around her speaking in hushed tones, those who understood translating for those who did not.

'Lately escaped from Freygard,' Sarin informed Ragnor. 'Queen Danara reported me dead, slain by bandits, but at the time I was her prisoner. Lady Rianna knew full well I was alive, but it did not suit her purpose to reveal that fact as she was determined to legalise her adulterous relationship with King Tarn of Kabra.' He smiled cynically. 'I regret coming to you, Lord Ragnor, without the necessary pomp and circumstance. Unfortunately, I find my situation somewhat lacking at present. My people have been told I perished and a usurper sits upon my throne.'

Sarin was not foolhardy, and he did not appear to have lost his mind, yet Niska couldn't understand why he had come to Ragnor alone and unprotected. Strangely enough he appeared quite composed and unafraid as he looked thoughtfully at Ragnor and his followers. When he caught sight of Niska, however, his lips twisted in the semblance of a smile.

'Why do you come here, Sarin?' Ragnor asked, not even affording the former monarch the respect of his title. 'For your wife, mayhap?' he asked, grabbing hold of Rianna's hand and pulling her close.

'My wife?' Sarin gave a harsh laugh. 'Which one? They are both here.'

'Both?' Ragnor frowned.

Niska had never bothered to inform Ragnor she was once married to Sarin, as it had seemed unimportant when she thought him dead. Also she would have been obliged to explain that Sarin set her aside when he took Rianna as his wife and that would have been demeaning.

'Your sister, and of course Rianna, although Niska was only a secondary wife,' Sarin said, pursing his lips. 'Clearly neither placed much importance on the union, especially Lady Rianna.' He shrugged his shoulders dismissively. 'Perhaps I'm well rid of them both, Lord Ragnor. I've nothing of substance to offer any woman at present, other than myself.'

'Yet you still have rights to them both?' Ragnor growled, glaring furiously at Niska, then back at Sarin as he played pointedly with the dagger at his waist.

'Rights I am only too happy to forego,' Sarin said quickly. 'Your sister makes her own choices and who can blame the noble lady. While you're welcome to Rianna. She deserted me, cuckolded me, ran off with my worst enemy. She ceased being my wife the moment she entered into her adulterous relationship with Tarn. She's yours, Lord Ragnor, to do with as you will.'

Judging by Ragnor's expression he rather resented the magnanimous gesture. 'If you did not come to claim what was once yours, then why did you come?' he asked curtly. 'Would it not have been wiser to return to Percheron and lay claim to your throne?'

'Indeed it would, but circumstances prevented me,' Sarin replied with a heavy sigh. 'I could explain all, if you would find the time to listen. Also I wish to ask for your aid.'

'Aid,' Ragnor repeated in amazement. 'Why should I even consider helping you, Sarin? We are strangers to each other. Percheron and Vestfold have never been allies. I see no reason to give you aid, no reason at all.'

'You'll find a reason soon enough,' Sarin said confidently. 'Especially as I have something to give you in return,' he confided with a sly grin. 'Something which will please you greatly, no doubt. Dismiss your men and we can discuss the matter in private.'

Tarn lay wrapped in both his cloak and a blanket, staring up at the star-spattered sky, willing dawn to come and with it a little warmth. Moonlight filled the snowy clearing, and it was a beautiful sight, but the cold clawed its way into his limbs and every few minutes he had to move to stop his extremities from growing numb. There were no fires here to warm them, no tents to shelter them from the bitter cold. They were close to Ragnor's stronghold and had to be ready to move at a moment's notice.

Around him some of the soldiers were snoring and Tarn wondered how they could sleep in such conditions. He must be growing weak, he thought, as he glanced towards the trees ringing the small clearing. One of the guards was sitting against a tree-trunk, and looked to have fallen asleep. His head was lolling forwards and his sword had slipped from his frozen grasp.

Tarn stood up anxiously, stamping his numbed feet, hearing in the distance the howl of a lone wolf calling to its mate. He walked across the freshly fallen snow, intending to berate the sleeping guard. Suddenly he heard a faint crackle and saw dark figures start to emerge from the trees creeping menacingly towards the sleeping men. In his mind Tarn saw daggers flash in the moonlight, the blood of his soldiers flowing, spreading like scarlet blossom across the white snow.

'Jentius! Faros!' he yelled, drawing his sword. 'We're under attack!'

Tarn ran towards the dark figures as they pounced on his men, before they were even fully awake, let alone had a chance to struggle. Some of the attackers were tall blond northmen. Others were the feared Berserkers, their bare bodies decorated by strange patterns, their only garments wolfskins wrapped around their waists.

Lunging at one group, Tarn swung his sword in a shining arc, slashing and cutting at the attackers. Blade clashed against blade, the sharp metallic sound reverberating through the clearing. One huge Berserker gave a maniacal laugh, swinging his huge sword at Tarn. He parried the blow, his muscles straining under the weight of the attack. As they struggled, their blades locked in mortal combat, the Berserker stared Tarn full in the face. Muttering something, he anxiously drew back, stepping away from Tarn, appearing unwilling to continue the fight.

There were many more to contend with, Tarn thought, as, keeping his balance with catlike skill, he turned and parried another blow from a northman. Tarn slashed aside the attacker's sword, cutting through flesh and bone. Warm blood sprayed his face as he fought like a man possessed. Yet even as he advanced on the enemy they tried to back away from him, parrying his thrusts and darting aside to avoid his angry blows.

Frustratedly he swung round, seeing even more men stream into the clearing, their heads covered by helms decorated with horns. His men were outnumbered more than five to one, and had little chance of survival. He saw a huge northman, just about to slam his axe into Jentius's back. 'Jentius,' Tarn yelled, leaping forwards, his blade biting into the attacker's arm.

The northman screamed as he dropped his axe and backed away, clutching his bloody, near-severed limb. Grabbing the axe, Tarn swung round, determined to try and protect his men until he'd breathed his last breath. He heard fearful cries, saw figures dart about like rats, as a number of his soldiers tried desperately to escape but they were ringed by the enemy and could do nothing but stand and fight to the death.

'By the gods, kill me too,' Tarn screamed as he hacked at the attackers with axe and sword, but as he forged bravely forwards they all drew back as if fearful of challenging him.

Faros, Jentius and the men still standing, retreated, clustering together in a group in the centre of the clearing, while Tarn strode round them, wildly swinging his weapons, taunting their assailants, daring them to fight, but still they all seemed reluctant to do battle with him.

'Damn you,' he yelled as every one, Berserker or northman drew back at his approach. 'Cowards! Fight me!'

By now they ringed the clearing three or four men deep, yet they still made no attempt to touch Tarn or charge the remaining men. 'Surrender and no more need die,' said a gruff voice.

Tarn had no wish to surrender. He had been selfish enough to force these men to follow him into Vestfold and risk their lives to save Rianna. If anyone should die in this frozen land it should be him. 'And if I don't?' he challenged, pointing his sword at the man who had spoken.

'Then we'll kill every one of your men, but not you,' the man replied. 'Lord Ragnor wants you alive, King Tarn.'

Tarn knew there was no decision to be made, the bitterness of defeat soured his mouth as he lowered his sword.

This was not the way he had planned to enter Ragnor's stronghold, Tarn thought, as he plodded through the wide gates. He had been stripped of his armour and weapons, left wearing only boots and breeches, his hands tied behind his back. It was a chill morning, but he was immune to the cold now as he was led deeper and deeper into Ragnor's lair.

Oddly enough there was no hatred or resentment in the eyes of Ragnor's followers as he was led past them, just a grudging respect. All warriors, friends or enemies, were revered in Vestfold.

'Faster,' one of his captors growled as he shoved Tarn in the back, almost making him lose his footing. 'Lord Ragnor is waiting.'

'My men?' Tarn asked the tall brown-haired warrior to

his right, the man who he'd been forced to surrender to. 'How many of them are dead?'

'Less than you think,' he said in a thick guttural accent. 'We had orders to take as many as we could alive.'

'Why?' Tarn asked, relieved that some had survived.

'They are worth far more to us alive than dead. We are always in need of new thralls,' he added, grinning.

Instead of leading his men into death, he had led them into slavery, Tarn thought. By now Rianna was most probably Ragnor's slave and, instead of rescuing her as he hoped, he would join her in bondage. Would Ragnor try to ransom him he wondered? He knew that many Kabran nobles would be willing to part with what wealth they had managed to retain to ransom their king. But the thought of the sacrifices they would be forced to make in the process made him feel even more guilty.

Someone must have told Ragnor where he and his men were. They'd been captured like rats in a trap. That someone could only be the weasel Sarin. But how could he have brought himself to betray his own soldiers? He should never have chanced trusting Sarin, even for a moment. He was the scum of the earth, Tarn thought bitterly, as he was led through the gates towards Ragnor's longhouse.

He was escorted into the hall of the longhouse, and led towards the throne where a tall man, with hair almost as pale as Niska's, sat. When he saw Tarn approaching he grinned in a sickeningly self-satisfied way. 'King Tarn,' Ragnor acknowledged sarcastically. 'What brings you to my lands?'

'You know full well,' Tarn replied coldly. 'Your bitch of a sister. She kidnapped my betrothed.'

'Rianna is no longer yours. Forget her,' Ragnor snapped curtly. 'Now she is mine.' He snapped his fingers and Rianna stepped forwards looking as gloriously beautiful as ever and, to Tarn's relief, unharmed. She was dressed in an elaborate gown, with a barbarous gold ornament hung around her neck. As she looked at

Tarn with anguished eyes her face drained of colour, yet she did not speak. 'The lady has consented to marry me,' Ragnor announced.

'Now that I have given up all rights to her myself.' Sarin stepped into view, not dressed as Tarn had last seen him in clothing fit only for a mercenary. He was now clean-shaven and clad in fine garments of fine wool and velvet, reminding Tarn of the monarch Sarin had once been.

'I thought *you* were the traitor. You son of a cur,' Tarn grated, lunging threateningly forwards, desperate to throttle Sarin. 'I'll kill you!' The guards pulled Tarn back and roughly forced him to his knees in front of Ragnor and Sarin.

'I had no choice, Tarn,' Sarin said calmly, appearing unmoved by Tarn's loathing. 'You'll come to understand that in the fullness of time,' Sarin added, glancing at Rianna.

Her green eyes filled with hatred for a brief moment, then she turned away from him and stared entreatingly at Tarn. He knew then that she still loved him no matter what, and he also knew he could bear her no ill will for whatever she had been forced to do in order to survive.

'You should be slithering on your belly, like the snake you are, Sarin,' Tarn spat. 'Not masquerading as a man. How could I ever . . .' He shook his head. 'May the gods strike me down for trusting you.'

'They do not appear to want you dead, Tarn. Why else would you be kneeling here before me, instead of lying in the snow, your lifeless body stiff and turning black in the icy cold.'

'When I'm free I'll kill you with my bare hands,' Tarn growled.

Sarin seemed amused by the empty threat as he turned to look enquiringly at Ragnor.

'Have the prisoner taken to the cell that has been prepared for him,' Ragnor ordered. 'Ensure any wounds he has are properly tended. I want him to remain in good health.' He chuckled. 'He is worth a king's ransom, is he not?'

Niska was wishing that Chang would return soon as she left the refuge of her room, as she always felt so much more secure when he was around. Sarin's unexpected appearance had unsettled her, especially as Ragnor had been so ready to welcome him into the longhouse as an honoured guest.

She still found it difficult to accept that Sarin was alive, and wondered why he had come there instead of returning to Percheron and attempting to regain his throne. Also she had no idea what Ragnor was planning. She was more than certain he would either try to ransom Tarn, or use him to gain control of Kabra. Niska preferred the latter plan, because once Ragnor ruled Kabra he would have no need for Tarn. Then she might be able to convince Ragnor to give her Tarn as her slave. That had been her ambition ever since she had first laid eyes on him in Percheron. Owning Tarn would be the perfect way to hurt Rianna. Revenge always did bring with it the sweetest meat.

She was so caught up in her thoughts that she failed to notice Sarin walking up the corridor towards her, until he was standing in front of her. 'So, Niska?' He smiled in his usual rakish fashion. 'We are alone at last.'

'Sarin,' she acknowledged, not offering him the respect of his former title. In Vestfold he was no better than any other man. He was no longer the omnipotent monarch she had once willingly served. 'Your fortunes have changed yet again. Not only does my brother feed you and your whore, he clothes you as well, in garments befitting your former status.'

'Your brother has been more than kind. But his kindness comes with a price,' he added wryly. He looked Niska up and down, admiration lighting his dark eyes. 'Fate has been kind to you, Niska, so it seems.'

'Luck has no part in where I find myself,' she said

dismissively. 'And little in yours I'd wager. You were travelling under Tarn's protection, yet you were only too happy to betray him when it suited you. Do you betray all who place their trust in you?'

'What do you think?' he challenged.

'That perhaps I should warn my brother,' she retorted.

'Ragnor is well able to look after his own affairs. He values the prize I have given him.'

'After all that has happened between you in the past, how did you ever persuade Tarn to trust you?' she asked curiously.

'Trust wasn't the point,' he told her. 'Convenience was the motive when we started out. We were both searching for you. It seemed wiser to do so together.'

'Tarn was following me intent on rescuing Rianna. But why were you doing so?' she asked innocently.

'You know full well why,' he growled.

'Because you adore me so much you could not live without me,' she suggested with a cynical smile. 'You flatter me, Sarin.'

'You always were a devious bitch.' He grabbed her arm as she tried to brush past him, and slammed her against the wall.

'Desist,' she hissed. 'How dare you lay hands on me!'

'How dare you steal what is mine.' Sarin pressed his body close to hers and the heat grew between Niska's thighs. The animal magnetism was still there; time had not diminished the intense attraction between them.

Niska tried to remain immune to Sarin's charms although it was far from easy. He had always held a seductive power over her. It was Sarin who had first introduced Niska to the varied delights of the more erotic and bizarre sexual practices. He was a master at his art and had excited her more than any other man could, even Chang.

'Steal?' She smiled sweetly. 'Why should you think such a thing? I did not steal from you, Sarin.' A wild excitement filled her veins, and Niska was filled with the sudden need for Sarin to pull up her skirts and fuck her.

'You broke into my treasure vault and stole my jewels. Lesand sent a troop of men after you, Niska. You're a thief pure and simple. No one takes what is mine and gets away with it.'

A frisson of fear slid down Niska's spine and the sensation was invigorating. Sarin's obsidian eyes bored into hers, and she could feel the hard muscles of his belly, and the firm line of his cock pressing up against her pussy. Sarin was no more immune to her attractions than she was to his.

'The only thing of yours I took was Rianna. You should bless me for ridding you of the adulterous bitch,' she ranted, her need for him growing stronger. Warm liquid seeped from her cunt, dripping teasingly over her denuded lips.

'Lies trip off your viperous tongue so easily.' Sarin forced her even harder against the wall, trapping her there with his muscular frame, grinding his pelvis against hers. A warrior walked by and glanced at them curiously but they both ignored him, too wrapped up in one another to care what he thought.

'No better than they do yours,' she countered, shuddering as he sensuously licked her cheek.

'Does your quim still taste as sweet?' he whispered as his hand slid under her skirt. Sarin's expression changed, lust lighting his dark eyes as he found her naked pussy. 'So you still keep yourself denuded there, just as I commanded?'

'Not for your sake, Sarin. For the sake of all my other lovers.'

Niska gave a soft growl as his fingers probed her sex, sliding deep into the soft, wet channel.

'Your brother doesn't know what he's missing.' Sarin's lips caressed her earlobe, then he nipped it with his teeth. 'I've seen the way you look at him. Yet he rejected you,

235

Niska. He prefers Rianna and that sickens you, doesn't it?'

'All men are fools – my brother one of the biggest because he trusts you!' She shivered as his fingers dug deeper, twisting and teasing until hot waves of need consumed her. 'By the gods, Sarin,' she groaned rubbing her belly against his.

'No one can satisfy you like I can Niska,' he grunted. 'Your brother may have refused to bed you, but he's still no fool.' Sarin bent his fingers so that his knuckles brushed a sensitive spot. The pleasure was so intense that Niska's knees almost buckled. 'Ragnor demands much in return for his help. More than I wish to pay: all of Kabra and near a third of Percheron.'

'Will you give it him?' she asked as the burning heat turned her sex into an aching furnace. 'Or take my help instead.'

Sarin froze at her words, then to her disappointment and despair withdrew from her. 'Your help, Niska?' he asked, running his sodden fingers tantalisingly across her mouth. She could smell the odour of her own juices, taste their unique, musky flavour on her lips.

'I have a large force of mercenaries at my call, and the funds to employ many more. Baron Crissana left me well provided for.' She pressed her thighs together, fighting the need for him to fuck her, longing to feel his thick cock piercing her hungry flesh. They stuck together, slick with her juices, her entire groin an engorged, aching mass of desire. Yet she would never lower herself to plead for anything from Sarin. 'We could raise an army big enough to allow you to regain control of Percheron, without my brother's involvement.'

'And the price?' Sarin took a step back and stared enquiringly at Niska.

'You are the price, Sarin.' She glanced down at his prick bulging lewdly against his fine cloth breeches. 'Agree to make me Queen of Percheron and promise that you'll never even consider taking another wife. If you do that, then I'll help you to depose of Chancellor Lesand.'

Sarin's expression told Niska that he was interested and intrigued by her proposal. She knew he would not give her an answer yet. Truthfully she had not even decided if she wanted to help him, but it was always wiser to keep a number of different options open.

# Chapter Eleven

Niska's pussy still ached and her engorged nipples rubbed against her satin gown as she walked towards Ragnor's strongroom, where Tarn was confined. Prisoners were usually lodged in the cells attached to the slave quarters, but Tarn was far too important a prize for that.

Her brief encounter with Sarin had been arousing and had left her hungry for fulfilment, just as it had him. It was a delightfully titillating sensation and would give her confrontation with Tarn an extra edge of excitement, she thought, as she brushed past the sentry on duty outside the strongroom.

Jorvik was inside talking to the other guard. He smiled warmly at Niska as she sidled up to him. She asked, 'Is the prisoner confined as I suggested?'

'Yes, but are the chains really necessary?' he enquired. 'It would be impossible for him to escape.'

'Necessary,' she insisted. 'If I am to venture into his cell. My brother wishes me to examine him and ensure he has no wounds that need attending to. He appears to be a noble warrior, but he is also very dangerous. With my own eyes I saw him attack his cousin Cador for no reason at all in Sarin's palace in Percheron.'

Out of the corner of her eye she saw Tarn tense angrily at her words. At the time he had just discovered that Cador had betrayed him and he'd had every right to attack his cousin, but Niska was not about to tell Jorvik that.

'Most likely he had good reason,' Jorvik replied, glancing at Tarn. 'It's a fact of life that men do battle to settle their differences.'

While women attain their goals in more devious and infinitely more successful ways, Niska thought as she smiled sweetly at Jorvik. His presence was beginning to irritate her. She was eager to be rid of him and confront Tarn in private.

'I must be about my business,' she pointed out. 'As you must yours, no doubt. If I decide that the prisoner needs medical attention, I'll send for Gunnar – she's well skilled in such matters, I hear.'

Jorvik gave a sly grin. 'Gunnar is well skilled in *many* matters.'

'Indeed,' Niska said tartly.

'I'll leave you to your task.' Jorvik ignored her sour expression as he smiled at her, then he left the room.

Thick bars divided off the far end of the windowless chamber. The barred room usually contained gold and other booty, but that had been moved to the adjoining strongroom so that a secure prison could be available for King Tarn. He was by far the most important captive Ragnor had ever laid hands on.

Tarn's blue eyes coldly surveyed Niska as the guard unlocked the door and she stepped inside the cell. 'You may return to your duties,' she told the guard. 'The prisoner is securely confined. I'll be quite safe.'

The brute nodded and returned to his bench to resume sharpening his sword, while Niska looked thoughtfully at Tarn. Tarn was one of the most handsome men she'd ever laid eyes on and she'd always desired him. There was a purity and nobility in Tarn that fascinated her, and her pussy ached even more as she thought of owning him as her own personal body slave. He had a few bruises and scratches on his gold-tinted skin but apart from that he appeared to be unscathed.

'I'm reminded of another occasion, much like this,' she said with a teasing smile.

Tarn tensed, but could not draw back as she stepped closer. His arms were chained above his head, and chains fastened his feet to rings bolted to the floor. Confined and helpless he was hers to do with as she wished.

'Would that it had also been the last,' he grated, watching her warily.

'Then you were my husband's newest captive.' Niska ran her hands over his superb pecs, feeling them tighten at her touch. 'Now my brother holds you prisoner. The gods do not appear to be on your side, do they, Tarn?'

'The gods had nothing to do with this. They did not betray me. It was Sarin,' he said through gritted teeth.

The pain and hatred he felt for Sarin was mirrored on his face. Tarn's relationship with Sarin had always been an enigma to Niska. They professed to hate and despise each other, yet they were constantly drawn together, and there was always an underlying tension between them as if powerful emotions they didn't want to surface were constantly held in check.

'Your chains enhance your beauty, Tarn,' she taunted, her lust for him growing by the moment. 'Slavery suits you, it seems.'

'Damn you to perdition, Niska,' he growled, staring at her with loathing.

Niska smiled, running her hands teasingly up and down his arms and over his chest. 'Ragnor asked me to come here and ensure you were unharmed. You're worth much to him, he wants to ensure his prize is safe and well cared for.'

'Call this well cared for?' Tarn gave a harsh laugh. 'Your brother saw for himself that I was unhurt in the battle when his men attacked us.' He shuddered as her fingers pulled at his nipples. Niska played with them,

240

pulling and twisting them until they turned an angry red. 'How could I be harmed when not one of his men would come near me?' he asked bitterly.

'They had precise instructions. They were to bring you back alive and unharmed no matter what.' She stroked his flat belly, her finger playing with the buckle of the belt that held up his thick leather trousers. 'The King of Kabra is worth far more to him alive than dead.'

Niska glanced towards the guard. 'Go find Gunnar. Tell her to prepare a drawing poultice of arnica for the prisoner.'

He rose to his feet. 'I have orders not to leave you alone, my lady.'

'There's a guard outside the door, I'll come to no harm. Whereas if I do not have the poultice . . .'

'As you command.' He pushed his sword into the worn scabbard at his belt, and left the room.

'Alone at last!' Niska purred. 'Better to conduct this interview in private, don't you think?'

'It is never better to be alone with you, Niska,' Tarn said with a twisted grin. 'I've learned that lesson to my downfall before.'

'Yet you enjoy what I do to you, don't you, Tarn?'

'Never,' he groaned as she unfastened his belt and eased his leather pants down over his lean hips.

Lust lighted her eyes as she exposed his generous sex and muscular thighs. 'And my memory does not deceive me,' she murmured, her fingers brushing his cock, then cupping his balls. 'Yet you have more scars than I recall.' She rubbed the paper-fine skin of the soft sac and Tarn shuddered. Even the most reluctant lover could be turned on by such a caress. Tarn was no exception and his cock twitched and began to stiffen, even though Niska knew that he was doing his best to fight his arousal. 'No doubt you fought many battles.' She rubbed her satin-covered tits against his bare chest, still stroking the tender patch of skin that set his senses alight whether he wanted it or not.

241

'Few so difficult as this,' he gasped, as she began to wank his cock.

It grew hard, the skin on its shaft smooth, too delicious to resist and Niska rubbed it harder. 'Tis so large,' she said with a breathy sigh.

'Leave me alone, bitch,' he growled, his muscles straining as he tried to pull away from her and was brought short by his chains.

'Why resist now when you were so willing in the past?' she reminded him.

'I pleasured you then because you ordered it and I was weak,' he replied, staring at her with disgust as she pulled back his foreskin to reveal the succulent plum beneath, one sparkling dew-drop trembling at its tip.

'Ordered it?' she repeated. 'Why did you not refuse me? Did I beat you? Did I have the gaolers hold you down? You wanted me, Tarn, you're just not willing to admit it even to yourself. You desire me and in time you'll come to enjoy being my slave, just as you enjoyed serving Sarin.'

'Ragnor has his uses for me. He'll not give me to you, madam.'

'He will in the fullness of time. When your usefulness to him is at an end.' Niska longed to spear herself on Tarn's cock and feel it piercing her vitals. Her knees felt weak at the thought as she ran her thumb across the straining head, feeling it twitch powerfully in her hand. But there was no way she could carry out her desires when he was chained like this. 'Then you'll be mine completely.'

'I'll never be yours, Niska.' Tarn shook his head, yet his belly trembled and his cock leaped in her hand.

Niska pressed herself closer to him, inhaling his masculine scent, which was intensified by the odour of battle still clinging to his flesh. She felt Tarn strain against his fetters again, trying to pull away from her as she lifted up her skirts and straddled his bare thigh, rubbing her denuded pussy against his leg. Liquid seeped from her

242

cunt, streaking his golden skin with its sticky wetness. The pleasure of being so close to Tarn increased her arousal as she wanked his cock harder.

Power was a glorious aphrodisiac, she thought, her sense focused on a knife-edge of lust as he strained to pull away from her, while she pressed her quim harder against his leg. The soft hairs on his thigh rubbed against her hungry clit, as she watched his face twist in a rictus of agony at the effort of fighting his impending climax.

His shaft pulsed in her hand, and she heard his despairing groan. His thigh muscles contracted against her open pussy, as great goats of spunk spurted from his cock, covering her hand with translucent pearls.

Niska moaned and pressed her fingers against her quim, anointing her sex with Tarn's leavings. His chained body pressed close to hers, and the smell of him surrounding her, increased her desire as she rubbed his creamy offerings round and round her clit until she came, in a long drawn out shudder of bliss.

'Mayhap I should have you chained to my bed, then I could take you whenever it suited me,' she said with a soft laugh as she pulled down her skirts and daintily licked her fingers clean.

'Even if you possessed my body, you'd never posses my mind. So you'd never truly own me, Niska. No one ever will, only Rianna,' he said, his voice hoarse with emotion, his face flushed.

'You will be mine,' she insisted, pulling up his breeches and refastening his belt. 'And Rianna will belong to my brother. Think of it Tarn. You may well both reside in the same longhouse, yet you will be forbidden to touch or even speak. You'll be so close, yet so far, spending every night knowing that your beloved is sharing Ragnor's bed, just as she does now.'

'Never, Niska. I'll die first,' he spat, staring at her with such hatred it took her breath away.

\* \* \*

Sarin slipped silently into his bedchamber, his heart still pounding. He had almost been caught in Niska's chamber by Tanith, but she had come and left never realising he was hidden under the bed. Zene was already in the room anxiously pacing the floor. 'Did you find them?' she asked agitatedly.

'I did.' He grinned as he poured the contents of the leather bag he was carrying on to the bed. Strands of gems, bracelets and diadems landed in a tangled mass along with a plethora of loose stones. The morass of colour sparkled in the lamplight and Zene gave a soft gasp of surprise.

'They're so beautiful,' she said, picking up a ruby the size of a pigeon's egg.

'They come from every corner of the known world. Lands few have ever heard of,' Sarin said proudly. Some were collected by his ancestors, the majority of them by him. Sarin owned them and they would always be his, no matter what. 'That's the Eye of Ashra,' he told Zene.

'It's so big,' she said and peered through the blood-coloured stone. 'And flawless.'

'Legend says it has magical qualities.' Sarin grinned. 'An entertaining story with not one grain of truth I'd wager.'

'Will you tell it to me some day?'

'Yes.' Sarin was proud of himself. He'd employed his fledgling abilities as a locksmith to open the chest that Niska foolishly kept hidden under her bed. Ragnor believed that all her wealth was stored in his strongroom but she'd kept the jewels hidden even from him. With luck it would be some time before Niska discovered that they were missing.

'So many beautiful pieces,' Zene said in awe as she examined the jewels.

'Many of them will adorn you if you wish it, when we return to Percheron.' Sarin stuffed the sparkling mass back into the bag. 'You must leave now, Zene, and hide them in the cave I told you about.' He slipped the precious bundle into her saddlebag. 'Here,' he said handing them to her.

'I'll return before dusk,' Zene replied, smiling as she hiked the bag over her shoulder.

'Be careful,' Sarin warned.

Most of the men here were unsure how to treat Zene. They respected her as a warrior, yet couldn't treat her as a fellow comrade because she was female. Mostly they avoided her, and she had a freedom of movement that was denied to Sarin. No one would think it odd for her to leave to go hunting, but Ragnor insisted that Sarin stay close to the longhouse purely for his own safety. Ragnor treated Sarin as an honoured guest but it was obvious he still didn't trust him. However, Sarin trusted Zene: she was a friend as well as a lover. He had never been so sure of a woman as he was of Zene.

'Take this as well.' He removed a small bag of gold from his doublet. 'The jarls here are notoriously careless with their money when they're drunk,' he said with a smile.

Zene had already bribed the gaolers to ensure that the captured Percheron and Kabran soldiers were well cared for. The wounded as well as Leon were recovering under the loving attentions of the gaoler's plump daughter who was skilled in the use of herbs.

'What would you have me do with the gold?' Zene asked.

'If the plan fails then you are to bribe the guards to let the men escape.'

'But it must not fail,' she said as she put a hand on Sarin's arm.

'That all depends on Tarn,' Sarin replied with a troubled frown.

Tarn's arms had grown numb, but his legs still ached as he'd been standing now for hours, and was no doubt destined to remain in this uncomfortable position for much longer. Stoicism had deserted him after Niska's visit and he'd begun to believe he was destined to perish here in Vestfold.

He tried to tense and relax his muscles but nothing helped and he gave a heavy sigh. He heard a loud creak as the door opened and turned his head, fearing it was Niska come to humiliate him again. It was not. If anything it was worse, he thought, as he saw Sarin enter the room.

Sarin spoke to the guard, it was doubtful the man understood what he said, but he soon made it clear he wanted to enter Tarn's cell. At first the guard refused, but when Sarin grabbed him and hauled him over to the cell door he reluctantly got out the key and pulled the barred door open, muttering under his breath.

'What a surly fellow,' Sarin said cheerfully as he confronted Tarn, totally ignoring the prisoner's expression of loathing.

'Mayhap he didn't like the smell in here: it stinks of traitorous scum.' Tarn's lip twisted in disgust. 'First Niska, now you!'

'I've not come to gloat,' Sarin said in a low voice.

'Why else would you be here?' Tarn challenged. 'I've no wish to see you.'

'In the circumstances your foul mood is understandable.' Sarin looked Tarn up and down, frowning when he saw the cruel way he was confined, his arms stretched tight above his head. 'Why did they chain you like this? There's no way you could escape.'

'Ask Niska.' Tarn turned his head away from Sarin, filled with such hatred for the man who had betrayed him, he felt he might explode. 'Why not free my arms then?' he asked, turning his head back to grin evilly at Sarin. 'Then I could lock them around your throat.'

'You'd be too weak to do anything at first,' Sarin said thoughtfully. 'The pain when your arms are eventually lowered will be intense as the blood starts to flow freely again.'

'I'll stand it, if it gives me the opportunity to kill you,' Tarn growled. His blue eyes were glittering.

'I'm pleased to see you have not lost your determination or your fire. You'll need both if we are all to survive this,' Sarin said cryptically as he looked around the cell. There was a bucket and a low stool in one corner, both out of Tarn's reach. 'This will do.' He picked up the stool and placed it behind Tarn's legs.

'Is this another method of torture?' Tarn asked.

'Torture? Do not be so foolish,' Sarin muttered as he looked at how Tarn's chains were fastened. They were looped through rings high in the wooden wall, then fed downwards to be wrapped around a low bar, thus allowing the chains to be tightened or loosened at will. 'Lift your arms as high as you can, so that I can get some slack on the chain,' Sarin ordered. Convinced that he was foolish even to think of trusting Sarin again, Tarn obeyed. To his amazement Sarin began to unwrap the chain until it was slack enough to let Tarn's left arm fall limply by his side. It felt numb, yet the lacing pain started almost at once and he gave a soft groan. Sarin freed the other arm, then stepped forwards and helped Tarn to sit down on the stool, leaning his back against the smooth wooden wall. 'Is that better?'

'I don't know why you did this,' Tarn said, filled with relief to be a little more comfortable even if his arms still pained him.

'You need to be in good health when we execute the next step of my plan.'

'Plan?' Tarn queried frowning. 'I know of no plan, except the one to preserve your wellbeing and safety at all costs.'

'It was Zene's idea. She suggested it when I returned to camp and told her it would be near impossible to get into Ragnor's stronghold and come out alive.'

'Well we are here now and both very much alive,' Tarn said cuttingly. 'But I doubt I'll ever leave in one piece and neither will Rianna . . .' he faltered. 'She'll be forced to wed that barbarian.'

'Not so,' Sarin said grinning. 'I revealed your whereabouts to Ragnor for a reason, Tarn.'

'To ensure that Ragnor helped you regain your throne,' Tarn replied in disgust.

'Far from it. Ragnor's price is way too high,' Sarin said, and he appeared to be speaking the truth. 'I did it because there was no other choice.' He sighed heavily. 'I regret the loss of the three men, and the number who were wounded.' He paused and looked Tarn straight in the eye. 'I had no wish for you to die, or come to any harm. Believe it or not, I have changed.'

'I see no sign of that!'

'You will.' Sarin bent closer to Tarn. 'There is an ancient rite in Vestfold, that has probably not been carried out for a century or more, but it still exists, still remains part of their law. It's the right of conflict between two adversaries, when one takes another's woman. They call it Baldnarok. You can challenge Ragnor, Tarn. Claim that Rianna is your wife and therefore she cannot marry him. To wed her Ragnor must do battle, as the rite says, and kill you first.'

'Even though it pains me to say so, she is your wife, not mine. You have the right to challenge Ragnor, not I,' Tarn replied in confusion.

'You may distrust me still, but I have done this for you. I'll admit in the past I've thought always of myself and not others, and you may still think of me as your enemy. But I care for you, Tarn; deep down I always have. Also I'm certain of one thing.' Sarin put his hand on his heart. 'If anyone can best Ragnor, it is you not me. You're the stronger and better warrior.'

'Maybe so,' Tarn agreed. 'But however much I may wish to fight Ragnor, surely he can refuse the challenge because she is not my wife. I never had the chance to wed her.'

'You took her virginity,' Sarin said with an uneasy

grin. 'Cador told me you did, but I refused to believe him at the time. I have discovered that the ancient laws of Vestfold decree that, as you took her maidenhead after she plighted her troth to you, then you are handfasted. In their eyes my union with Rianna meant nothing because she was already yours. Ragnor believes he is safe because I have washed my hands of her. Yet if the truth be known he cannot keep Rianna as his thrall or wed her until you have given up your rights to her.'

'And I'll never do that,' Tarn said determinedly. 'Not while I draw breath.'

'Then all we have to do is issue a challenge to him. If he wishes to keep her he'll have to agree to the challenge.' Sarin put his hand on Tarn's shoulder. 'Let us pray to the gods that you win, Tarn.'


'What is wrong? Where are you taking me?' Rianna asked the warrior who'd barged into her chamber, grabbed hold of her and dragged her along the corridor.

Gunnar and Ragnor had been teaching her this strange guttural language, but either she had formed her words wrongly or the guard was ignoring her, she thought, as she was bundled into a small room.

She was confronted by a table behind which sat Ragnor, Jorvik and an elderly white-bearded jarl. Sarin was sitting on a chair in the far corner of the chamber. He gave her a reassuring smile, which surprised her as she had deliberately walked away from him when he'd tried to talk to her only moments ago.

Ragnor, however, looked grimmer and even angrier than he had earlier today. She had been caught trying to sneak into the strongroom to see Tarn. Ragnor had been furious and threatened to beat her. Instead he had pulled her down on to the bed and made love to her, but she'd lain there unresponsive, unable to be aroused by Ragnor when her beloved was imprisoned so close. Confused and upset by her coldness, Ragnor had stormed out of the room.

'Lady Rianna,' the elderly jarl said. 'Do you swear by Thor's hammer that you will answer all questions put to you truthfully?'

'Yes,' she replied in confusion. 'Why am I here? Have I done something wrong?' She recalled the thrall's terrible death at the burial ceremony; justice here was swift and just as harsh.

'King Tarn has challenged me to the rite of Baldnarok,' Ragnor said curtly.

'Baldnarok?' she repeated. 'What is that?'

Jorvik glanced at Ragnor, expecting him to explain. When he said nothing he looked back at Rianna. 'Combat to the death, with you as the prize. King Tarn claims that he was handfasted to you before you wed Lord Sarin, thus making the subsequent union null and void.'

'I understand Lord Ragnor has expressed a wish to marry you?' asked the old man.

'Yes,' she agreed awkwardly. She'd had no choice but to say yes to the proposal even though she had no wish to wed anyone but Tarn.

'In order for Lord Ragnor to marry you King Tarn must be persuaded to relinquish his claim on you, Lady Rianna. He has refused to do that.'

Rianna's heart leaped; she couldn't believe this was happening.

Ragnor said furiously, 'Tarn lies. He has no rights to the lady. He took her only after she had already married Lord Sarin.'

'And Lord Sarin gave up all rights to the lady when he arrived in Vestfold,' added Jorvik, looking at the white-bearded jarl.

'Were you handfasted to King Tarn before you arrived in Aguilar to wed Lord Sarin?' the old man asked Rianna.

'I'm not sure what handfasted means,' Rianna said cautiously, wondering how Tarn had ever heard of this rite. She glanced over at Sarin and he nodded and gave her a brief meaningful smile. Surely not, she considered, as she looked back at the old jarl.

250

'It is when you plight your troth and gift your maiden-head to a suitor. Tis an ancient and venerable custom here in Vestfold, one designed to protect the virginity of our maidens. Were you a virgin when you took part in the ceremony to marry Lord Sarin?' the jarl asked.

'No.' She clasped her hands and lowered her eyes, not wanting Ragnor to see how happy she was. 'I know now that by the laws of Vestfold I was already handfasted to Tarn.'

The icy air was as still as death itself as the sun rose over the mountains. The golden rays hit the snow and the blanket of white began to melt. It turned into slow streams of water, which heralded the approach of spring at last in the lush valley surrounding Ragnor's stronghold.

Most of the large flat area between the adjacent long-houses had been swept clear of the snow already, and a circle of pale stones had been set out on the hardpacked ground. A crowd was already gathering fast, all of those who had a right to be there were eager to witness their lord and master vanquish the foreign king. There had never been a Baldnarok of such importance; so much rested on this one brief battle between two men.

Few of the crowd had laid eyes on King Tarn and most were surprised when the two men appeared and they saw him for the first time. He was as tall as Lord Ragnor, just as muscular, just as broad-shouldered and, some of the women whispered quietly, even more handsome then their own ruler. They were equally matched and it should be a good fight, most thought, as excitement grew among the lower ranks.

The expressions of most of the jarls were grim, as they already knew the strength of the man their master was about to face. They were gathered in a tight group close to the edge of the ring, Rianna and Sarin among them. Tarn and Ragnor stepped forwards. They were both naked, apart from a small breechcloth around their hips.

251

Yet neither shivered as they walked towards Rianna. She knew why as the strong odour of seal oil drifted towards her. It had been plastered on their bare skin, as the Vestfoldians believed the oil protected man from the cold, just as it protected the seals from the chill waters of the lakes and open seas.

Rianna glanced nervously at Sarin. He'd spoken to her in private after the questioning by Ragnor and his jarls. Sarin had told her that he wanted to help them and it was he who had suggested the challenge to Tarn. She still didn't trust Sarin, still loathed him, but at this moment he felt far more familiar and far more comforting that anyone else in the damnable place.

Ragnor paused as he reached her. 'Rianna.' He handed her a small sharp-pointed dagger. 'A rune to give me strength?' he asked, looking at her almost appealingly. It was the first time she'd seen him since she'd admitted she was handfasted to Tarn.

She swallowed hard and shook her head. 'Do not ask this of me, you know I cannot,' she whispered.

'Allow me, brother.' Niska brushed past Rianna, holding out a larger and more vicious-looking dagger. Taking hold of Ragnor's arm, she carved a rune denoting courage into his forearm. The blood streamed from the cut flesh, standing out like tears on his oiled skin. Niska used a silk scarf to stem the flow, then lifted the bloodied scarf to her lips. 'My prayers are with you brother,' she said in a loud voice.

'I have no need of prayers, for I shall win.' He stared straight at Rianna as he spoke and she shivered when she saw the steely determination in his eyes. Her knees felt weak and she might have faltered if she hadn't felt Sarin's supporting hand on her arm.

Tarn, escorted by two guards, was led past her. She pushed Sarin aside and rushed forwards to grab hold of Tarn's arm.

'Tarn,' she said smiling at him lovingly. 'You should not have put yourself in such peril to save me.'

'I just thank the gods you're unhurt,' Tarn replied. His blue eyes were full of love.

'The runes have great importance here. I cannot deny you what I have, Ragnor,' she said softly, fighting back her tears. Rune scars meant nothing to her or Tarn, but they had meaning for Ragnor, and that was the reason she had to do this.

The watching crowd held their breath as Tarn nodded and held out his arm. 'I'll carry your mark with pride,' he said with a reassuring smile.

Feeling nervous and sick to her stomach, Rianna dug the point of the knife into his skin and carved the selfsame propitious pattern into his arm as Niska had for Ragnor. She shuddered as she saw blood flowing from the wound and down his arm. Anxiously she stemmed it with the skirt of the velvet gown. 'Win, my love,' she said, rising on tiptoe to kiss his cheek.

'You're a fool,' Jorvik growled as he grabbed hold of her and wrenched her away. Tarn looked at her for a long meaningful moment and then moved forwards with his guards, stepping into the circle of stones where Ragnor was waiting. 'Ragnor will never forgive you this slur on his honour,' Jorvik told her.

'If Tarn dies, then so do I,' she told Jorvik as he pulled her back to stand by Sarin.

Tarn had never felt fear before a battle but he did so now. It wasn't only his fate that rested on this encounter. If he lost, Rianna was destined to spend the rest of her days in the barbarous land. Ragnor was a dangerous and unknown opponent, Tarn thought, as the two men faced each other in the small stone-ringed circle.

An elderly jarl stepped forwards and handed each a long, curved, wickedly sharp dagger, almost two-thirds the length of a sword. The weapon was unfamiliar to Tarn, but it was well balanced and expertly made. As the jarl left the ring, Tarn held the dagger loosely in his hand, swinging it slightly as he moved warily on the balls of his feet, his gaze locked on Ragnor's pale eyes.

Tarn detected a faint flicker in their cold depths, a millisecond before Ragnor leaped towards him. He jumped back, but as he moved Ragnor's razor-sharp blade left a thin red line across his bare chest. The wound was barely a scratch, and did not deter Tarn. Employing his dagger like a sword, he lunged at Ragnor and their blades clashed with a metallic scream, which sounded overloud in the silence as the watchers held their breath.

Tarn attacked again, his expression cold and fearless, his lips drawn back in a tight smile. His blade flashed, leaving a wide gash across Ragnor's upper sword arm. Ragnor drew back, his blood flowing freely from the wound, mingling with the crusted blood of his rune. His face set in a mask of fury, Ragnor gave a loud roar and struck wildly at Tarn. If the blow had caught him it would have near severed a limb but he parried it easily and danced back. He felt the stones against his bare heels, reminding him that he must at no time step out of the circle or the battle would be deemed lost.

The two men circled each other warily, waiting for the right moment to attack. Tarn's palms were damp with sweat and seal oil, and he tightened his hold on the leather-wrapped hilt of his dagger, waiting for Ragnor to pounce again. With a low growl, Ragnor attacked. Tarn bent and leaped aside, the blade whistling uselessly past his left shoulder. As he swung round, and faced his opponent again he saw a flicker of concern cross Ragnor's face.

'Did you expect the fight to be easy?' he taunted. 'I'll kill you, Ragnor. You'll never have Rianna, she's mine.'

'Mine now,' Ragnor retorted, lunging furiously at Tarn. Their blades clashed with a sharp scraping sound again and again, each attacking and defending, until they breathlessly drew back knowing that they were far too evenly matched. They fought on, both scarred by the battle now; blood oozing from the scratches on their flesh, neither badly wounded as yet.

Ragnor threw himself forwards again with such ferocity that Tarn crouched and threw himself into a dive, rolling and springing lithely to his feet, landing almost behind his attacker. Tarn lunged and before Ragnor could turn and parry the blow, Tarn's blade cut deep into his side. Tarn pulled the dagger from Ragnor's flesh, the blade scraping jarringly against his victim's ribs.

Uttering a loud groan, followed by a grunt of painful fury, Ragnor held his arm against the wound and backed away. 'You'll die for that,' he shouted as blood dripped from the wound on to his legs and feet.

'First you have to catch me, Tarn taunted.

'Now, Jorvik,' Ragnor yelled, gripping his weapon so hard that his knuckles turned white as he circled Tarn.

There was a dull thudding sound as an axe landed at Tarn's feet. Jorvik threw the other axe more carefully, guiding it straight into Ragnor's left hand. Bending to grab hold of the axe, Tarn backed away as Ragnor advanced. He held the weapon for a second to gauge its balance and weight, edging cautiously around the ring. With an ear-shattering roar, Ragnor lunged, wildly waving both dagger and axe. Tarn parried the blade with his, deflected the axe blow with the haft of his weapon and managed to swing Ragnor's hand aside with a display of sheer brute strength.

Ragnor angrily lunged again, Tarn parried and the two men struggled, muscle straining against muscle. Blood dripped from Ragnor's wound on to Tarn, the seal oil making their skin stick slickly together as each battled to defeat the other. Using every ounce of strength he had, Tarn shoved Ragnor away. He began to move slowly round the circle again, anticipating the next attack. Ragnor was losing a lot of blood from the wound in his side and he would soon grow weaker. All Tarn had to do was bide his time and wait.

With a blood-curdling battlecry Ragnor threw himself at Tarn, brandishing his axe. Tarn parried the axe blow, smashed aside Ragnor's dagger and kneed him in the belly. Ragnor grunted in pain, and staggered back. Tarn advanced, hit him hard across the shoulder with the haft of his axe and followed it up with a blow to the side of the head. The sickening crack reverberated round the bailey as Ragnor crumpled to the ground.

Tarn kicked Ragnor's weapons away from his slack hands, dropped the axe and kneeled across his victim's chest. He held the blade of the dagger to Ragnor's neck. He looked barely conscious, but his eyes flickered open as Tarn said, 'Submit. Admit I've won, and I'll not kill you.'

'No,' Ragnor hissed.

'Do it – no more need die,' Tarn said softly as he pressed his blade to the pale skin until it brought forth bright beads of blood. 'Submit. Allow me to take Rianna and depart. She loves me, not you.'

Ragnor's eyes were filled with pain, and the depth of his emotion surprised Tarn. 'I'll never accept that. I'll not lose her,' he gasped.

'Your law says you must submit,' Tarn replied, pressing the dagger harder to Ragnor's throat. 'Unless you wish to die and let Jorvik rule in your place. I demand that you agree to free my men and Lord Sarin.'

'It appears I have no choice,' Ragnor muttered resentfully as he closed his eyes.

Relieved the battle was at an end, Tarn stood up and tossed his dagger aside. He wasn't badly wounded, but the cuts he had were bleeding quite profusely now and he felt weary. That mattered not. All he wanted to do was gather up Rianna and leave this barbarian stronghold as swiftly as he could. He smiled as he saw Rianna lift up her velvet skirts and run eagerly towards him.

'Tarn,' she gasped, rushing to the edge of the stone circle. 'You are hurt, my love?'

'A few scratches,' he said, pausing his side of the stones, waiting for the jarls to announce the combat was ended. 'It's nothing,' he added and smiled lovingly at her.

'Tarn,' she screamed, her eyes widening in fear.

He felt a muscular arm grab his throat, and the point of a dagger press into the small of his back.

'I'm not finished,' Ragnor growled, pulling Tarn hard back against his bloodied form. 'I'll kill you, Rianna is mine!'

'I'm not yours, I never will be,' Rianna said, her face tight with concern. 'Tarn bested you Ragnor, and gifted you your life. You cannot do this.'

'I can and I will,' he grated.

Tarn felt Ragnor lean heavily against him, warm blood dripping on to his legs. Ragnor was making an odd rasping sound, as if he was having difficulty breathing. Yet he still held the dagger pressed hard against Tarn's back.

Rianna lifted the small dagger she was carrying, and for a moment Tarn feared she was going to lunge at Ragnor. Instead she pressed the point to her neck, just above her collarbone. 'Kill Tarn, and I'll die too, Ragnor,' she threatened. 'If he dies I no longer wish to live.'

'You would not,' Ragnor growled, his voice sounding weaker.

'I would,' she insisted shakily. 'It is your choice; do I die or live?'

'Ragnor,' Tarn said calmly. 'Your people witnessed you lose our fight. Do you wish them to witness you losing your honour as well?'

'Honour,' Ragnor gave a chuckle that ended in a disgusting gurgling sound. As he loosened his hold a little, Tarn moved as fast as he ever had – turning and twisting, feeling the blade slither cuttingly across his back as he threw Ragnor to the ground. He landed flat on his back half out of the circle of stones, clutching at his wounded side as he struggled to draw breath.

'It is finished,' Jorvik said and strode forwards. 'Lord Ragnor has left the circle. The law of Baldnarok says he must surrender to you, King Tarn.'

'Are you sure you wish to do this?' Tarn asked Rianna.

'I am certain,' she replied, squeezing his hand.

'I'll check on the men to make sure they are ready to depart,' Tarn replied.

'And I will see you outside.' She smiled at him reassuringly then followed Jorvik into Ragnor's chamber.

Ragnor was lying on the bed, propped up by pillows, his side heavily bandaged. His face was pale, but it grew even paler as he caught sight of Rianna.

'Why have you come?' he asked breathlessly, still having difficulty breathing because of his wound.

'I've come to bid farewell to you, Ragnor.' She sat on the stool beside the bed and took hold of his hand.

'Why?' he rasped. 'I believed after all that had happened you would never wish to lay eyes on me again.'

'I have regained what I thought I'd lost. Why should I allow bitterness to sour my happiness?' she said gently. 'I was so frightened when Niska brought me here, yet you treated me with kindness. You loved me, wished to marry me – how could I despise you for that?'

'I tried to kill the man you love,' Ragnor groaned, his face twisted in pain. 'Is that not reason enough to hate me?'

'Tarn loves me, so he can understand why you acted as you did.'

'Then he's more magnanimous than I.' Ragnor gritted his teeth as he sat up. 'I've lain here far too long.'

'Not long enough to recover. It is a bad wound,' she said, pushing him gently back against his pillows. 'Your land is in safe hands,' she added, glancing meaningfully at Jorvik. 'All I ask is that you consider Tarn's proposal of a peace treaty between Vestfold and Kabra.'

'My people are warriors,' Ragnor frowned. 'They may not welcome peace.'

'Ask them,' she challenged. 'Ask them what they truly want.'

'Why does King Tarn allow a woman to involve herself in matters of state?' Ragnor coughed.

'He trusts me more than most,' she replied. 'Has your sister not proven to you that women can be far from weak.'

'Niska is a law unto herself,' he muttered. 'I never understood her when we were children and I do not now. She left early this morning, slunk away with her men. Off to find some man she calls Chang,' he added, then grinned. 'Jorvik said that she was in such haste to depart she left all her treasure in my strongroom.'

'She will have difficulty paying her mercenaries,' Rianna commented, knowing that Sarin had the jewels she'd stolen. Niska must be unaware that the booty she carried with her in the locked chest was nothing but a worthless pile of rocks. 'But she'll survive, she always does.' She paused and looked thoughtfully at Ragnor. 'Just think of Tarn's offer. Send word to Kabra if you decide the answer is yes.'

Ragnor nodded but said nothing more as Rianna rose to her feet and Jorvik escorted her from the room.

Tarn was waiting along with Sarin and all the surviving soldiers who had accompanied them into Vestfold. It appeared that the two men had made a peace of sorts but how long that would last Rianna didn't know. She smiled at Leon, who sat a little unsteadily on his horse beside Zene. The men all looked happy to be returning home at last.

'Let us hope we never see Vestfold again,' Tarn said as his hands clasped her waist and he lifted her on to her palfrey.

'Who knows what the future holds,' she said as he swung into the saddle of his white stallion and manoeuvred it beside hers.

Tarn turned to look at Rianna, his love for her reflected in his blue eyes. 'Whatever it is we'll face it together,' he said. 'Now let us return to Kabra. We have a coronation to attend.'

# Visit the Black Lace website at
**www.black-lace-books.com**

FIND OUT THE LATEST INFORMATION AND TAKE
ADVANTAGE OF OUR FANTASTIC FREE BOOK OFFER!
ALSO VISIT THE SITE FOR . . .

- All Black Lace titles currently available
  and how to order online
- Great new offers
- Writers' guidelines
- Author interviews
- An erotica newsletter
- Features
- Cool links

BLACK LACE — THE LEADING IMPRINT
OF WOMEN'S SEXY FICTION

TAKING YOUR EROTIC READING
PLEASURE TO NEW HORIZONS

# Black Lace Booklist

Information is correct at time of printing. To avoid disappointment, check availability before ordering. Go to www.black-lace-books.com. All books are priced £7.99 unless another price is given.

## BLACK LACE BOOKS WITH A CONTEMPORARY SETTING

| | | |
|---|---|---|
| ☐ ALWAYS THE BRIDEGROOM Tesni Morgan | ISBN 978 0 352 33855 6 | £6.99 |
| ☐ THE ANGELS' SHARE Maya Hess | ISBN 978 0 352 34043 6 | |
| ☐ ASKING FOR TROUBLE Kristina Lloyd | ISBN 978 0 352 33362 9 | |
| ☐ BLACK LIPSTICK KISSES Monica Belle | ISBN 978 0 352 33885 3 | £6.99 |
| ☐ THE BLUE GUIDE Carrie Williams | ISBN 978 0 352 34131 0 | |
| ☐ BONDED Fleur Reynolds | ISBN 978 0 352 33192 2 | £6.99 |
| ☐ THE BOSS Monica Belle | ISBN 978 0 352 34088 7 | |
| ☐ BOUND IN BLUE Monica Belle | ISBN 978 0 352 34012 2 | |
| ☐ CAMPAIGN HEAT Gabrielle Marcola | ISBN 978 0 352 33941 6 | |
| ☐ CAT SCRATCH FEVER Sophie Mouette | ISBN 978 0 352 34021 4 | |
| ☐ CIRCUS EXCITE Nikki Magennis | ISBN 978 0 352 34033 7 | |
| ☐ CLUB CRÈME Primula Bond | ISBN 978 0 352 33907 2 | £6.99 |
| ☐ COMING ROUND THE MOUNTAIN Tabitha Flyte | ISBN 978 0 352 33873 0 | £6.99 |
| ☐ CONFESSIONAL Judith Roycroft | ISBN 978 0 352 33421 3 | |
| ☐ CONTINUUM Portia Da Costa | ISBN 978 0 352 33120 5 | |
| ☐ COOKING UP A STORM Emma Holly | ISBN 978 0 352 34114 3 | |
| ☐ DANGEROUS CONSEQUENCES Pamela Rochford | ISBN 978 0 352 33185 4 | |
| ☐ DARK DESIGNS Madelynne Ellis | ISBN 978 0 352 34075 7 | |
| ☐ THE DEVIL INSIDE Portia Da Costa | ISBN 978 0 352 32993 6 | |
| ☐ EDEN'S FLESH Robyn Russell | ISBN 978 0 352 33923 2 | £6.99 |
| ☐ EQUAL OPPORTUNITIES Mathilde Madden | ISBN 978 0 352 34070 2 | |
| ☐ FEMININE WILES Karina Moore | ISBN 978 0 352 33874 7 | |
| ☐ FIRE AND ICE Laura Hamilton | ISBN 978 0 352 33486 2 | |
| ☐ GOING DEEP Kimberly Dean | ISBN 978 0 352 33876 1 | £6.99 |
| ☐ GONE WILD Maria Eppie | ISBN 978 0 352 33670 5 | |
| ☐ HOTBED Portia Da Costa | ISBN 978 0 352 33614 9 | |

## BLACK LACE BOOKS WITH AN HISTORICAL SETTING

☐ THE AMULET Lisette Allen      ISBN 978 0 352 33019 2   £6.99
☐ THE BARBARIAN GEISHA Charlotte Royal      ISBN 978 0 352 33267 7
☐ BARBARIAN PRIZE Deanna Ashford      ISBN 978 0 352 34017 7
☐ THE CAPTIVATION Natasha Rostova      ISBN 978 0 352 33234 9
☐ DARKER THAN LOVE Kristina Lloyd      ISBN 978 0 352 33279 0
☐ ELENA'S DESTINY Lisette Allen      ISBN 978 0 352 33218 9
☐ FRENCH MANNERS Olivia Christie      ISBN 978 0 352 33214 1
☐ LORD WRAXALL'S FANCY Anna Lieff Saxby      ISBN 978 0 352 33080 2
☐ NICOLE'S REVENGE Lisette Allen      ISBN 978 0 352 32984 4
☐ THE SENSES BEJEWELLED Cleo Cordell      ISBN 978 0 352 32904 2   £6.99
☐ THE SOCIETY OF SIN Sian Lacey Taylder      ISBN 978 0 352 34080 1
☐ TEMPLAR PRIZE Deanna Ashford      ISBN 978 0 352 34137 2
☐ UNDRESSING THE DEVIL Angel Strand      ISBN 978 0 352 33938 6

## BLACK LACE BOOKS WITH A PARANORMAL THEME

☐ BRIGHT FIRE Maya Hess      ISBN 978 0 352 34104 4
☐ BURNING BRIGHT Janine Ashbless      ISBN 978 0 352 34085 6
☐ CRUEL ENCHANTMENT Janine Ashbless      ISBN 978 0 352 33483 1
☐ DIVINE TORMENT Janine Ashbless      ISBN 978 0 352 33719 1
☐ FLOOD Anna Clare      ISBN 978 0 352 34094 8
☐ GOTHIC BLUE Portia Da Costa      ISBN 978 0 352 33075 8
☐ THE PRIDE Edie Bingham      ISBN 978 0 352 33997 3
☐ THE SILVER COLLAR Mathilde Madden      ISBN 978 0 352 34141 9
☐ THE TEN VISIONS Olivia Knight      ISBN 978 0 352 34119 8

## BLACK LACE ANTHOLOGIES

☐ BLACK LACE QUICKIES 1 Various      ISBN 978 0 352 34126 6   £2.99
☐ BLACK LACE QUICKIES 2 Various      ISBN 978 0 352 34127 3   £2.99
☐ BLACK LACE QUICKIES 3 Various      ISBN 978 0 352 34128 0   £2.99
☐ BLACK LACE QUICKIES 4 Various      ISBN 978 0 352 34129 7   £2.99
☐ BLACK LACE QUICKIES 5 Various      ISBN 978 0 352 34130 3   £2.99
☐ BLACK LACE QUICKIES 6 Various      ISBN 978 0 352 34146 4   £2.99
☐ BLACK LACE QUICKIES 7 Various      ISBN 978 0 352 34147 1   £2.99
☐ BLACK LACE QUICKIES 8 Various      ISBN 978 0 352 34133 4   £2.99
☐ MORE WICKED WORDS Various      ISBN 978 0 352 33487 9   £6.99

To find out the latest information about Black Lace titles, check out the website: www.black-lace-books.com or send for a booklist with complete synopses by writing to:

Black Lace Booklist, Virgin Books Ltd
Thames Wharf Studios
Rainville Road
London W6 9HA

Please include an SAE of decent size. Please note only British stamps are valid.

Our privacy policy
We will not disclose information you supply us to any other parties. We will not disclose any information which identifies you personally to any person without your express consent.

From time to time we may send out information about Black Lace books and special offers. Please tick here if you do <u>not</u> wish to receive Black Lace information. ❏

Please send me the books I have ticked above.

Name ....................................................................

Address .................................................................

...........................................................................

...........................................................................

...........................................................................

Post Code .............................................................

**Send to:** Virgin Books Cash Sales, Thames Wharf Studios, Rainville Road, London W6 9HA.

**US customers:** for prices and details of how to order books for delivery by mail, call 888-330-8477.

Please enclose a cheque or postal order, made payable to Virgin Books Ltd, to the value of the books you have ordered plus postage and packing costs as follows:

UK and BFPO – £1.00 for the first book, 50p for each subsequent book.

Overseas (including Republic of Ireland) – £2.00 for the first book, £1.00 for each subsequent book.

If you would prefer to pay by VISA, ACCESS/MASTERCARD, DINERS CLUB, AMEX or SWITCH, please write your card number and expiry date here:

...........................................................................

Signature ..............................................................

Please allow up to 28 days for delivery.